Dear,

Honor & Haven:

The Letter Chronicles

Marqua'lla

SOUL Publications

Dear, Honor & Haven   Marqua'lla

SOUL Publications

Find Marqua'lla

Facebook: Marqua'lla L. Thomas, Author Marqua'lla

Group Marqua'lla's Reading Parlor

website: www.soulauthors.com

Part 1

Dear Honor

SOUL Publications

Prelude

Haven

"Haven, never let anybody fuck over you or your family without showing them that vengeance is always the Stones' for the taking. You make them feel a worse pain then they caused you or your family and make them regret ever fucking with a Stone." I heard the words my father spoke to me almost every day since I started school play in my head, as if he was whispering them in my ear again. As my fingers traced along my father's name engraved in his headstone.

It was my first time seeing where my parents were buried. One of my father's friends paid for my parents to be buried next to each other, since neither of my parent's families bothered with it.

"I read the letter that was crumbled in your hand on that day. After reading it all I could focus on is the anger and need for vengeance that filled my heart. Don't worry dad, revenge will be the Stone's soon." I told his headstone as I angrily ripped out the weeds surrounding his grave.

SOUL Publications

"I won't be back until I make sure the people who ever crossed us will never forget the Stone's name and regret fuckin' wit' us." I kissed my fingertips on both of my hands, then placed them on my parent's graves.

I stood up and walked to the car where my best friend since high school, Amity was waiting for me. As she pulled out of the graveyard all I could think about was making my next move, my best move.

Honor

January 9ᵗʰ, 2011

"Truth, Honor," it's time to come in. Our mom yelled out of the living room window to us.

"Kendrix get your ass back over here." Truth, my older brother called out when Kendrix tried to walk down the street as he caught the football, I tossed to him.

"Truth, I was just going down the street to the store really quick." Kendrix said as he walked back towards the front of our building where me and Truth was. Kendrix was our mom's client's son, that Truth was stuck watching while his mom was in the house getting her hair done by ours.

"Nah man later we 'bouta go in the house and eat, then you and your moms should be leaving." Truth answered.

"Aight, damn man," Kendrix said as me and him walked over to where Truth was standing waiting on us. Kendrix was pissed we had to go in, so he ran in front of the both of us and was already heading up the stairs.

"Get down!" Truth shouted right before he fell on top of me causing my body to fall slightly on top of Kendrix right as the shots started firing.

"Truth, get your heavy ass the fuck off me," I told Truth after laying there for a few seconds and realizing he wasn't moving. He needed to get up, so we could get in the house before they came back around.

I turned around to push him off me and the first thing I noticed was that blood was seeping from his mouth and side. The next thing I noticed was a man walking up behind us with a ski mask on and a gun in his hand.

"Kendrix run inside!" I shouted when the man started to lift his gun.

"Brah, come on get the fuck up man." My heart was pounding in my chest as I scooted back on the ground and tried to pull Truth with me by the collar of his shirt.

Tears pooled in my eyes as my brother opened his mouth and blood poured out, he lifted slightly just as the man squeezed the trigger. The bullet pierced through the back of Truth's head and came out through his forehead and grazed the left side of my cheek. The pain on my face didn't even register as my brother's blood splattered on my face and the dead weight of his body fell on top of me.

SOUL Publications

Kendrix tried to get up and run but the gunman shot him in the back then turned the gun on me.

"Shit!" the gunman shouted and started ducking as someone started shooting towards him. He started shooting back towards the other gunman as he ran off towards the waiting car. Whoever it was started shooting at the car as it pulled off.

"Are you hit lil nigga?" I heard someone ask but I couldn't see their face because Truth's body was laid out on top of mine.

"Yeah," I said right before the person who saved my life moved Truth's body off mine. When I was finally able to see the person standing before me, I realized it was Patch who had saved my life. He was a stickup kid from the neighborhood that stayed to himself. He never got into shit that had nothing to do with him. Hell, two niggas from our hood could be stomping one another out, Patch would walk by like he didn't see the shit instead of stopping to watch like other niggas. But if someone from our hood was getting jumped by someone from another hood ours had beef with, then he was jumping in. It didn't matter if he didn't fuck with the nigga or not.

"I gotta get out of here but from now on keep one of these on you." He gestured to his gun then took off running as the sirens got closer.

July 05, 2017

"Fuck!" I screamed as I woke up in a cold sweat. The dream made it seem like my brother being killed in front of me had just happened.

I headed straight for the shower, I could feel my brother's blood on my face, and the smell of the gunpowder was as fresh as it was six years ago. I turned on the shower as hot as it could get, and it got scorching in the hotel. I scrubbed my face and body until the smell and feel of the blood went away.

"Damn it!" I yelled out in frustration.

A nigga mind needed to be straight, so I could be focused on the final day of testing for the California Bar Exam I had in a few hours. I had been living out of a hotel in the City ever since I graduated, studying my ass off because I had to pass the exam on my first try. I barely had any sleep and I think the delirium from studying all day and the testing the day before had my mind in a fucked state.

Dear, Honor & Haven   Marqua'lla

I took a Vicodin out of the small zip part of my suitcase and bit a small piece off with the back of my teeth. I just needed enough of the pill to get me some sleep, but not too much that I missed the test. I swallowed the small piece before the nasty taste of the pill could linger on my tongue. Visions of Truth and I over the years played through my mind as I laid back on the bed with my right forearm covering my eyes.

"I'mma do this shit for you nigga," I said to the ghost of my brother that had been with me since his death. A flashback of my brother nodding his head at me was the last thing I saw before I passed out.

I was just on the verge of falling into a deep sleep when knocks at the door woke me. My body felt sluggish as I made my way to the door. Whoever was at the door knocks were getting louder.

"What!" I barked when I opened the door.

"Didn't you order a pizza from Pizza Hut?" the delivery girl said. I had forgotten that I had even ordered a pizza over an hour ago.

"My bad," I took my pizza from her sat it on the counter. I noticed something about her looked familiar as I handed her the receipt back. I remembered her face from somewhere, but I didn't know where.

"Can I have that back?" she asked pointing to the receipt.

"Could've at least gave me a bigger tip," she mumbled as she rolled her eyes then walked off. I slammed the door behind her and went back to bed.

****

Five hours later…

It seemed like my alarm went off an hour after I passed out. I slipped on my clothes, grabbed my briefcase and phone then headed to the coffee shop down the street from the hotel. Although I wasn't from the City, I could tell you everything that was in a mile radius of the hotel.

Since my father believed it was the streets or nothing my uncle helped me pay for college. He even footed the bill for me to stay in an expensive hotel for two months. My uncle did all of that from behind bars and my father wouldn't even slip me a dollar, because I was doing something he was against. I drank two large coffees as I poured over the exam material. I packed up, left the coffee shop, got in my car, and headed to the building where the exam was being held.

****

I walked out of the building where the exam was held eight hours later. I had a two-hour break from twelve to two, I used that time to nap and get a quick bite to eat and another coffee.

"Congratulations," a girl that took the exam with me said as we walked to the parking lot together.

"Nah, don't speak nothing but positivity into the universe, if you believe you passed it'll more than likely happen. If you believe you failed, then you'll just stress about the test results before you get them." She added when she saw the look on my face.

"Good lookin', congrats to you too." I told her.

She was five feet nothing and hella skinny, her breasts were huge and looked like they weighed more than the rest of her. I couldn't help but to stare at her breasts as they bounced while we were walking. If she was thick in all the right places and her ass was a tad bit bigger, I would've been on her.

"Thanks, and don't forget to keep thinking positive." She said right after I pushed the alarm to unlock my car.

"I look forward to seeing you in the courtroom." I told her as I stopped beside my car.

SOUL Publications

"See, now you get it," the woman said before she walked away.

"Don't forget to celebrate!" she yelled out while getting into her car. Her whole vibe screamed free spirit, and that she didn't give a fuck about what anybody thought of her.

Speaking of celebrating, Patch was meeting me at my hotel room with a few strippers. I told him I didn't want to celebrate until I got the results back, but he said bullshit he was bringing a few bitches through and we were going to get fucked up. When Patch got something in his mind it was no changing it. If I didn't cave in, he would've just been at my hotel room banging on the door; possibly getting me kicked out for disturbance. Plus, I needed something to relieve the pent-up stress.

I started my car and let it warm up, then reached for my phone in the glove box. I ignored all the texts from my Pops and went to compose a new text message to Patch. I told him I was about to pull out of the parking lot and head over to the hotel. He texted back saying he was already in the City and should be pulling up at the same time as me with the strippers.

I rubbed the top of my head and clinched my teeth as I ignored another call from my father, his call had interrupted me from reading the second message from Patch. I had told my Pops I would call him a few hours, after I got done taking the final part of the Bar Exam. But that nigga didn't give a damn about anything I had going on, unless it had to do with the streets. My father and I didn't get close when I started holding back on how smart I was and turned to the streets. He hated that I wanted to become a lawyer when I was a child and punched me in the chest every time, I said that shit. To him me becoming a lawyer was like me turning into a sellout. Truth was opposite, he thought anybody that didn't make a way out of the streets to help their city was stupid. In Truth's mind the only thing staying in the streets would do was lead to destruction, so he worked his ass off in sports for a scholarship, since my father wasn't willing to help him pay for school.

I was just shy of being fifteen when my brother died and already in community college. My mother had put me in concurrent enrollment which meant I was able to attend high school and the local community college at the same time.

Ring. Ring.

The sound of my Pops calling me again snapped me out of my thoughts. I hit ignore again then dropped my phone in the cup holder and pulled out of the parking lot.

"Yeah Pops?" I wasn't even two blocks away from the testing site and he was already calling me again. Shit, you would think he was a worried mother as much as he called my ass.

"What's this I hear about Patch throwing your ass a party at a hotel," all that nigga wanted to know was, why he wasn't invited.

"Man, it ain't even like that, just a few of our niggas coming through for a drink or two." I told him leaving some shit out so he wouldn't want to come through.

"And a few bitches, stop lying," my pops said. He was acting like he was pressed or some shit to hang with me and my niggas.

"Man, I don't know what the fuck Patch got going on when he leaves my room, but ain't no bitches gon be there."

"Man see that's why I didn't want you to go to school, you come back on some gay shit. You 'bouta hang in a hotel room full of niggas, with no women around. What part of the game is that?" If stuff didn't go my Pops way, he said shit that he thought would degrade a nigga until he got his way.

"Aye, the police behind me," I said then hung up the phone. It wasn't like I lied to him, there wasn't gone be any women there, but a few strippers were rolling through.

Honor

Thirty minutes later, I was pulling into the parking lot of the hotel. My Pops was still calling me back to back after I hung up in his face. So, I put his ass on the block list as soon as I parked close to the elevator of the hotel.

I texted Patch to let him know that I'd be waiting for him at the elevator on level one of the hotel parking garage before I got out of the car.

"See I told you I saw his ass up here the other day, girl," I heard a familiar voice say as I pulled my briefcase out the trunk of my car.

"Honor! Honor! Muthafucka you hear me!" Nicki yelled. She was someone I used to fuck a couple of years back. Back then I didn't give a damn that she was nothing I wanted in a woman. All I could focus on was that I was having sex with someone that was a few years older than me.

Nicki took my virginity when I was fourteen and she was around eighteen or nineteen at the time. I thought she was the love of my life, only to realize that she slept with anybody that tossed a few dollars at her. The entire time I thought we were in a relationship. The thing that made me walk away from her without looking back was on the day my uncle got arrested. I went to her house to be with the person I thought was in my corner, only to walk in on her fucking another nigga on her couch like it was nothing.

Nicki jumped off the couch when she saw me heading back out the door and ran behind me. She didn't reach me until I was already walking out of the front door, she tried to pull me back into the house by my shirt. I turned around and grabbed her right wrist and squeezed it until she let me go then pushed her back hard enough for her to stumble backwards.

That was the last day I saw her ass, because I had changed my number and left for college in another state a few months later. My mother had already applied for me to attend the University of Michigan and I didn't even know it. That night I came home after walking in on Nicki and with another nigga, my mother gave me my acceptance letter. I wasn't gonna go at first but then my moms, Patch, and uncle Rocky talked me into it. I left for school two months later and only visited a handful of times a year.

"Where the fuck you been at for the last four years?" Nicki asked when she walked up on me, as I walked towards the elevator. I didn't even answer her I just nodded my head in the direction of the parking lot exit, letting her ass know to take that noise back to where she came from.

The chick she was standing next to was the same girl that had delivered pizza to my room the night before. I thought I had recognized her from the hood, but when she didn't say anything, I thought the sleepless nights of studying had my eyes playing tricks on me.

"So, Honor, your bitch ass can't answer me?" Nicki screamed loud enough for the whole hotel to hear her.

"Oh, so you gone ignore me like you been ignoring our daughter for the past three years." I stopped in my tracks to face her.

"Man quit all that bullshit, you know damn well me, and you don't have no damn kids." I had to stop myself from snatching her dumb ass up.

"If she ain't your daughter, tell me why your father is paying me to take care of her and stay away from you?" She had her hands on her hips with a smirk on her face. She thought she was getting a point across, not realizing she told on herself.

"I'm not that desperate lil' nigga anymo'. Me and you both know damn well my father payin' your ass because it's a possibility the kid is his. Why else would the nigga want you to stay away from me, dummy?" The look on her face let me know she didn't know I found out, she was fucking my father behind my back. He knew I was having sex with her and even encouraged it. The nigga showed me what type of nigga he really was and that he'll do anything to make me feel less of a man.

"Damn bitch, you fucked the nigga daddy too, tho? You been sayin' she looks just like the nigga, neva said she look like him because he could be her brother." Her friend said without looking up from her phone, she was probably texting someone everything she heard.

"Nigga I told your ass just fuck these hoes not wife them, but you wanted to listen to your bitch-ass father instead of me. Shit, I know Truth ass told you to stay away from bitches like her too," Patch said as he walked up with the strippers following him.

"You must be fuckin' one of those lil bitches and that's why you are acting funny. You 'bouta get one of those lil hoes fucked up out here. And since we're mentioning Truth and all your family members I fucked, might as well add him to the list. I fucked Truth before I was fucking you or your limp dick daddy. I should've kept fuckin' him instead of you and your dad, then maybe you would take care of your blood. The way you takin' care of your brother's girl, hell you must be fucking with her ass;

shit probably started as soon as he got put in the ground."
Nicki bringing up my brother made the little bit of control I
had left leave my body. I dropped my briefcase before I
wrapped my hands around her throat. I slammed her against
the wall next to the elevator as I clenched my teeth.

"Bitch, if my brothers name ever comes out of your
mouth again, I will forget I don't hit women and beat your
ass to death."

With each word I said, I squeezed her neck harder.
Nicki was clawing into my hand and arm trying to get me
off her. I was so far gone that I couldn't feel her nails
tearing at my skin, almost drawing blood.

"They have cameras in here and she's not worth losing
your blessings. Let her go before you catch a domestic
violence charge. For what she said I wouldn't blame you if
you sliced the bitch neck right now but do that shit in the
hood where there's no cameras." One of the girls that came
with Patch said.

The stranger gently placed her hand on my arm to calm
me down. I squeezed Nicki's neck one last time, before I
loosened my grip. Nicki slid down the wall next to the
elevator. I reached over her to press the button and she
flinched.

23

"So that's the bit-" Nicki said in between deep breaths while gasping for air.

"Shut the hell up bitch and be glad I gave your dusty ass a chance to live by pulling him off you, hoe." Said the brown-skin stranger. The top of the stranger's hair was light green and the ends were a darker green.

"Bitch, I'mma beat your ass next time I see you." Nicki stressed in a hoarse voice. She reminded me of those people who talked with a tube in their throats on the tobacco commercials; she sounded like a robot.

"You've called me a bitch one too many times, so you don't have to wait! I'm bouta beat your ass. I saved your ass and you're still coming for me," Green hair stranger replied as she walked towards Nicki.

I had to catch her around the waist with my free hand to hold her back. Nicki was the type of bitch that start shit then play the victim. I also didn't want the green haired stranger to catch a charge over a broad like Nicki.

I held onto the girl, all the while Nicki was saying what she was gone do, but she was still on the ground.

"Lil' mama leave that scary ass girl alone and come on," Patch told green hair. The other girl he was with picked up my briefcase and handed it to me.

"Come on y'all let's go get this party started." Patch said, wrapping his arm around the girl who handed me the briefcase.

"You can let me go now, I am calm." Green hair said once the elevator dinged and I let her go. She playfully jumped at Nicki and just like I thought, Nicki flinched. The girl who came with Nicki was still on her phone and ignoring everybody. Nicki friend started all that shit and almost got Nicki killed.

"If I was a petty ass nigga, I would call Pizza Hut and tell them you gave my address out. You foul as fuck for this," I told Nicki's friend.

"Whateva, nigga. Nicki, let's go!" her friend yelled at her as the elevator door closed.

Damn, I regret fucking that bitch. I should've merked her dumb-ass.

Honor

Twenty minutes later me and Patch were sitting on the couch in the living room of my suite, while the ladies were in the bathroom. Patch pulled a bottle of Hennessy, Crown Apple and Gin out of his bag along with a sprite, ginger ale and cranberry for mixers.

"What the fuck is that Gin for?" I asked him as he pulled a speaker and red plastic cups out of his backpack too.

"Them bitches, they not getting none of this shit your ass tripping if you thought they were." Patch told me as he filled one of the red cups with Hennessy.

"You think your ass slick. I see you brought two of the skinniest strippers you could find, and it's supposed to be my celebration." I told him

"Man, nigga when you win I do too, this a celebration for the both of us. And my baby mama been on my ass 'bout settin' a good example for my son and all that other shit she be spittin'. So, I had to get me two bitches to make up for that naggin' shit a nigga been hearing, and you see I was generous and made sure to find you the thickest stripper they had." He told me as he shrugged his shoulders then turned on the speaker.

A little nigga from our hood named Lil' S music came from the speaker. He was talking about his patna that was killed and it reminded me of my brother, every word he spit made me reminisce about my brother. My head started involuntarily moving as I thought about what my life would have been like if he was still alive.

"Let me Bluetooth something from my phone to the speaker, we can't dance to that." One of the girls peeked around the door frame and said.

"Man, don't nobody wanna hear that shit your ass wanna play." Patch told her as she walked out of my room.

"We can't dance to this, we made a whole playlist and you fuckin' up our performance." She told Patch as she stood in front of him with her arms crossed and her lip poked out.

"It might not be, but y'all can take turns bouncing your asses on this dick to it." The girl bit her lip and side eyed Patch as he looked her up and down.

"You're tryna have a repeat of last month, I see." The other girl said as she walked out of the room and headed straight for Patch.

"We can have our own party in the room, just grab some drink and a few cups." Green hair girl said as she stood in the doorway separating the living room from my room. Her eyes went wide when she looked over and seen Patch and the other two girls kissing each other at the same time.

"There's another room over there," I told Patch as I grabbed the Hennessy and a few cups.

"Nah we good, I got everything we need in this room, condoms, drinks, and a couch. We good fam go in the room and have some fun." Patch knew I was a more private person, I didn't have a problem with us both getting lap dances in the same room. But what I wasn't gone go for, was my boy fucking on the same couch I was going to be getting a lap dance on. That's where a nigga drew the line at.

"Man, nigga we were supposed to be talkin' and celebrated not separated by closed doors." Patch said as I got up off the couch.

"Boy you be wildin' Patch we ain't teens anymore, I'm not 'bouta be passin' the blunt and shit." When me and Patch were teens before I left for college, we had no problem fucking in the same room. We'd be passing the blunt back and forth or the dirty sprite as some chicks rode us. Patch always found two friends that were willing to do anything with each other, we had some wild times.

"Man, you went off to school and came back a sucka." Patch said as I followed the green haired chick into my room.

"Nah, I just grew up," I said loud enough for him to hear before I shut the door behind me.

I sat in the chair next to the nightstand and sat the Hennessy and cups on it.

"You want some before you start?" I asked her because she looked nervous as she fumbled with her phone.

"Yeah, just a shot," I could hear the tremble in her voice.

"This your first time?" I asked her as I poured her a shot.

"Yeah doing a private show, and I only went on stage a handful of times. I just moved back out here and couldn't find another job and you know rent is due." She said as I handed her the shot. I watched as she took the shot to the head like it was nothing.

She clicked some buttons on her phone after handing me her empty cup. I let my eyes roam her body discreetly. Green hair had smooth light-brown skin without a blemish in sight. Whenever she blinked, I couldn't help but to be drawn into her onyx colored eyes surrounded by her long eyelashes. She looked as though she held a lot of secrets within those black almond shaped eyes. And at the same time, she looked and acted so innocent.

When *So Anxious* by Ginuwine started playing from her phone, she started to fumble with the knot of her short black silk robe. When her robe finally slid down, I could see a tattoo covering her body from her right shoulder down to her right hip. She started to move seductively to the music, winding her hips and letting her hands roam up and down her body.

Green hair was thick below but when it came to the top half, her breasts looked as though they were barely a C cup and she was a pack or two away from having a six-pack. She had an oval shaped face with slightly strong cheekbones and her big tooth at the top had a small chip in it. Her face was round and a little chunky, with a nose that was a tad bit wide. She had some full lips that had me picturing her wrapping them around my dick. The lower half of her was shaped like Raven-Symone when she played on That's so Raven, but green hair had thicker thighs and a rounder ass.

"So, you want that rough type lap dance or you want the seductive type?" she asked me as she stood in front of me and demonstrated both.

"Give me a lil of both," I told her.

Juvenile's Back That Azz Up started playing and she turned around. Her ass cheeks started to move to the beat one at a time and a nigga just sat back and enjoyed the show. When the music changed to Ginuwine's Pony, she dropped into a split then slowly bounced up and down as her ass cheeks continued to move one at a time.

I had to bite my bottom lip when she moved to her knees, so they were on either side of her and all I could do was picture her riding. All I could do was picture her bouncing up and down on my dick as I sucked the hell out of her titties.

"Aye, come here a second and try that on me." Even if I didn't get the pussy, I know I was going to be rubbing one out later to this scene.

"Keep your hands on the rail at all times no touching the ride." She said as she stood up and walked towards me. Green hair licked her lips when she looked down and seen my dick was semi hard through the slacks I had on. She turned around in front of me, bent down a bit and put one hand on each of my forearms as she sat in my lap with her back towards me.

I gripped the side of the chair as she bounced and grinded on my dick. She groaned and clutched my forearms as my dick started to twitch beneath her pussy. Her panties were so thin, I could feel the heat from her pussy engulfing my dick as her juices coated my slacks. Green hair got lost in pleasuring herself on my dick and forgot all about me. She was grinding her pussy onto my dick aggressively as her nails dug into my arm and her moans bounced off the walls over the music.

"Nah, bitch you can't do that shit. Fuck it, I need it." She said to herself. I wasn't even able to register it or blink my eyes, she surprised me when she pulled down my boxers and briefs in a quick motion.

Damn her ass needed it more than I did.

She moved her panties to the side then placed the tip of my dick at her opening. She wrapped her legs around me when I scooted up just a bit in the chair and laid back so only my shoulders were pressed on the back of the chair. She leaned forward and grabbed the back of the chair for leverage as her pussy slid down my dick inch by inch. Her breasts were pressed against my chest and I could feel her swollen nipples as they grazed up and down my chest as her pussy slid up and down my hard dick. She started moving her hips in a figure eight motion. I grabbed her right breast and sucked her nipple gently between my teeth. She grabbed my shoulders for support and started bouncing up and down on my dick like her pussy was starving and my dick was its last meal.

I pinched her right nipple between my thumb and pointer finger. I pulled my head slowly back until her nipple popped out of my mouth. I moved her legs from around me and sat them on either side on the chair. I grabbed her hips and drove deeper into her pussy. She leaned back and gripped my forearms as I pierced deeper and deeper into her as she moaned for more.

Bang. Bang.

"We out nigga I'mma hit you up later, I gotta go get PJ!" Patch yelled through the door an hour later.

"Shit! A'ight nigga." I stammered out as she gripped my dick with her pussy muscles then released.

"Keep celebrating 'cause nigga we made it." I heard Patch yell through the door then chuckle.

"They're gone now, you can speed back up." I didn't even notice I had stopped drilling into her hard after Patch knocked on the door until she spoke up.

Her wish was my command as I slightly stood up and penetrated her. I slammed into her harder and harder making her breasts bounce up and down. She reached between us and started massaging her clit. Somehow, she maneuvered her legs between the crooks of my arms causing my dick to ram deeper into her. I hammered my dick deeper and deeper inside of her trying to see just how loud I could make her scream. Her screams and the sounds of my balls smacking against her ass drowned out the music still playing on her phone.

I stroked into her deeper and harder until her pussy began to spasm around my dick. She clawed at me as she shut her eyes tight and her body shook. Green hair's pussy squeezed me as she came, and her juices gushed onto my dick the deeper I went. My body jolted as I emptied myself into her.

I collapsed back into the chair with her body still on top of mine. We both sat there catching our breaths until she placed her hands on my shoulders and slowly lifted her pussy from around my softening dick.

"You go shower while I check my phone to see if I have to work tonight. If not, we can go for round two before I go." She said as she headed to her phone.

I stood up, made my way to the bathroom and jumped into a hot shower. As I stood in the shower, I realized that I had just fucked a bitch I didn't know raw. Hella scenarios started playing in my head about all the clichés of sleeping with a stripper. From me getting an STD to her becoming a full-blown stalker for the dick.

"Damn it took you long enough," Green hair said as she stood in front of me in a different bra and some boy shorts. She had a drink in her hand as she sat on the bed with her legs crossed.

"You were in there so long I showered in the other bathroom, and went to the ice machine across the hall. I put some ice in your cup when I heard the water turn off a few minutes ago and poured you another drink." She said and motioned towards the drink on the nightstand.

I picked up my drink and sat next to her on the bed. We made small talk until we finished our drinks. I tossed my cup into the trash from the bed and she cheered me on when it fell into the trash.

"You okay?" she asked me when I grabbed my head and laid back.

"Yeah, I think all the shit I been doing these few months is catching up to me." I told her.

"Turn around and I'll massage you, you're looking hella tense over there." Green hair said as she got up and headed to her bag. I watched her rummage through her purse until she pulled out some lotion. I turned around onto my stomach and waited for the feel of her hands, but it never came because a nigga passed out from sleep deprivation, I think.

Patch

I pulled up in front of my baby mom's house thirty minutes after I left Honor's hotel room and dropped the strippers off. I sat for a moment, so I could fire up a blunt. Her ass swear she needed to save my soul for our son sake, whatever the hell that meant. A nigga had never heard no shit like that until I met her ass. We weren't even together, and she was tryna change a nigga to meet her standards. She started that nagging shit when my son was a few months old and I had to take a few puffs before walking into her house just to deal with her. I ain't fucked with nothing but strippers ever since I slipped up and nutted up in my baby moms.

I put my blunt out in the tray then sprayed the smoke odor spray. The weed smell went away quickly making my car smell like strawberries and mangos.

"Aye, my nigga Patch we over here," Truly son, Truvon, called out to me when I stepped out of my car.

I saw Truvon walking down the steps to Truly's house holding Pj's hand. My baby mama swore me and Truly were more than best friends. She thought she could just take my son next door to Truly place whenever I didn't call back in time for her.

"My mom said she gotta study." Truvon told me as he climbed into the back of my car after helping PJ in.

I popped my trunk and got Truvon's booster seat out. When I opened the backseat the lil nigga wasn't back there anymore, he had his lil ass in the front seat.

"Get your lil ass in the backseat and watch your motherfuckin' mouth." I told him and watched as he turned around and looked at me.

"I gotta tell you somethin' really quick, then I'll hop back there." Sometimes a nigga forgot his lil ass was a kid with how he talked to me. That was my bad though, when he was a youngin' I spoke to him like I was speaking to a nigga my age whenever Truly wasn't around; I spoke real shit to him about the streets.

"So, my mom said I can't tell you, but my Pa-Pa said that since you pay the bills you the man of our house. And he said to tell you or him stuff like this even if my mom says she gon' beat my motherfuckin' ass if I do.

"Yesterday this big nigga came through and was hitting my mama. I went and got the bat you gave me and whacked him in the head with it when he slipped on the floor. He told her if he finds out she told somebody, his niggas gone come shoot up our house with us in it. He said he'll be back, so she is making me stay with you." Truvon said then climbed into the backseat.

"Who was it, her boyfriend?" I asked him wondering if that punk ass nigga had got out of jail already.

"Nah it was another dude, but I don't know who he is," Truvon answered.

"Stay yo ass in the backseat, and make sure both of y'all are buckled up." I told him as I texted his mother and told her to bring her ass outside.

She texted back that she wasn't going nowhere with me. She came flying out of her house after I told her I was going to post a picture of her on Facebook to embarrass her ass. Truly easily got embarrassed about the smallest things and I knew the picture would get her. I was in the room when she had Truvon and I snapped a picture as he was coming out of her pussy. I always threatened to post the picture on throwback Thursdays. She did everything I wanted her to because of it.

"You's a dirty bastard Paevon." Truly climbed into the car slamming the door behind her. I chuckled as I pulled off while looking in the backseat to make sure the boys had on their seatbelts.

"Man, I should toss your ass out this car for using my government name," I told Truly.

She sometimes used my government name to get underneath my skin to make me mad. She knew I hated that shit. I didn't even want my baby mama to name my son that, but my moms and Truly ganged up on me and I gave in.

"Where are we going?" Truly asked.

"To my mama's house to drop the boys off."

"Oh, hell no, I'm not going with you to your moms she's worse than your ass." Truly had a black eye. She also had a cut on her bottom lip which was swollen.

"That's what your ass gets for trying to hide that shit from me," I replied.

"Didn't I tell your lil' ass not to tell him nothing?" Truly turned around in her seat and asked Truvon.

"Pa-Pa said Patch is the man of the house and I have to tell him everything." Truvon told her because of what Truly's grandpa told him.

"That doesn't even make sense, Patch doesn't live with us, so he is not the man of our house."

"He pays our bills though, so Pa-Pa said he is," Truvon said.

"Who the hell told you he pays our bills?" Truly asked him.

"Pa-Pa did and I'm tellin' him you got mad at me for telling Patch." Truvon said and I knew his lil ass was telling the truth. I knew he was gone snitch to Truly grandpa because he snitched on me and Truly to my mom.

"Man nigga, quit fuckin' cussin' at him. That's why his ass just got in trouble at school for talking grown." I told Truly as we turned onto the street my mother lived on.

"You cuss way more than me in front of him and your mama do too, it's y'all fault not mine." Truly said as she rolled her eyes at me.

"Roll them motherfuckas at me again and I'mma knock those bitches outta your head." I told her. Truly and my mother only lived a few minutes away from each other, so we arrived at my mother's house two minutes later.

"Aye grandma, some man punched my mama in the eye and lip! Patch got robbed by two strippers who he wasn't supposed to be with, and PJ's mama sleeping with a married man at her church!" Truvon yelled out my window when he saw my mama sitting on the porch with her friends.

"Man, I should hire his ass as a lookout, he sees and hear everything, ole ear hustlin' ass lil motherfucker." I mumbled underneath my breath. I've never wanted to strangle a lil kid more than his ass at the moment.

"I told your stupid ass to stop fuckin' with those bitches and get with Gertie's daughter, Tasha. Since you and Truly keep acting stupid like y'all not in love and shit. Truly, I made pepper spray and sent you home with two socks filled with rocks the other day; for your ass to use, not for them to collect dust while you get your ass whooped." My mama said as she walked to the car.

"It was Tasha hoe ass and her friend that robbed me, while you tryna get at me mama." I told her.

"Oh, that bitch robbed you? Don't worry I'mma fuck her mama up then rob both of their dumb asses!" My mama said as she made her way over to Truly side of the car.

"What nigga I gotta fuck up behind you now, Truly?" my mama asked as she opened the door.

"Don't worry 'bout that moms I'mma handle that, just get the kids and take them to my house." I told her.

"Give me some money so I can take them to the Chuck E Cheese since your retarded baby mama be depriving my grand-baby of fun." My mama said as she leaned over Truly with her hand out. I reached in my pocket and handed her a knot of money.

"Aye yo Grams, that means we got enough money to buy me those headphones and a new Playstation 4, huh? Oh shit, we're winning." Truvon said as he unbuckled PJ out of his car seat. Truvon was a sore loser and had already broke two PS4's and countless controllers. Me and Truly told him the only way he can get a new one is if he saved up his allowance.

"Your ass not bouta get nothing after I beat the shit out of you for cussin'." Truly said to her son.

"Yep, we bouta go ball out, let's go," my mother told the boys. She helped them out of my car then they walked to hers.

"I apologize for blaming you for Truvon getting in trouble at school. Your mother is the reason he keeps getting into trouble, the next time the school calls I'm sending her ass up there." Truly said as my mom and the boys pulled off.

"Fuck all that, tell me what the fuck happened to your face." I demanded.

"Truvon's father have been writing me, demanding that I take Truvon up there to visit him, but I ignore it. He sent one of his cousins to my house to make me take Truvon to visit him. His cousin did this to my face. He said he'll come back to my house if I don't follow their orders." Truly folded her arms and huffed—she was pissed off.

Truvon's father was this nigga from the other side that played football at our high school. He raped Truly, and nobody wanted to do anything about it, everyone pretended like they didn't know what that nigga did. They started fucking with Truly at school by calling her names. So, I caught up with that nigga one night and beat the hell out of him to the point where I thought he was dead, so I left him in a ditch. After everyone in school heard he was found half dead in a ditch they stopped fucking with Truly. Two months later Truly found out she was pregnant and since she wanted to keep the kid of her rapist, her parents kicked her out of the house. She went to live with her mom's parents. Truly's story reminded me of my mother's, so I vowed to make sure she was straight.

When my mom was at her friend's house, her friend's older brother raped her, and no one believed my mother. When I was born nine months later, everyone close to her tried to sweep it under the rug, including her parents. Since my mother didn't have anyone to help her or tell her it wasn't her fault, she put all the blame on herself. And after I was born, she got addicted to drugs; I had to take care of myself most of the time. My mother was what some called a functioning fiend. Don't get me wrong, she was a damn good mother when she was on drugs. But she would disappear for days when she was high out of her mind; she didn't want me to see her like that. On those days and sometimes weeks a nigga had to fend for himself.

"Who are you telling my business to?" I snapped out of my thoughts and looked over at Truly who was staring at the text I received on my phone. We were still sitting in front of my mother's house as I texted someone from her son's father old neighborhood. I wanted to know who all was related to that nigga before I made a move.

"Man sit the fuck back and let me do me!" I barked.

"This him?" I asked, showing her a picture of some fat nigga, my homeboy sent me.

"Yeah that's him," she replied. I sent my homeboy a text back asking for the address.

"You still got those steel toe boots from that stupid ass job you use to work at?" I asked her as I pulled out of the driveway.

"Oh, you mean the boots I spent hella money on? Only for your ass to come to my job on the first day. Then you proceeded to fuck it up by saying things that shouldn't have come out of your ratchet mouth. Yep, I remember that day like it was yesterday. I was only working for four hours before they fired me. Let's not forget the other job you got me fired from, too, for yoking up my boss." Truly was getting hyped from bringing up old shit.

"Your ass acting like you needed those jobs. You should be focused on finishing school. We need that business degree, so you can wash my dirty money. I'm trying to get out of the game and you're the only person I trust enough to help me. Besides, I only came to your jobs because you were complaining about your bosses acting racist. I was looking out for you.

"I can't help but to be happy that you care a lot about me. But I just don't like how you're planning what I'mma do with my degree without me." She kicked her feet up on my dash like it was her car.

"Man, this not your fucking ride, put your damn feet down."

"You treat me like I'm a child." She said as we pulled into her driveway.

"Man shut the hell up and go change into those boots. Put on a longer shirt too." I called out to her after she got out of the whip.

While I was waiting on Truly to come back out, a car pulled up into my baby mama's driveway. I watched as she climbed out of the car with her hair all over the place. She looked as though she had been crying and when our eyes locked, she put her head down.

"Don't be ashamed now for sleeping with a married man!" I shouted out the window. She ran into the house and the car quickly backed out of the driveway.

"See that's where Truvon get it it from." Truly said when she got back into the car. I started backing out of the driveway while she still had the door opened.

"Asshole," Truly said and whacked me in the arm after she closed the door.

Twenty minutes later...

It was eight o'clock at night when we pulled up on the nigga who fucked up Truly's face. He was standing on the corner in his cousin's neighborhood serving a fiend. I waited until he was by himself before I stepped out the whip. I took the safety off my gun then shot the nigga in the leg and motioned for Truly to get out of the car.

"Go kick that nigga's face in! He put his hands on you in front of Tru. Your ass betta think about that and go fuck him up or I'mma fuck your ass up!" I told her.

He was on the ground crying and moaning like a little bitch, his screams had gathered a small crowd.

"Y'all just gone let a nigga from the other side come over here and shoot me?" he yelled.

"Man, your bitch ass ain't even from here and you already know you violated when you did that shit for your fam. You know we ain't with that shit. But just like that ain't our business this ain't either." Said a girl in the crowd who was dressed like a dude.

I didn't stop Truly from stomping the nigga until he passed out. We rushed to my car after we heard sirens. We didn't have to worry about anybody snitching because niggas who worked for me had a strong pull in the neighborhood. The mall didn't close til' nine so I took Truly to her favorite store, Nordstroms. Truly was spoiled and I think that was why I treated her like a kid sometimes. She had clothes in her closet with the tags still on.

"How do you like this?" Truly asked while I was sitting in the dressing room. I was texting this broad I met the other night at the liquor store. She wasn't talking about much other than sucking my dick in the back seat of my Mercedes.

"PATCH!" Truly spat.

"Oh, my bad. I don't know about that. It's too short. What you tryna show pussy and ass?" She rolled her eyes and I chuckled because she already knew how I felt about her wearing tight clothes.

I know I shouldn't look at her like this, but her ass is looking juicy.

I caught a slight erection and cursed myself from looking at my homie that way, but I couldn't ignore her beauty. Truly was dark-skinned, with almond shaped eyes and full lips. She reminded me of Lauryn Hill in her younger days. Her wavy sew-in reached to her succulent backside. At twenty-three years old which is one year younger than me; she had a face of an eighteen-year-old. Truly was perfect and I don't think she realized it. She was a solid size twelve and her round breasts sat perfectly without a bra. My erection hardened while imagining if her nipples looked like Hershey kisses.

"Help me take this off please," she said with an attitude. I placed my phone inside my pocket before I walked into the dressing room with her. I towered over her short body, she was around five-foot-three and I was six-foot-two.

"Don't break the zipper," she scolded.

"Man, I got this. You shouldn't have put this tight dress on anyway. I think you're trying to date a nigga or sumthin." Truly sucked her teeth as I unzipped her dress. She turned around and faced me, staring into my eyes.

"What you want?"

"You're too handsome to be a jackass," she said.

"Just hurry up because the store is ready to close," I replied. I leaned in and pecked her lips. It wasn't nothing sexual. We have been doing it for years. Sometimes I thought she wanted more even though I couldn't give her more. She had been through a lot and niggas like me wasn't good to women. I left out the dressing room and went to the register to pay for the items she wanted.

I need a break from her before I end up fucking the shit out of her.

Honor

When I opened my eyes the next morning the sun was shining through the blinds. It felt like someone crushed my skull with a hammer. I tried to roll out of the bed to close the blinds, but I realized something was holding me back.

"Aye yo lil' mama get up and untie a nigga," I told the girl who was lying on my arm. I lifted the crook of my arm to shake the chick, but she wasn't moving. I didn't plan on getting that drunk the night before, but things happen.

I looked in the mirror in front of me and could see that my arms were handcuffed to the bottom of the bedpost, where the bedpost and the top of the mattress met. My legs were tied to the bedpost at the foot of the bed just the same. I would have been completely naked if it wasn't for my boxers. I also noticed the lipstick kisses on my body.

"Oh shit!" I realized the chick next to me wasn't responding because she was dead.

"Fuck, they gon think I somehow killed this bitch last night, ain't no way them motherfuckas gon' believe I don't remember what happened and woke up next to a dead woman." I said to myself as I tried to remember the night before. All I know was I somehow left my room last night and ended up cuffed to a bed.

A lump formed in my throat as I realized that even if I didn't kill her, some of my actions from the night before could've. I had done a lot of shit in my life but killing a woman was never part of it.

"Whoever you are I'm callin' the police on you, I seen what you did to that poor girl last night. I had to chain you up before you could do the same to me." A woman's voice called, and it reminded me of the intercoms in school.

I closed my eyes and said, "tell me what I did!"

This can't be real. There is no way in hell this is happening to me! All my life I have been lucky.

"You were fuckin' her brains out, then she screamed out that your dick was even better than your brother and father's. The next thing I know you was choking the girl and I was yelling for you to stop. You wouldn't let go until she stopped breathing. I hit you over the head with a lamp then cuffed you to the bed and placed her next to you, so you could see what you did when you woke up." The voice echoed throughout the room.

This gotta be a prank. Ain't no way this shit is playing out like I'm in a thriller movie.

"The only person you could be is that green haired girl Patch invited to my party. Just call Patch instead of the police and let me go. Tell him to come through and clean something up for me. I'll pay you." I told her, hoping she believed me. I was planning on killing her too because I couldn't leave a witness behind.

"Guess again. I hired that girl with the green hair. She's dead right next to you. That's what she looks like without her wig and makeup. I'm not letting you go. I believe people should pay for their crimes, not with money." The chick said nonchalantly, like my freedom wasn't already on the line.

"At least let me use the bathroom before they get here, I promise I won't move until you are out of the room."

"I guess I can do that." The voice said, and I got a little anxious, to get out of the house before the police arrived.

The room went pitch black, the sun had somehow been blocked from shining light through the blinds. The door squeaked just a bit and that was the only indication I had that someone else entered the room.

I felt something cold hit my legs, then a finger drawing circles around my right hand.

"Bitch give me the fucking key!" I yelled at her.

">53

53

Dear, Honor & Haven   Marqua'lla

"Fuck," I felt something prick me in the arm and seconds later I began fading out.

"I'll see you when you wake back up," was the last thing I heard.

"Son you gotta prove that you can be on my team before I let you on." My Father told me as we walked into the warehouse him and my uncle used. At fourteen years old, my father had me doing criminal stuff.

"What the fuck is he doing here Richy?" my uncle Rocky asked my father when he saw us walk in.

"He wanted to join the team, so he gotta get on just like any of these other lil' niggas." My pops answered.

"Richy I get that man, but he 'bouta accomplish sumthin' we neva could which is graduating. I want him to have a better life than us and have a chance of getting out of here without a record." Rocky said.

"Man, this my son, worry about your own kids whenever you have them but quit speakin' on mine. But if you wanna do this, we can do this back and forth shit without all these lil' niggas around." my father said.

I took a step away from my pops when I seen my uncle reaching behind his back, because even I knew what my dad said was fucked up. My uncle had a temper and certain shit a nigga just couldn't say to him, brother or not. My uncle's wife and kids were killed when the nigga she was cheating with decided if he couldn't have her nor could my uncle. A dude broke into their house and shot them up before setting them on fire. The man who was responsible for their death anonymously paid a someone to give my uncle a note explaining why he had to do it.

"Speak on my kids again nigga and the next bullet won't miss. The only reason you're still breathing right now is because you're my brother." He said after the bullet he fired from his gun whizzed past my dad's head.

"What's your name and why did you come alone when you know we work in teams of two here?" my father asked Patch.

"I don't trust niggas. I can move by myself and still get everything done," Patch replied.

"You're with my nephew since you two are the youngest ones and least expected to move hustle the corners. Just remember, time is money and not a day late. I will be expecting my profit tomorrow night. Do y'all lil' niggas understand? Don't fuck up!" Rock barked. Basically, my uncle wasn't giving me an easy pass because I was family.

"Don't worry nigga we 'bouta make every nigga that came before or after us look like bitches." Patch said and that was how we became like brothers.

Bang. Bang.

I woke up from my dream when someone pounded on the door.

"POLICE!" a woman shouted. The door was kicked in and someone barged into the room. I tried to escape but only my right hand was free from the cuffs. I frantically tried to free my left hand but it wouldn't budge. A sadistic laugh echoed throughout the pitch-black room as I heard footsteps coming closer towards me.

"Freeze, get down on the ground! Nah I'm just playin'. It's time to wake up and eat," the woman said.

"Psssst, eat your food. I'll clean you up soon if you big a good boy." I realized it was the bitch from the intercom.

"Where's the police?" I asked her.

"They'll be here as soon as I give them the right address and that could be today, tomorrow or the next day." She said before she walked out of the room and closed the door behind her. As soon as the door closed the lights came back on.

My eyes burned from the brightness; it felt as though I was looking at the sun for first time in a while. I blinked my eyes for a few seconds until they adjusted to the light. The dead body was on the floor; it must've fallen when I tried to escape. There was a urinal pan on the nightstand next to me along with a half loaf of bread and a glass of water. Next to the glass of water was a small tube of hand sanitizer. I used the sanitizer before I ate the stale bread. It felt as though I hadn't eaten anything in weeks due to the massive hangover, and the drugs she gave me to knock me out.

My throat felt raw as I swallowed but no matter how bad it hurt, I couldn't stop myself from devouring it. I picked up the tall glass of water seconds later and choked as I guzzled it down.

Fuck! She must've put something in the water. I'm ready to black out again...

Two days later...

The smell of what could be described as rotten metallic woke me. It took a minute for my eyes to adjust to the room, yet, again. My eyes roamed the room looking for the cause of the smell. There was blood splatter on the wall next to the door. A body of a white police officer was sprawled out on the floor with a bullet in his head next to the dead woman.

"Fuck, this crazy bitch killed a police officer too. She's trying to frame me," I panicked.

"I didn't kill the officer, you did," she said.

"How the hell did I kill him when you had me chained to the bed?"

"You don't remember waking up to the officer uncuffing you from the bed? You thought he was ready to take you to jail so you took his gun out of the holster and shot him. Maybe you don't remember it because you were still delirious from the pills I crushed into your water."

"You passed back out with the gun still in your hand," she added after a long pause.

How did I miss the gun lying next to me?

"I'll pay you whatever you want to make this go away. I can't believe I'm being held against my will by a bitch," I spat.

"First off, I don't know who the hell you're callin a bitch, but you got the right one! I will cause hell in your life nigga. And you nor one of your niggas can ever give me back what I need!" she screamed. A sliver of light came through a tiny crack in the blackout curtains, and I was able to get a good look at the bodies and blood.

"I don't know who the fuck you think you're talking to, but you better lower your motherfuckin' voice and come uncuff a nigga. You got me in this bed practically naked and chained to the bed, just admit that you had the dick a few years back and wanted more, you didn't have to kidnap me to get it."

"Man, nobody fucked you years ago so get over yourself. You really think too highly of yourself and you the one who needs to watch who the fuck you are playing with. I got you on tape committing not one but two murders so you're at my mercy now." She said with a bit of cockiness in her voice. Her arrogance would've been sexy if I wasn't chained to a bed.

"As you see I got no problem choking a bitch the fuck out for disrespecting me. I'mma get out of these cuffs one way or another and when I do that's your life. So, if you don't wanna end up like the bitch on the floor, come let me out of these motherfuckin' cuffs." I told her to get a reaction out of her.

"You talk a lot of shit for a nigga that can't move an inch, but maybe that's because you have killed two people," she said.

"Me and you both know I can't kill mannequins, dummy! Bitch, gig is up so let me go! You got me good I'll admit but game over!"

From the sliver of light, I was able to see that the bodies on the ground weren't real. The cotton in the cop's neck was exposed. She must've bought the fake bodies from a high-end costume store.

"I guess the jig is up, those are two mannequins with fake blood on the walls." She only admitted to it because the cat was out the bag.

"What's that smell since it's not dead bodies in here?" I asked her because the smell was getting stronger than a motherfucker.

"I planted catfish guts under the nightstand," she answered between her giggles.

"So, tell me why you put on this ruse and kidnapped a nigga?" I asked her.

"It's not something you did per say, but you kind of have something to do with it," she answered.

"So, you kidnapped me for something one of my patnas did to you?" Patch was the only nigga I was cool with. So, if she wasn't holding me hostage because of something I did it had to be because of that nigga,

"Nah it's not because of your patna. You'll find out soon, but I'm letting you go."

"I've been told I'm a good listener and that I give good advice. Just tell me what's going on and I can help you out of it, before you get in too deep and can't come out intact. Is somebody helping you or are you doing this alone?" I asked her. I figured I could talk her out of it if she was alone, but if it was a nigga behind it then I might be dead soon.

"Nope. I'm not tellin' you anything else. I already told you too much, night night."

A minute later, she walked into the room with a hoodie on her head and a bandana around her face to keep her identity hidden. She jammed a needle into my arm and stood over me until I'd fallen back to sleep.

Honor

I was on the verge of waking up, but I wasn't quite there yet, my eyes were still closed, and my mind was still in a dream like state. There was a lump in my throat, the kind that made you feel as though you had to throw-up. At that moment I would do anything for a glass of water.

When I finally opened my eyes, I was surrounded by nothing but darkness. My hands moved around feeling for anything to indicate where she put me. My right hand bumped against something. I brought it to my eyes and from the feel of it I realized it was a lighter.

"What the fuck! Let me out of here you crazy bitch." I yelled out. I flicked the lighter and realized I was locked in a coffin. I hated being locked in confined spaces, especially when it was dark and hard to breathe. When I was a kid, I had nightmares of being buried alive—my nightmare was coming true. Me and Truth had seen a horror film with someone being buried alive when we were kids; our father thought that would discipline us. He locked me and Truth up in a small shed in the back of an abandoned house years ago. I was only six at the time and Truth was ten. We were in there for ten minutes, but it felt longer because of the rats. I could still smell the pungent smell of their feces and hear them scurrying around us. A pregnant rat crawled up Truth's pants and he peed himself.

"Aye ma, let me out of this shit." I kicked and punched at the coffin and nothing budged. I hyperventilated as my throat was closing up on me. The more I gasped for air the angrier I got, wanting to kill that bitch. I could hear what sounded like rats scurrying around me.

Calm the fuck down and control yourself, stop acting like a little bitch.

I thought of ways to get out as I tried to control my breathing but it didn't work. My heart started to race, and I could feel myself about to pass out, when suddenly, I felt like I was free falling. My body jerked, and my eyes popped open.

I laid there trying to process what happened as I looked around me.

Fuck that was just a dream.

I opened my eyes and realized I was still chained to the bed.

I had blocked the bad memories of my childhood which was easily triggered by certain smells and images.

****

Dear, Honor & Haven   Marqua'lla

The sun was beaming through the window and caused instant pain behind my eyes. I wanted to shield my eyes from the sun, but I was still in handcuffs.

"There's water and bread next to you," the woman said from somewhere outside of the room.

"How I'mma reach it with my hands cuffed to the bed?"

"I cleaned you up after I got those awful rats out of the box and changed your cuffs to longer ones while you were sleeping. You must be a ninja turtle. You had an interesting conversation with a rat while you were dreaming. You were screaming like a little girl," she teased.

She only made the chain longer for my left hand, so I could reach the dresser. For a second, I contemplated drinking the water since she drugged me the last time. I knew I couldn't hold out and had to take a chance because of how dry my throat was.

My throat ached every time the water traveled down it. I didn't care because I felt dehydrated. Every swallow of water made the nauseous feeling disappear for a few seconds at a time.

I had already beat the odds with the first and second glass of water and I didn't want to push it with a third nor the bread.

"You know my niggas gon' be causing hell in the Bay lookin' for me." I told her trying to appeal to a side of her I didn't even know if she had, a cautious side.

"Patch started gettin' suspicious of me answerin' his texts with just emojis. I had to look through y'all texts to mimic how you respond to him. He thinks you're on vacation with some chick and won't be back for a few weeks."

"This crazy girl you went to college with has been texting your ass too. She's pissed you haven't responded to her since a few months before graduation. She goes from texting you to DMing you on all your social media sites. She also sent you videos of her fingering herself. I see why you haven't responded to her. Her pussy look like it was pulverized by a meat grinder and she was extra dry. And don't get me started on her extra porn moaning. I was tempted to send her a video of my own pussy in a text saying, 'this what a real one looks like.' She's straight trash."

"I wouldn't do that if I was you, her ass like bitches too. If she sees your pussy she might start stalking your ass too. Nah never-mind, send it to her," I chuckled.

"Your dad was texting you too with his crazy and annoying perverted ass. I photoshopped a random girl in the pictures I take of you to send to him. Your dad asked for more, he even asked for a video of you fucking the girl with shots of her pussy. He said you was a gay bitch boy since you didn't send it to him. If I was you, I wouldn't trust him as far as I could throw him. He seems like the type to probably fuck your bitch in your bed, then smile in your face."

She wasn't as deranged as I thought she was because she was able to see through my dad's bullshit through a couple of texts.

"Shit, a lot of people don't see it, just the ones he fucked over."

I don't know why I was opening up to her after all the things she did to me, but she was surprisingly easy to talk to.

"At least you realized it before it was too late, unlike some of us. I found my parents dead in our home when I was in high school," she replied.

Before I could respond she quickly added in, "Let's stop talking about that and watch a movie." She said, and the movie Reasonable Doubt started playing seconds later. I could tell she was watching the movie in another room, because every so often I heard the echo from the TV in the distance.

Sleep took over me when the next movie came on. Whatever sleeping pills she gave me must've still been in my system.

Honor

A couple of hours later I woke up when I heard a door close.

She must've just left out.

I went to move my left hand and noticed I was no longer cuffed to the bed. I got out of the bed and my legs buckled underneath. The bed post I grabbed kept me from falling on the floor. I regain my footing, there was no telling how long I was in that bed. I headed to the door once I regained the strength back in my legs. The lever to the door wouldn't budge. I tried to yank it open with both hands to pull it open but that didn't work. She must've had someone use a special kind of door.

The door was steel with four nice size square glass panels. I walked over to the nightstand closer to me, picked it up then rammed it into the glass, but the glass wouldn't break.

My arms started to burn, and I couldn't hold the nightstand any longer. I sat the nightstand down and realized the door knob was electric. To unlock the door a fingerprint or code was needed.

With my back against the door, I thoroughly scanned the room to see what else I could use. There was a tray with two plates of turkey wings, rice, cornbread and greens on the nightstand along with two sodas and a water. A towel and a washcloth were on the edge of the bed along with a change of clothes.

My eyes landed on the window and the sun was shining through. I couldn't see a latch or anything else that could've helped me pull the window open. I tried to break the window with the nightstand. The glass wouldn't break because it was hard plastic, the same as the door panel.

I gave up trying to escape. When I sat on the edge of the bed I reached over and picked up a plate of food. After I was finished, I washed it down with a grape soda then I grabbed my things for the shower.

Thirty minutes later, I walked out of the bathroom with my towel wrapped around me. I sat on the edge of the bed and picked up my last plate and ate it. I got dressed after polishing off my plate; Crazy Girl knew how to cook if she made the food. Hell, the food was so good I might kidnap her ass and make her cook for me for the rest of her life.

I searched the room and bathroom for anything that could give me information I could use to escape. All I could find were two intercoms in the room and a few cameras in the bathroom and bedroom. I tried to pull the cameras out of the wall, but they were encased inside of something that I couldn't break. I had to hand it to the psycho, she had thought of everything. The way she thought and planned everything, had me curious about what else she had in store for me.

"I'll let you go but first I'mma need a little show of Simon says," she said.

"I'll do whateva I need to to get out of here," I told her.

"Reach into your pants slowly and pull out your dick then squeeze the tip," she replied. I did what she said.

"Now close your eyes and picture my hand curling around the middle of your dick. You groan as the feel of my hot breath cascade around your tip. You're anticipating feeling my waiting mouth engulfing around the top of your dick as my tongue flicks against your tip." I begin to move my hand sliding it up and down my dick to the sound of her voice.

"The feel of my mouth sucking the top of your dick as my tongue swirls around it enticing the precum out of you. You moan out my name as my hand bumps over your raised edge. I can feel your fist tighten around my hair as you deep throat me." I stroked my meat to the sound of her voice. Her soft and low voice alone was enough to make me bust a nut.

"The pants of our breaths could be heard as the pleasure your feeling starts at your toes. You're on the edge of no return as the feeling travel through your body. Suddenly, I stop pleasing you," she said.

"Looks like you're staying her because Simon never 'said', and you still moved," she laughed.

This bitch played me. I'll get her back soon.

I laid back on the bed and closed my eyes. I ignored her as she teased me through the intercom. When she stopped talking to me, I closed my eyes and went to sleep.

Patch

I sat in the car smoking a blunt waiting for Truly to come out of the jail from visiting Honor's uncle Rocko. Rocko had something to tell me but I didn't do that visiting shit so Truly went in for me. Honor was supposed to visit him with her, but I hadn't seen him since three days ago at his hotel room. He was supposed to be out of town or something, but knowing him he was probably laid up with a chick.

I hadn't worked for Richy and Rocko since Honor went off to school all those years back. When Honor left, he gave me half of the money he saved, and I combined that with my money. Rocko put in a word for me to his connect and after that me and Honor were in business for ourselves. Richy thought he could intimidate people into giving him their money because he was going broke.

One of my workers called my burner phone and I answered on the second ring.

"Wassup?" I answered.

"We need to up that situation." He was letting me know that my traps needed to re-up.

"A'ight I got you when I come back that way, but it should be something to hold you over in the back room." I told him letting him know I had left a lil bit of extra there and he could find it in the back room until I came through.

"After you get that straight go make the pick-ups for a nigga and meet me at the spot." I told him then hung up as Truly walked out the visiting building.

Twenty minutes later me and Truly was down the street from the jail at this food truck she followed on Instagram. I think she only said 'yes' to the visit, so I could take her to the food truck. We ordered our burgers then sat down at one of the picnic tables while waiting for our order. The person who took our order brought our food and drinks out a couple of minutes later.

"I told you they were good," Truly said when we were both halfway done with our food.

"So, you gon' continue ignorin' my calls and act like we didn't fuck." This chick I didn't even remember meeting let alone fucking walked up to me and said. The chick was pretty in the face but she was a little busted. She was light-skinned with blonde jumbo braids. She was almost dressed like a hooker.

Dear, Honor & Haven   Marqua'lla

"Man gon' somewhere with that bullshit, I don't know you." I waved her off.

"You niggas not gon' keep playin' me," the girl said then slapped the hell out of me.

I didn't have time to react because Truly jumped up and punched her in her nose.

"Get up and put your hands on him again so I can knock you the fuck out!" Truly yelled in her face.

"I'm not 'bouta fight a bitch over a dick everybody else practically had," the girl said.

Truly kicked the girl in the stomach and was about to punch her again but I snatched her up. I rushed her to my car before the police came. It was something about the way she defended me that turned me on. Soon as we got inside my car, I pulled her face to mine and slipped my tongue between her lips for the first time. She moaned and wrapped her arms around my neck as I reached under her shirt and cupped her breast. I deepened the kiss as my hand massaged and tweaked her nipples. I pulled away from her breasts and reached for her pants.

"Stop I can't do this with you because I'mma be the only one hurt once we cross that line. You think it's okay for you to fuck whoever you want to and for me to be locked in the house waiting on you. I have these feelings for you that won't go away, and you keep brushing them to the side. Just take me home and after that don't call me or come by my house, I don't want to see you again." Truly said.

I never wanted her to be hurt by something I did so it was time for me to give her a little bit of space.

Honor

Two hours later...

I woke up and realized my arms and feet were chained to the bed again. I yanked on either side of me trying to get the cuffs to break. I winced in pain when the cuffs scraped my skin.

"You keep betraying me after I give you a little freedom, you tried to escape and didn't play my game right. Stop fighting this and deal with it like a man. I'm not trying to hurt you, hell I let you shower and made you a home cooked meal. Now you're back to eating bread and sponge baths." She said over the intercom. Sure enough there was bread and water on the nightstand next to me.

"So, you're telling me, if somebody kidnapped you and chained you to a bed in an unfamiliar house, you would just eat instead of trying to escape?" I said while looking directly into the camera in front of me.

"That's the problem with men, they try to use brute force all the time when it's uncalled for. I would've built an emotional relationship with my kidnapper to play off their emotions. There are so many potential ways to get out of this, you have to make the best of it. You're going to kill yourself from doing all of this dumb shit, knowing there is no way out unless I let you out," she told me.

"That's how that Stockholm syndrome stuff happens. Pretending to care for the kidnapper, only to find yourself actually caring about the muthafucka. Bitch, you lost yah damn mind!"

"You don't know shit! If you did, we wouldn't be having this conversation. Call me a bitch again and I'll put something in your food that'll put you to sleep forever! This is your last warning!" she screamed through the intercom.

"Sounds like somebody don't like to be proven wrong. And you'd never know what you'd do until you find yourself in my shoes. Stop pretending like this shit is cool and you don't know how I'm feeling. I want to go home!" I barked.

"Watch a movie while I go visit my brother's grave," she replied with sadness in her voice. I was beginning to think my kidnapper was using me to get over something she had been through. She was a complete stranger, but judging by actions she wasn't the type of chick to go around kidnapping niggas.

After the first thirty minutes of the movie I eagerly drunk the water and ate the bread hoping she had drugged one or the other, but she didn't. The movie was called, *Hostel.* The gore scenes were making my stomach turn. The kidnapper was warning me through the movie, basically telling me she'll torture me if I don't obey her. When the movie ended almost two hours later, it started over.

Great! The bitch didn't put anything in my bread because she wants me to keep watching this bullshit ass movie.

It was the only time where I wished the crazy chick had drugged me.

****

I closed my eyes when the movie went off for the third time and tried to fall asleep, but I started to hear sniffling.

"I'm so sorry brah I should've stayed with you that night no matter what you said," I heard her sob. Hearing her cry out for her brother touched me a little. For a second, I wanted to hold her in my arms as she cried but then I remember she was my kidnapper and snapped out of it.

"What the fuck!" I heard her yell out. She must've realized she had pushed the intercom on accident and I heard her crying.

A couple minutes later she stormed into the room she was holding me in. She had something wrapped around her head so only her mouth and eyes were showing other than that she was completely naked.

"So, you like to listen to private moments," she said as she walked over to the bed. I watched as she climbed on the bed then crawled towards me. Before I knew it, she was straddling my face and her pussy was pressed firmly against my lips.

"Eat me you know you're hungry," she said. She spread her juicy pussy lips then grinded her pussy against my lips. I kept my mouth closed as she got her rocks off until a slither of her juices seeped into my mouth. When I tasted her essence all I knew was that I wanted more.

I opened my mouth and swiped my tongue around her clit a few times before I sucked it into my mouth as she moaned in ecstasy.

"Shit, right there, don't move!" she moaned out while grinding against my tongue as I pressed it firmly against her clit.

"Yes, I'm coming!" she shouted as her juices gushed on my tongue.

My dick started to get hard as I pictured it being my dick sliding up and down her clit as she came instead of my tongue. I had to shake that shit off because I shouldn't be getting hard for someone holding me against my will.

"You're not going to return the favor?" I asked her as she climbed off my face after I sucked up everything, she had to offer me. Like I was a bear and she was my honey.

"No, that's your punishment for listening to shit you had no business listening to. You could've told me the intercom was on." She said then walked out of the room.

I had to be fucked in the head to want to fuck her but just thinking about the way she tastes gets me hard. I wanted to ram my dick so deep in her that she could feel me inside of her every time she took a step for days.

I had to stop thinking like that, I shouldn't want to know what she feels like when her pussy is wrapped around my dick.

Patch

Two days later...

Me giving Truly space only lasted for one night. I gave her that night to cool down then I picked her up the next morning from my mother house and took her to this African American Museum she had been wanting to go to. She was still acting like she wasn't fucking with me anymore after we left the museum. But I had one of the niggas that worked for me find that bitch and made her apologize to Truly. I still don't know who the bitch was every female I fucked knew not to approach me when I was with Truly. If I had lost Truly behind that bitch bullshit her family would've woke up to her head being their new yard ornament.

"Order a pizza we gonna be here for an hour or two," I told Truly when the two women who usually helped us count the money didn't call back after thirty minutes.

"I'll order us a pizza from that new place down the street and have them deliver one to your mother's house," Truly said. I appreciated my mother watching the kids because she didn't have to. Just like I appreciated Truly helping a nigga out whenever I needed.

When Truly moved in with me and my mom, she made sure to contribute somehow to the house since she didn't have any money. She made sure the house was clean and we had a meal on the table for breakfast, lunch and dinner. Then when Truvon was old enough to go to daycare she started selling weed to my weed clients while I was out peddling other shit.

She only did that for a few months though, because when I started working for Rocko and Richy a few months after she moved in; a nigga started really making money. I made her stop, but she didn't want to feel as though I was just giving her handouts, so she started counting my money. She even started calculating how much money I needed to set aside to reup for my side hustle. And when we started making more money, we hired on these twin girls that lived down from my mom building to help us count.

"Next week I'mma need you to take Tru for me for a few nights, my summer finals are the following week, I need to study." Truly looked up at me when I walked into the living room from the basement with another duffle bag of money we needed to count.

"Tell me what that nigga Rocko was talkin' 'bout." I told her as we pulled out the money counting machines, rubber bands and notepads to keep track. I didn't get to hear it from her the other day because of that shit that happened after the visit.

"That somebody need to start lookin' for Honor, because ain't nobody heard from his ass since that night you seen him. And no matter what he has always answered y'all calls, even if he didn't answer his dad. Rock thinks something is wrong. Shit, I told him that Honor just finished getting more than one degree, he just took the bar as well, so give him at least a few weeks before y'all start going crazy looking for him. If I was him, I wouldn't even be texting y'all back. Everyone would be on DND for two months.

"He said that no matter what Richy says, he's not fucking with him on the business tip anymore. So 'ice that nigga out' and he'll let you know why when he gets out. He found a guard in there that will be bringing the stuff in for him. He needs you to find someone to meet the dude and do the hand off.'"

"Shit, I wish your ass would put me on DND for two minutes let alone two months. I'll track your ass down like last time and embarrass you, try that shit on me at your own risk." Truly ignored me and kept talking like she didn't hear what a nigga was spitting.

"Oh, and he said since Richy is no longer with him he wants you and Honor on his team as equal partners. He needs y'all to watch out for his blocks until he gets out. He got a dude on his team named Eagle that he wants you to contact. He said just supply that nigga Eagle, and Eagle would do the rest. If Eagle has a problem, then he wants you and Honor's team to back him up. Rock already contacted the connect and told him you and Honor would be picking up his shipment. So, you got a few weeks to make Honor come back to the real world." She said just as someone knocked on the door.

We both took out our guns and looked at each other before I went to answer it. "It's just the pizza." I opened the door, signed the receipt and took the pizza, Pepsi and the Sprite he had. I handed her the Sprite and sat the large pizza in the middle of the table. Half the pizza was plain cheese like she liked, and the other half had pepperoni, sausage, olives and mushrooms on it just like I liked it.

"Hey, I was saving my last two slices for later." Truly said ten minutes later, when she noticed I had polished off her last two as well.

"I'll grab you a peach cobbler from Mrs. Daliah," I told her, then asked her a few things about how school was going before we got back to counting the money.

We were almost through with the count two hours later, when my phone started to ring back to back.

"You need to get to the block before your mama get locked up." I heard the lil nigga that called me yesterday say, with Truvon's voice in the background cheering my mother on.

"I'll be there in five, just in case the police come make sure you swoop up my kids if I'm not there." As soon as he said he would, I hung up the phone. I didn't even have to say anything to Truly, she had already slipped her coat and shoes back on and was waiting at the door for me by the time I got mines on. We locked up then headed to my mom's without saying a word, as we sped to my mother's house.

We were a block away from my mother's, coming up the hill when I noticed a crowd surrounding a front porch. I didn't realize it was my mom's place until we got to the top of the hill.

It looked like the whole hood was either inside of her gate or in one of the gates next door.

I could hear, "get her Granny!" being screamed over the noise of the crowd in Truvon and PJ's voices when I stepped out of the car.

Dear, Honor & Haven   Marqua'lla

My mother was sitting on top of Gertie catching her breath as Gertie struggled to get up. Gertie's breasts and the top half of her shoulder and arms were pinned to the ground because of the way my mother sat on her. Truvon was standing at my mother's back with a bat in his hands with PJ standing slightly behind him.

"That lil nigga funny. Every time somebody looked like they were getting too close to your mama that lil nigga started swinging that bat telling them to stay away from his granny." One of the homeless niggas that use to be the man to see when I was younger said from the crowd.

"Shit nah, the funny part was when that bitch Tasha tried to jump in it and his lil ass hit her in the leg with the bat, now that shit took me out." Someone else in the crowd that I couldn't see said.

"Whoever recorded this shit better delete it out of their phones, let me see my mama or kids face on social media. I'mma be at your house and have someone record me beating the shit out of your ass then upload it. And if I don't feel like it, I'mma just shoot your ass and send the video of you takin' your last breath to your family." I saw hella niggas and bitches in the crowd deleting shit out of their phones.

"Ma you know damn well you're on probation and shouldn't be out here like this. You should've just dragged her ass in the house and beat the shit out of her in there." Truly finally said when she snatched the bat out of Truvon's hand.

"We were in the house and I was fuckin' this bitch up, then she ran outside, and I had to catch her. The bitch tried to steal from me," moms reached down and slapped Gertie.

"She tried to steal the Playstation me and Granny just bought and Granny's money. She snatched the controller out of PJ's hand when I was in the bathroom and Granny was in the kitchen. I caught her and told Granny." Truvon said and PJ was standing next to him nodding his head.

"It's your fault that my mother was tryna steal from yours, Patch. Those girls you had jump me told me I had to pay you double and come work for you for free or my mama would find my body hanging in front of her door. I told my mother and she said she'd help me get the money," Tasha said as she stood from her position on the ground.

"Your bad for reaching into cookie jars that don't belong to your ass," I told her.

"What, I ain't reach into no damn cookie jars, I was in your pockets." Tasha's eyebrows raised.

"You know like that saying, who stole the cookies from the cookie jar, he was saying you shouldn't have stolen his money out of his pocket." Truly rolled her eyes at Tasha and mumbled idiot at her. "You need to stop fucking with bitches that can't comprehend simple facts." I ignored Truly. I didn't want to tell her that was the reason why I fucked with bitches like Tasha.

"Ma get your ass up, you 'bouta make the block hot and we're going to lose money because of that shit. Go lock up your house because you are staying a few days at my house." I told my mother as I helped her up.

I had to get my mom's away from her house for a few days, or she would be fighting Gertie's ass every time she seen her. The last time someone stole from my mom she ended up in jail for a few weeks. The woman finally called the police on her after she beat the woman's ass every day for a week straight. She made the block hot and I ended up losing money and I couldn't have that.

"Truly take the kids to the car," I told her as some of the crowd started to leave. Gertie was still on the ground and Tasha was struggling to help her big ass up.

"Anybody seen the twins?" I asked the crowd of people that was still around. I was looking for the two girls that was supposed to be counting my money.

88

Dear, Honor & Haven   Marqua'lla

"My sisters' went to the hospital because our parents overdosed." The twins lil sister stepped out of the crowd with the twin's kids on either side of her. She couldn't have been more than twelve and had four kids with her.

"Here take this money and get y'all something to eat and tell your sisters to hit me when they get back." The girl took the money from me, stuffed it in her pocket and grab the two youngest kids hands and walked off with the oldest two following behind her.

My mom came out of the house twenty minutes later with a duffle bag of stuff she didn't need. She had clothes at my house in one of the spare rooms, her ass always had to be extra. I dropped her, Truly and the kids off at my house then headed back to the spot and counted the rest of the money. While I was counting the money, I sent a text to a few key players from my hood, to meet me at the spot I always held my meetings at. It was just an old abandoned building on the docks that looked like it would cave in at any moment.

****

I walked out of the bathroom in my room with a towel wrapped around me after I got out of the shower. I went straight home and showered after I left the warehouse after the meeting. I dismissed what Truly said earlier and called a meeting with a few of my workers and Rocko's. The meeting was to let them know whoever found Honor's location and gave it to me would get a few racks.

"Truly, why the fuck you over there eating in my bed, I told your ass not to do that shit." I said to her as I snatched the ice cream sandwich out of her hand, then tossed it out my open window before I closed it.

"Hey, it was still half of the ice cream left and that was my reward from all the studyin' I did today, bastard. You eat in my bed all the time and I don't snatch your plate and throw it out the window." Truly protested.

"I eat in your bed because your ass does, and you know that shit. We eat in your bed not mines and you know it." She rolled her eyes and scowled at me as I walked towards her.

"Hand me the blunt you rolled for a nigga," Truly always had a blunt rolled for me when I came home to her house or mine.

Truly handed me the blunt and I handed her the lotion. I lit the blunt and started smoking as Truly stood on my bed and put lotion on my body, as I stood on her side of my bed with my back turned to her. I smoked as her smooth hands rubbed lotion all over my body. I opened my towel when she got to the lower part of my body and she got down off the bed, so she could get a nigga legs and shit.

"Here get your two puffs in," I handed her the blunt after she got finished rubbing the lotion into my body. I walked over to my side of the bed and slid in naked. Truly got into the bed on her side after she hit her two puffs then put it out.

"Roll over here and quit playin', you know I can't sleep without your head on my chest girl." I told her as I grabbed my shirt, she had on and tried to yank her towards me.

"Nope, I'm still mad 'bout my ice cream and sleep how you sleep when you're here or somewhere else without me." Truly told me.

"Man quit playin', when you're not sleepin' on me a nigga don't sleep, I just be out workin' until I stop by your spot and crash on you for a few hours." I told her the truth and it made her smile. She scooted closer to me and laid her head on my chest. My hand went to her bare ass under my shirt. I palmed it as I always did before we went to sleep.

Honor

For the past two weeks I hadn't seen the woman who kidnapped me. I tried to stay up to catch her when she came into my room to leave food for me but I never could.

I didn't realize I had fallen asleep until I felt something cold trailing down my stomach. When I opened my eyes all I could make out was that the crazy chick was straddling me naked and something was in her hand. The only light in the room was a small flicker from two candles on the nightstand to the left of me. When my eyes adjusted, I could see there was a knife in her hand from her shadow that bounced off the wall.

I could feel the tip of the knife press deeper into my stomach and it halted my breathing. She started to draw imaginary pictures on my stomach with the knife, at times the knife against my skin felt like it did when I shaved my beard.

"F. U. C. K. M. E. fuck me," looking at the shadow on the wall, I could see her using her wrist to turn the knife to draw. She used her wrist to guide the tip of the knife against my stomach to spell out some words. I called off each letter of the words she spelled that I could make out.

"That's all you had to say," she said, then dropped the knife on the ground. She reached for one of the candles on the nightstand, picked it up and brought it close to her lips before she blew it out.

I laid there with her just straddling me for a lil minute, when all of a sudden something hot splashed against my stomach.

"Ssssss," I hissed when another splash of a hot sensation coated my stomach, then an enticing smell hit my nostrils.

"What the hell is your crazy ass trying to do to me." I questioned her as I jerked the lower part of my body trying to jolt her off me. She didn't move though, all she did was press her thighs into my legs and let another drop land on my stomach.

"Dropping candle oil on you." she said like it was no big deal to drop hot candle wax on me.

"Did you enjoy that movie Hostel two weeks ago?" she asked.

"Why would you even think I enjoyed that movie?" I asked her as I looked up at her shadowy figure. I could only see a tattoo near her right breast when she leaned in.

"Because it shows just how good you got it here and how it could really be." She answered as she let another bit of the candle wax me.

"Shit, girl quit dropping that candle wax on me before you burn me to death." I didn't want to give her the satisfaction of knowing that after the slight burning sensation a spark of pleasure shot through my body. The smell was doing something to me as well.

"I'm not using a regular candle, this is a massage candle that's made for this, it has a low melting point. What you feel is oil dropping on your skin not wax. Just sit back and relax," I swear this chick was like Dr. Jekyll and Mr. Hyde.

I felt my dick start to jump beneath her with every drop of hot wax, oil or whatever it was. I watched as she leaned over and sat the candle on the nightstand then she reached underneath her and pulled my boxers down. She placed one of her hands on my stomach and used the other to spread her pussy lips over my dick. My dick was hard and pressed against my stomach I was eager to see what she was going to do next.

My dick twitched making her let out a needy whimper, as she slowly started to grind her wet pussy against my dick. She threw her head back and guided her clit up and down my throbbing dick. Her moist clit slid up to the tip of my dick as her nails dug into my stomach. She began to move her hips, gently rocking forward and back, causing her slick pussy to slide along the hard edge of my dick. The slickness of her juices and the feel of her slit rubbing over my engorged dick head made me groan.

"Fuck," I grunted.

"Umm," she moaned out as she kept grinding her needy pussy faster and faster against my tip. She kept her hips moving, coating my dick with her slippery core. My dick was getting harder and harder from the feel of her hot wet pussy massaging it.

"Oh damn, I'm 'bouta come, I need to feel you inside of me." She moaned out as she gripped my dick, lifted and placed me inside of her. She pressed down gently, and my dick nuzzled in the mouth of her pussy. Her pussy clamped down around me and her juices gushed down my dick. The sounds she was making and the feel of her pussy gripping my dick was taking a nigga over the edge.

"This is another part of your punishment for not being grateful about not being handcuffed." The chick told me as she hopped off my dick seconds after she came. I was still rock hard and needed relief, and she was acting like she wasn't going to give it to me. I can't believe I fell for her shit again.

"Come on just put the tip in your mouth for a second, hell I'll even settle for you just squeezing the tip with your hand a few times. I'm almost there," I told her, she laughed and walked towards the door. I looked over at her and noticed she pressed a one on the keypad before she covered my view of the keypad with her body.

A few minutes later, moans and the sound of a bed squeaking invaded my head. I looked up to see a porn on the tv with a thick brown chick getting her pussy pounded. Damn, her ass knew how to torture a nigga; my dick was aching to the point of pain.

"What the hell did I do to you to deserve this?" I asked her, and I knew she could hear the frustration in my voice.

"Who said you did anything to me?"

"If this is what you do to someone who hasn't done nothing to you, I don't want to see how you do someone who has." She could make a living out of torturing the truth out of men.

Thirty minutes later...

Suddenly, the porn was shut off and the room was pitch black, except for the light coming from the candle.

"Today was my brother's birthday," her voice had a slight stutter in it. I remembered she said she was going to visit her brother's grave weeks ago.

"Tell me about the best memory you had with your brother." I knew what it was like to miss a sibling on their birthday.

"In elementary school my mom grounded me for some reason and it was my best friends sleepover that weekend. My brother helped me sneak out of the house and into the window of my best friend. I had so much fun that night. Maybe because of the fear of getting caught or maybe it was just fun. He came the next morning before my parent's or my friend's parents could get up and snuck me back home."

"The first thing I remember my brother doing was coming to my classroom. When I started school, I started to get teased by the other kids because I was smart. When I told the class that I wanted to be a lawyer on my first day the boys in class started to call me a snitch and a nerd. I told my brother and he came to my class the next day pretending like I forgot my lunch. He stared the ringleader down and the teasing stopped for the rest of kindergarten and first grade.

"In the fourth the teasing started again, and Truth no longer went to the same school as me, so I had to start fighting back. Just picture a nerdy kid with glasses that had a slight stutter trying to fight back, and that was me. At first, I was losing fights back to back, but the more I stuck up for myself the more I learned to duck their punches and throw harder ones. It wasn't until my stutter went away and I started fighting back that people stopped picking on me." Truth was only four-years older than me, but he always made sure I was straight. I hadn't thought about that day he came to my class in a while.

"Let's watch a movie with some action, it's getting too emotional for me. Let's just say we both had the best older brother and leave it at that." She said then turned the TV back on.

"Have you seen Sleepless yet?" she asked.

"Nah, I ain't seen none of the movies that came out this year," I told her. She started the movie then quickly paused it, and it made me think it was just another one of the games she was playing with me. A few minutes later she walked into the room with two long bags of kettle corn and a grocery bag with sodas in it.

"I decided to come watch the movie with you, since you shared something real personal about yourself with me." She gave me one of the bags of kettle corn and handed me two cokes. The girl laid on the bed, so her feet were pointed towards my head.

"This is going too slow and it's not enough action for me," she said. It wasn't action for me either. Instead of watching the movie, I had been watching her ass and how it slightly moved every time she moved.

"Let's just watch a few episodes of The Originals again," I told her just as an alarm on her phone started to go off.

"I have to go get ready for work, but I'll put it on for you," she said. I watched her out of the corner of my eyes trying to see if I could catch another number in the code, but I couldn't because she used her fingerprint to open it that time.

I never thought I'd watch a show like The Originals. The more I watched the show with her the more I realized that The Originals was just like everyday life, only with paranormal creatures. The show had the witches, vampires, and werewolves beefing with each other over territory just like the hood. Somebody was always hating because another person made moves, they wish they could.

I must've nodded off for a few seconds, because I slowly woke up to an enjoyable feeling of pleasure at the tip of my dick. When I opened my eyes all I could see was her pussy hovering over my face. She had released my right hand while I was sleep, so I used it to spread her pussy lips and swiped her slit with my tongue. She moaned around the tip of my dick and her body shuddered a bit.

I hovered the tip of my tongue over her clit, so she could feel the presence of it there but not feel the pleasure of it. I wanted her to beg for me to use my tongue. She was playing with my dick by barely swiping her tongue over it, and I needed her to know two could play that game. My tongue slid just to the edge of her clit and added a bit of pressure before releasing. She tried to hump my tongue but all she got was air when she bucked her hips.

"Come on, stop being stingy with the tongue," she groaned.

"When you stop being stingy with that mouth my tongue will bless your pussy." I wasn't even finished with what I was saying, before I felt her lips stretch around my dick and one of her hands squeeze the base.

Her juices gushed onto my tongue as I applied pressure with the tip of my tongue. I sucked her clit into my mouth and flicked my tongue against it.

"Fuck!" I grunted when my dick hit the back of her throat. Her hand gripped the base of my dick with just the right amount of pressure then released. As her moans of pleasure sent vibrations around the tip of my dick, that caused me to pump into her hot waiting mouth. The more I sucked and licked her pussy, the more she sucked the skin off my dick.

"Shit," I said when she started to massage my balls with her free hand.

My finger entered her a little bit and she squirmed around it jamming her pussy against my tongue. She started humping my tongue in a frenzy as I stuck another finger into her. The faster I pumped my fingers into her, the faster she sucked my huge shaft. She bobbed her head up and down my dick, and every time she reached the tip her tongue slid across it. I pulled my mouth away from her pussy and groaned. My nut exploded into her mouth and she didn't stop sucking until she swallowed everything, I gave her.

I pulled my fingers out of her and wrapped my arm around her waist. I wasted no time finding her opening with my tongue, it brushed against her entrance before I shoved it inside of her. My tongue twirled and flicked around until I found her G-spot. She started to whimper and bounce her pussy aggressively on my tongue. Her pussy clamped around my tongue as her body shuddered and her pussy nectar streamed onto my tongue as she came.

She thought I was done when I extracted my tongue from her pussy. She tried to climb off me, but my hand around her waist prevented her from doing so. I sucked her clit into my mouth and twirled my tongue as she screamed like someone was killing her.

"Oh my, stop, it's too sensitive," she moaned out as she shuddered another orgasm into my mouth. I didn't listen to nothing she said. I closed my eyes and continued my feast on her pussy. She kept trying to lift off me, but I ignored her as my tongue slid up and down her clit. I could feel her nails digging into my skin as I sucked her clit into my mouth. I finally let her go after the third climax.

She fell onto the bed next to me and curled up into the fetal position. Her head landed on my left hand that was still chained to the bed.

"I bet you won't try to torture a nigga again by not letting him come." I heard her whimper a bit when I said that, but that was all I got from her right before I heard her snoring. I went back to sleep with a satisfied grin on my face.

When I woke up a couple of hours later, I noticed that she was still lying next to me. With the sun shining through the window I could see her tattoos. I could finally see her green hair in the light and knew it was the stripper that Patch had hired.

She had a tattoo of a panther crouching in a hood jungle that went from her ass to the start of her knee. In each one of the eyes of the panther was a bloody crime scene that I couldn't make out.

****

"I can't tell nobody 'bout what happened to me in this house. I swear niggas gonna start testin' me again if they find out the shit that I let happen to me here," I said. I couldn't believe how my body kept responding to her and how I felt when she was near me.

"Oh well if they do just show them why they shouldn't be testin' you. Even I know you're the quiet type that observes first and has everybody thinkin' you're weak,. When someone pisses you off, there's no stoppin' you and how far you'll go. It shocks people and you love it when they're shocked for underestimating you." I was so caught up in scanning her body and voicing my thoughts that I didn't even notice she had woken up and was looking at me.

"How do you know?" I asked her.

"Because I do my research. I'm sort of like you, but I have the craziest thoughts and I have to hold myself back from acting on them. It takes me awhile to react to something someone did to me, unless they did it to my family. But like you, when I react it shocks the fuck out of people." She told me.

"What made you want to become a lawyer?" she asked out of the blue.

I told her about how I always thought they had a lot of power and money when I was a kid. Plus, when I was younger people told me, I should be a lawyer since I had an answer for everything and could make people see my point. I didn't know what I wanted to be, so I just went with it.

"When I was a kid, I wanted to be a labor and delivery nurse for the longest. But after some harsh life experiences and finding myself, I quickly realized that wasn't for me anymore. I want to still help people, just in a different way. I haven't found it yet, but I know I want to be in a role where I support someone else." Green hair said, got up then walked out of the room naked.

Patch

One week later...

I was on the corner next to a freeway entrance and exit, watching two homeless dudes argue over a corner close to the freeway. I had pulled over when I saw the two of them arguing over who's corner it was. A nigga had already polished off his chicken from my mom's watching those two fools.

"This my block, I been here for two days and I'm not givin' up my lucrative spot to nobody." The dirtiest one said as he took a big ass sniff.

"Well young buck this been my spot for years. I was just at that new shelter for those days. You can ask anybody and they'll tell you this crazy Billy spot." He said then pulled out a lighter. Crazy Billy wasn't lyin' though, that's been his spot for years. I could remember getting off the freeway when I was a kid and Billy being on that corner. I took out my blunt, so I could get high and crack up at those two niggas fighting about a corner they beg for money on.

I stopped paying attention to the two fools in front of me, because I could see a car with two niggas in it pulling up behind me. I watched as Richy got out of the passenger side of the car and walked towards mine. I reached under my seat, picked up my gun and placed it on my lap.

"Patch you're a hard man to find," Richy said.

"Nah, I'm not, for niggas that I want to find me," I told him.

"I just need to know where my money and son at," Richy said as he leaned into the car.

"Nigga I don't owe you shit, get your ass away from my car before you catch some problems you can't get out of." I told him.

"Nah, you already got problems you don't want to catch," Richy said.

"I smoke trees and sucka ass niggas." I told him as I lifted my blunt, then my gun. I didn't point my gun at him 'cause when and if I do, that meant I was killing that nigga right then and there.

"You don't know what you just started," Richy said.

"I never start shit I just finish it, just come at me when you ready to take your last breath." I watched as he mugged me, then turned around and headed for his car. Richy was one of those pussy ass niggas and I wish he would come at me. I kept my eyes trained on him until he pulled off and got on the freeway.

"Help! Help!" I heard a nigga yelling a few seconds later and looked back over to the two homeless dudes. Crazy Billy had set the other dude jacket he was wearing, and his belongings on fire. When that nigga told him, his name had crazy in it, he should've walked away. I pulled off after I seen that shit. I didn't want to get caught up with the police.

Honor

Two weeks later…

We quickly got into a routine with one another, even though three of my limbs were still cuffed to the bed. Green hair would come into the room every morning with coffee and breakfast for me. I learned that she didn't like breakfast, and only had black coffee in the morning. So, while I ate my breakfast, she would take pictures of me as she drunk her coffee. She would then post pictures of me on my social media before she gave me a sponge bath.

After spending an hour or two with me she would leave me in the room alone with the remote control. When she came back, we had dinner, then fucked and sucked each other's brains out for most of the night.

I asked her name almost every day, but she wouldn't give it up. We talked about everything we both had never discussed with anyone else before, but she would never give me her name.

"Did you ever change your mind about becoming a lawyer?" she asked after reading something on her phone.

"Yeah, I went back and forth with wanting to be a lawyer over the years. Truth made me feel as though I would turn out like my father, if I didn't become a lawyer and stay out of the streets. I just wanted my law degree to be able to help my uncle get out of jail, and I know Patch is gonna need a lawyer sooner or later. I got my business degree as well, because I want to open my own businesses. I can't work for another nigga. A nigga needs to be his own boss," I answered her.

"Why can't they both be what you wanted and who you are?" she asked.

"What?" I didn't understand what she was trying to say.

"Who is to say that ruling the streets while starting a business, and helping out your uncle or Patch with their cases are not all you. You're caught up in your Pops pulling you one way and your brother another. Have you ever thought maybe you're both sides, the side of both your brother and father's expectations?

"It seems like they only accepted a part of you, and it made you feel as though that both halves couldn't be you. I hate when people think you can't have more than one side and personality to you. You could want to rule the streets and save people at the same time. Hell, I'm the nicest person some people meet, and I'm the craziest bitch other's meet. Which side somebody gets depends on who they are to me and, or what they have done to me." Green hair's words spoke to me.

"Yeah when I was younger, I thought that one or the other had to be me. I didn't realize that they both could be me until I got to college, and figured out I couldn't live under my father's idea of me nor my brother's. So, I double majored, in Law and I got a Business degree as well."

"Wait, that just sparked so many questions I have for you. First off, how old are you and how the hell did you double major in law and business?" the look on her face when she asked me those questions let me know she thought I was crazy.

"I'll be twenty-two in a few weeks, I skipped some grades and did concurrent enrollment. I had an AA in business and a high school diploma by the time I turned sixteen. I was still in school when I started running the streets with Patch, working for my father and uncle." I told her the rest of the story of how and why I left for college.

"I still don't get how you was able to do all that. I love school, but that shit was and is hard." Green hair said.

"I been told I might be a genius and I got photographic memory," I told her.

"You know what, you can go now," she said as she stood from the bed and started to release the cuffs.

"Wait, what's the problem?" I don't know why but the feel of the room suddenly changed.

"Nothing, it's just time for you to go, I can't keep you here forever like this." She said as she stood in front of me with a sad look on her face, letting me know she didn't want it to end either.

"After I told you all this shit, ain't no tapping out of whatever this shit is, ever." I told her as I grabbed her and pulled her down on top of me.

She leaned down and kissed me with everything she had. I slipped my tongue into her mouth as I rolled over, so I was on top of her. She withered beneath me as I bit the side of her neck lightly, in just the right spot. The way she moaned as I kissed and bit that spot made my dick hard as a brick.

"Do that again," she grunted out as the tip of my dick touched her clit. I reached between us with one hand, and moved my dick up and down her slick entrance. She wrapped her legs around me and I could feel the heat from her pussy surround my dick. I kissed my way down to her breasts then sucked her nipple into my mouth, causing her hips to buck under me. The wetness of her pussy rained onto my dick as she bucked her hips, so her clit was grazing the tip of my dick repeatedly.

"I need you now," she whined as she reached between us and guided me to her opening. Her eyes locked on mine as I entered her.

"Fuck me with everything you got," she groaned and lifted her hips and spread her legs wide. I pulled all the way out of her until only my tip was still at her opening, then surged deep inside of her. Her nails dug into my shoulders while I drilled in and out of her. I rammed my dick so deep in her that she struggled to catch her breath. Her mouth remained open as she gasped for each breath, I felt her hand on my stomach as she tried to push me back. She stopped trying to push me out a few seconds later, when I didn't budge.

"Shit girl," I grunted when she squeezed her walls around me and started fucking me back. I had to let her know who was in charge. I pinned her legs down and slid all of me into her and hammered against her spot. She moaned louder and louder as her head thrashed from side to side The sounds of my dick slamming into her gushing pussy made a nigga even harder than he already was. She screamed as her body shook beneath me as she came. I rolled over, so she was on top of me, she laid her head on my chest as she panted for breath.

I grabbed her hips as she lifted her head and placed the palms of her hands on my stomach. She started to bounce on my dick like she was searching for something, and I knew exactly what it was. When she had a big orgasm and I kept fucking her, she had mini ones until she had another big one.

"Fuck," I groaned and tightened my hands around her waist as her pussy gripped my dick and spasmed. She threw her head back in ecstasy as I held her still and pumped into her viciously. I gritted my teeth as my dick twitched inside of her, and everything I had surged to the tip of my dick. My hands locked onto her waist as my nut rushed inside of her.

She collapsed on top of me and every so often, I felt her pussy twitch and her body shuddered a bit. My dick started to grow inside of her as her pussy continued to clench and unclench around me. I held her against me and rolled over, so she was on her back, she wrapped her legs around me.

I surged inside of her with a deep and slow grind. I bit my bottom lip as her pussy clamped down around me and she gripped the sheets. I knew she was almost there. I slammed into her deeper and harder with my twitching dick. My dick jerked inside of her while she clenched her walls. She whimpered my name as we both climaxed. I knew my body was heavy against hers, but I couldn't help but to lean my weight against her. She kissed the side of my face and wrapped her arms around me.

"Come on let's go hop in the shower," I said as I slipped out of her and got off the bed.

"I can't move," she told me.

"Don't worry ma, I got you." I told her as I picked her up and carried her to the shower. I kept her in my arms as I started our shower. I had to hold her up in the shower and wash the both of us off. She wasn't kidding when she said she couldn't move.

I carried her back to bed and laid her in the center of it. I looked from her lying in bed to the open door for a few seconds before I climbed into bed with her. If asked two weeks ago if I would have left at my first opportunity, I wouldn't have hesitated to say, hell yes. But now I just couldn't leave her. I didn't know if it was the pussy or the fact that I was able to tell her shit I couldn't tell anyone else.

Honor

Two Days Later...

I laid there admiring the body of the woman I think I was falling for.

"I got something we should use your skills on today." I looked over at her and told her.

"Hell nah, my pussy and jaws sore from last night and this mornin'." She lifted on her elbows and turned her head toward me and said. She continued to stare at me and licked her lips as if she was rethinking her answer.

"We can do that but that's not what I was talkin' 'bout, filthy mind." She rolled her eyes at me.

"You like this filthy mind tho, and all the things it thinks up to do to you." Green hair wasn't lyin'.

"Shut your ass up and go get dressed." I told her and smacked her on the thigh.

"You stupid motherfucks," she said and slapped me in the chest then rolled out of bed. I chuckled as I got out of bed and followed her into the bathroom. I tried to push her ass out of the way before she turned on the water, but she beat me to it. She liked the water scorching hot and I couldn't get with that. My whole back was tatted up and none of my tattoos ever felt like when blazing hot water hit my back.

"Reach over there and turn the cold water on a lil bit more." I told her when I climbed behind her in the shower and a little bit of the water splashed on my arm.

"You gone tell me where we're going?" she asked me, ignoring what I said, as she handed me the towel to wash off her back.

"To get me a new phone then after that it's a surprise." I told her.

I got my phone back from her the other day and went to the bathroom to piss. A nigga texted Patch, but my phone fell into the toilet with my piss before I could respond to him. I left that shit in there and didn't try to fish it out, until the toilet was flushed and I had on those thick ass cleaning gloves.

"It's a couple of phone places in the Plaza down the street from here, we can go there. But 'bout that other shit, my ass don't like surprises so if you don't tell me then I'm not going." She shrugged her shoulders. I mushed her in the back of the head a bit, causing the front part of her hair to get slightly wet.

"Stupid bastard," she screeched and jumped out of the shower making the hot water hit my body.

"Awl fuck!" I screamed and tried to hurry up and get the water down to warm after she flushed the toilet. I could hear her chuckling her little ass off from the other room.

"I'm beating your ass for that shit." I told her as I stood under the cool water and let it sooth my skin.

"Whatever, you betta hurry up because the phone store close early on Sundays and it's gettin' late." I heard her call out. I washed up quickly then got out of the shower.

We were both dressed thirty minutes later and heading out to her car. I snatched the keys out of her hand when she locked up and headed to the driver side.

"Who said you could drive my car?" she questioned.

"Myself," was my only reply as I got into her dark blue Honda coupe and started it.

"You need a damn bigger car. What the fuck is this shit." I had been driving for only five minutes and had already started to feel claustrophobic.

"You're only some inches taller than me and you're bulky, but not that damn bulky that you can't fit in my car. I love your confidence though," she rolled her eyes me.

"Man, you ain't gon' keep comin' for my height like that and shit like I'm not that nigga." I slammed on the brakes causing the top of her body to jerk forward then slam into the seat.

"Bastard," she yelled when a bit of the water splashed out of the bottle, and on her pants.

I pulled into the plaza and parked in the only open space in front of my phone carrier. She tossed my wallet at me before I got out of the car. It took over thirty minutes for me to get a new phone, because I had to get a new everything. They were talking about if I used my insurance then they'll have to mail me a new phone, and a nigga didn't have time for that. I just paid for an upgrade. I was back home, so it was time to get rid of that old number with my school area code anyway.

"Here's your new phone sir, just give me a second and I'll call it to make sure it works." I didn't have time for that, so I texted Patch instead to see if it was working.

Me:

Nigga I got a new phone and number this Honor.

Patch:

Blink three times if this really you nigga.

Me:

Nigga you dumb ass fuck I can't blink in a text.

Patch:

Aye this you nigga, whoeva got your other phone was texting back with emojis and shit. I knew that wasn't you.

Me:

Whateva, tell moms I'll be home this weekend and I'mma bring someone with me.

Patch:

Who the fuck you bringing home?

Me:

Ole girl from when I last seen you.

Patch:

Oh, hell nah, you bringin' that bitch Nicki to moms, she gon' fuck you and her up.

Me:

Nah nigga, ole girl with the green hair from that night. But speakin' of Nicki get me her address.

Patch:

You ole I fell in love with a stripper ass. And I got you blood.

Me:

Fuck you nigga, I'll tell you all 'bout it when I see you.

Patch:

A'ight, hit me up soon we gotta go over what Unk said.

Me:

I got u bro.

I put my phone in my pocket after sending the last text to Patch then turned around. I leaned back on the counter and watched her from the window. She was so into the game on her phone, that she didn't notice my eyes stalking its prey.

"Sir, is your phone ringing?" the worker finally asked.

"Yes, it is ringing." I turned around and answered. The phone was vibrating away in my pocket, until I answered her question.

"Okay, here's your receipt and the other phone is completely disconnected." She told me as she handed over the papers and the box where the rest of my phone equipment was at. My phone vibrated again a minute later, and I knew it was Patch giving me Nicki's address.

"Thank you for your help," I told her before I turned and walked out of the store. Green hair didn't even look up from her phone when I got in, nor when I plugged the address in the maps app on my phone. I started the car and pulled off without even an acknowledgement from her ass. Whatever game she was playing her ass was really into it, all I could see was her thumb moving hella fast out of the corner of my eye.

Twenty minutes later and we were parked a few houses down from our destination.

"So, what are we doing here?" she finally put away her phone and looked at me.

"This the girl from the parking lot of the hotel's house and I need your help gettin' some info from that bitch." I told her as I looked over at Nicki's house.

"What info you tryna get from her?" she asked as her right eyebrow raised a bit and her left one went down some.

"I need to know if her lil' girl is mine or my father's, because I can't have them fuckin' up my child or sibling, life." I told her.

"A'ight I got you, get my tool bag out of the trunk." H said as she started putting her hair in a ponytail. She reached into her backseat and grabbed the black pullover she had. I popped the trunk as she put the pullover on.

By the time I got the bag out of her trunk and walked over to her side of the car; she had already changed her shoes and had added some more rings to her fingers. Her face was hella shinny and I had no clue why.

"If the lil girl is in there just make sure she stays out of the room me and that bitch in. I'll get the answers you need. I been wanting to get my hands on that bitch ever since she called me out of my name that day." Green hair got out of the car and took the bag from me. I locked the car then led the way to Nicki house.

She stood behind me, so Nicki wouldn't be able to see her, as I knocked on her door and rang the doorbell. I could hear someone fumbling around as they made their way to the door, so I knew at least someone was in there.

"I knew you'd come back to me eventually, you were tryna act like you didn't want this in front of that bum ass nigga Patch and your bitch." Nicki said when she opened the door and noticed it was me.

"So, you gon' let me in?" I asked her since she had the door only cracked a lil bit and was blocking the door.

"Yeah, just give me like two mins and I'mma let you in." Nicki said then shut the door behind her. Seconds later, all that could be heard was thuds and bumps.

"Shut up before she hears your ass," I whispered to green hair when she snorted hella loud from giggling.

"Stop worrying 'bout me when your ass needs to be tucking your pants in your socks, so we won't leave out of here with her roach family. Don't act like you didn't smell the funk coming out of her house, and don't hear her ass tossing trash around in there." I didn't even respond, I just did what she said.

"You can come in now," Nicki swung the door open seconds after I finished tucking my pants into my socks. She was breathing hella hard. She must've thought she had got all the trash up out of sight, but I could see a slice of old pizza on the back of her brown stained couch before I walked in.

"Hold her right there for a second before you go," Green hair said as she walked in then walked into Nicki's kitchen.

"All you had to do was say y'all wanted a threesome with me, it didn't have to be all this." Nicki said then bit her bottom lip.

"Girl, don't nobody want a threesome with your nasty pussy ass, your house stank worse than the sewer, so I can only imagine what your pussy smell like." Green hair called from the kitchen.

"So, you just gon' let that bitch speak to me like that," Nicki said as the girl walked back into the living room.

"Shut your nasty ass up, I couldn't even find cleaning supplies in the kitchen, not even dishwashing liquid. It looks like shit is growing on your fuckin' plates in the kitchen." Green hair took out some hand sanitizer and napkins from her bag. She squirted the sanitizer on the glass part of the coffee table then used the napkins to wipe it off.

"Hey, don't be acting like my house is just a trash can." Nicki said when Green hair tossed the empty sanitizer and napkins on the floor.

"You can move now," she told me as she stood in front of Nicki. She cocked her hand back and punched Nicki dead in the nose as soon as I moved away from Nicki. Nicki reached for her nose as she fell back onto the couch, making the pizza at the top of the couch fall onto her head. That shit was nasty as fuck.

I walked out of the living room and went to search the house for Nicki's daughter. I didn't want her daughter walking in on her mother getting her ass beat. Nicki's muffled screams could be heard in every room I walked in looking for the little girl. It took me thirty minutes to search the house for the little girl, because she had so much trash everywhere. I was glad when I came up empty handed. I wouldn't be able to leave the little girl there if she was there with the way Nicki's house looked and smelled. The tub was more a blackish-gray color than it was white. I don't think she had cleaned up since she moved in. I hurried back into the living room after my search, because that was the part of the house that smelled the best.

"Now tell him what you told me." Green hair was sitting on the coffee table in front of Nicki when I walked back in. Nicki's shirt and bra were cut open and her titties were exposed.

"I didn't say nothing, stop lying to my man bitch!" Nicki screamed when green hair took a sock out of her mouth.

She stuck the sock back in Nicki's mouth then gripped Nicki's nipples with some pliers. Tears fell down Nicki's face and blood dripped from her nipples.

"Are you going to tell him now?" she asked as she squeezed the pliers harder. Nicki nodded her head quickly in response.

"I never fucked your brother, your dad bought me this house in exchange for me telling the hood that me and your brother was fuckin' years ago. He also told me if anybody, including you asked about him buying me this house, to tell y'all that it was because my daughter was yours. She's not yours or his, my daughter's father got custody of her and won't let me see her." Nicki sobbed.

"Man, quit all that fuckin' cryin' bitch. Tell me why the fuck he had you do that pussy shit?" I asked her.

"He never told me why, but maybe it was because somebody started a rumor that your brother was gay. No, it was not me. Your dad was pissed when he heard that shit, but I don't know why he wanted people to think my baby was yours." Nicki told me everything she knew.

"Now, you're not gonna tell nobody we were here or I'mma come back. And if you tell anybody else that your baby is his again Imma come back, matter of fact just post on social media that he's not the dad. And clean this house the fuck up and maybe your daughter's dad would let you see her." Green hair told her as she wiped Nicki's blood from the pliers while staring her down. Nicki's eyes kept going from green hair to the pliers.

"Your dad is going to kill me when he finds out that I posted 'bout my daughter not being yours," Nicki said.

"Just post that we took a DNA test and your daughter is not mine." I told her before I started sneezing.

"Let's get out of here before you sneeze to death." Green hair grabbed me by the hand and pulled me outside. My sneezing stopped when I got out of Nicki's damn house.

"I feel dirty from being in there and I'm starting to itch, let's go take another shower." She said as she scratched herself as we walked to the car.

"Yeah, we can do that, then go to this all-night cafe by the college that I want to buy into. You can tell me what you think and what upgrades I should have my partner do if I do buy it." I told her when we got into the car.

Patch

"The search for Honor is called off." I told the niggas standing in front of me. I called a meeting with a few important people from me and Honor's team and Rocko's. Along with a few others we used as look outs on our blocks.

"What happened, somebody killed that pussy ass nigga?" one of Richy's workers chuckled. He didn't know I knew he worked for Richy, because he tried to tell me he worked for Rocko.

"What's funny?" I walked up to him and placed my gun on his forehead then took off the safety. My eyes stared into his just daring him to answer me.

"N-n-n-n-nothing," he stuttered.

"I guess this bullet I'm bouta release is nothin' either." I smirked as my finger squeezed the trigger. I used the bottom of my shirt to wipe the blood off my face.

"This for whoever can get rid of his body without a trace." I placed a wad of money in the center of the table.

"My sister works at the funeral home; she can get me in when the place close and give me the keys to the hearse." Eagle, the little nigga that worked for Rocko said.

"Give this to your sister," I pulled a wad out of my pocket and pulled a few more bills out and handed them to him.

"Tell her if she wants more, there is more where that came from, all she needs to do is keep unlocking the door wheneva I hit you up." I told him.

"Shit we both down with whateva brings in the money." he answered.

"A'ight, I got a couple more people that would be interested," I told him.

"If anybody got a problem with Richy and his people no longer being a part of the team, then you can walk out now." I sat there waiting for one of them to make a move and none of them moved a muscle.

"We're closing ranks now and nobody from Richy's team can know shit or walk in nowhere we do business. You even see one of them at the door or on the block looking like they're gettin' off, kill 'em.

"The drop and pickup times are changing and there will be no more keeping extra product where it's too easy to gain access. Whoever oversees the block will receive a text from me about the location and drop time a few hours before someone makes the drop." I told them then dismissed them, a nigga had to go change his clothes.

Truly's house was the closest to the dock I was at, so I went there. I pulled into her driveway ten minutes later and let myself in.

Twenty minutes later after I was showered and dressed, I went to the office in Truly house where she usually was at that time. She wasn't in there, so I spent a couple of minutes searching the house for Truly and Truvon. It was damn near midnight and the house was empty, so I called Truly's phone. Her phone went straight to voicemail back to back. It wasn't like Truly to stay out this late unless she was staying at me or my mom's place.

I called my mom's phone and her phone kept going straight to voicemail. My mother and Truly both knew I didn't play that, not answering my calls. A nigga had no problem popping up on either one of them and embarrassing their asses. The last time Truly tried that I popped up on her ass while she was on her date and shut it down. Truly didn't talk to me for three days after that, but she did answer her phone for me though. She would answer the phone and sit on the line for a few seconds breathing before she hung up on me.

I knew what I had to do after waiting in Truly's house for twenty more minutes, without a call back from my mother. I left Truly house and headed straight to my mother's.

When I pulled up and parked, I could see my mom on the porch smoking a cigarette. She only did that when one of the boys were in her house, other than that she didn't come out of her house to smoke. She said she didn't want one of her grand babies getting second hand smoke.

"Hmm, all I had to do was not answer or return your calls for you to come see your mother." My mother said when she looked up and noticed me walking towards her.

"I was just ova here day befo' yesterday." She could never make up her mind. She complained when she thought I came over too much and when I went more than a day without seeing her.

"Coming over to steal some of my food or use my bathroom doesn't count as seeing me."

"Moms, Truly and Truvon in, there right?" I asked her.

"Truvon is here but Truly is not," my mom said that like it wasn't a problem.

"Where the fuck she at then."

"Paevon, you better lower your voice when speakin' to me boy." My mom stood up and put out her cigarette.

"But she's comin' back to get Truvon and no I don't know where she went. I think she went to one of those study groups or to the library."

"She doesn't be out studyin' this late without tellin' me. She must be tryna hide a nigga from me and you're helpin' her ass. I already told her ass, from now on I'm killin' any nigga she tries to fuck with before it gets that far. Every nigga she ever talked to, has caused her issues. She just made it worse for ole boy for not tellin' me, she must be tryna get to second base with the fuck nigga." My mother shook her head as if she couldn't believe what I said. It wasn't like she hadn't heard me say it before.

"Boy she don't give a damn who you fuck wit, so mind your damn business. And yes, she does study this late whenever she got a big test comin' up, we just don't tell your bothersome ass. Truvon be here until two in the morning sometimes while she's with her study groups." My mom folded her arms and dared me to say something more.

"Her ass better not be out there fuckin' unless she married. Truly know my rules and they go for you too."

"Boy I'm grown and so is Truly," moms said as she whacked me in the back of my head.

"Yeah a'ight, let me find out and we'll see just how grown the two of you and them niggas are. But I ain't ate since lunch, can you hook your son up real quick. I'm stayin' here until Truly walks her stupid ass through the door. I'mma park my car in the parking lot really quick then I'll be in." I waited until my mom's made it into her place before I headed back to my car to move it into the parking lot.

A few minutes later I walked into the kitchen and my mom was heating me up something. Truvon was standing in front of the fridge drinking straight from this big ass jug of fruit punch Minute Maid.

"Boy if you don't get a fuckin' cup." I told him, and he just looked at me.

"You betta leave my baby alone, and stop cussin' at him. That's his own juice he can do whateva he wants with it." Truvon smiled at me and licked around the rim of the jug. Then pointed at his name that him or my mom must've wrote hella big with a marker.

"You shouldn't drink the apple juice either, that's PJ's and the grape soda is Grams." Truvon said as he put the juice back in the fridge.

"Mom you let them get their own big ass juices and drink from the bottle, you would've smacked the shit out of me. You must want them to get diabetes or some shit."

"Boy, you got contact high from the fumes of my drug of choice and ain't nothin' wrong with your ass. Ain't nothin' wrong with them havin' their own drinks when they come to Grandma's, it ain't like they drinkin' it every day."

"The lies you tell, lady." She was lying about the drug fumes part. She didn't cook or do drugs in none of the apartments we lived in together. My mom like to go for the shock value at times, even if it wasn't true.

"So, maybe that comment was to lessen the blow of what I really had to say. I dropped you on your head when you was a baby and you turned out alright. There was this big ass lump on your head for a few weeks, you damn near looked like the Coneheads baby." My mother said to me as she put a plate of homemade chow mein and beef and broccoli in front of me.

"You told me I was just born like that when I saw the pictures."

"What can I say, I lied." My mama looked at me and shrugged her shoulders.

"Grams I want some more." Truvon said as he sat next to me at the table.

"Man, you always want some more." I told him.

"That's 'cause I be needing some more fuel to play the game. I'm tryna get good enough so instead of going to college I can play video games for a living. This one dude just got over fifty thousand from playin' a game so good." Truvon was so excited he didn't see the look on my mom's face. My mom stood behind him with one hand on her hip and the other holding his plate, as she stared him down.

"Boy if I hear that dumb shit again, I'mma beat your ass and make you live with Corner Joe for a whole week on them cold streets. 'Cause that's where you're gonna end up thinkin' like that." She smacked him in the back of his head then placed his plate in front of him. I remember when she told me that and I didn't believe her ass, so I did whatever it was again. My mom made me spend all day with Corner Joe for two whole days, I only got to come in the house late at night and a nigga couldn't shower. Seeing what Corner Joe did just to survive had made me realize, I had to do anything it took not to end up out there like him.

"I tell you what, we can go practice afta you eat because the gaming can be a side hustle, but you have to go to college or else you'll end up like me. Grandma can't find a decent job because I don't have a degree, and without a decent job I can't get enough money to buy a house. It's okay to want to do that on the side but you have to either go to college or get a trade." My mama told him, and I learned something about her that I didn't know she was feeling.

"Don't worry grandma, I'mma help you buy a house. We 'bouta go practice on the game and I promise I'mma go to a school." Truvon said before he started eating.

"You can have the rest of my plate, I still got some Snickers back there. Come on grams, so I can teach you how to play and we can win that money." My mom followed Truvon out of the kitchen. I finished his plate and mines then washed the dishes. I took one of the beers my mom had for me out the fridge, then headed into the living room to catch up on my show while I waited for Truly to get back.

****

It was damn near three in the morning and Truly still hadn't made it to my mom's. I was pissed when the first hour, then the next passed without Truly coming home. The more time that went by, made me want to choke her ass out because even my mother was starting to get worried.

"You need to go find her, this is not like Truly and you know it." My mom said as she paced in front of the TV in the living room.

I pulled into Truly's driveway ten to twenty minutes later, her car wasn't out front. I called the only other person

I trusted after speaking to my moms, and it took that nigga a minute to answer my calls.

"What nigga, damn," Honor answered.

"Truly not home and we don't know where she's at. I need you to come ride out with me and look for her while mom is callin' all the hospitals." I told him.

"You sure she just not out with some nigga that she don't want you to know about?" he asked me.

"Nah, she told moms she was studying and her midterms are coming up. Plus, moms is even gettin' worried and if she was just on a date and just stayin' ova with a nigga, mom wouldn't be worried." I told him.

"A'ight I'm bouta get dressed, then hit you back up nigga."

From Moms:

Don't you know one of the people she be studying with number?

To Moms:

Yeah, I forgot 'bout that. I'mma hit her up now.

T. Study Friend:

Aye dis Patch, is Truly with you?

My phone vibrated seconds later, but it was just Honor dropping me his location. I clicked on his location then backed out of Truly's driveway and went to scoop him.

When I drove into the neighborhood Honor was in, I realized Honor was down the street from Truly's grandparent's old house. Her grandparents sold their home and moved into a retirement community when Truly moved in with me and my mom.

I chuckled when I saw that nigga Honor standing on the lawn of a house with his bags in front of him. That nigga looked like one of them dumb niggas that got kicked out by their bitch and had all their shit packed with nowhere to go. I parked in the driveway of the house Honor was standing in front of and popped the trunk. While Honor was putting his shit in the trunk my phone vibrated back to back a couple of times.

From T Study Friend:

I had to work so she went with another group.

From T Study Friend:

Something happened with Truvon?

From T Study Friend:

I can contact the group she was with and hit you back if you want.

To T Study Friend:

Yeah hit them niggas up and see if she still with them.

To T Study Friend:

You know where they were studying at?

From T Study Friend:

Yeah, they were at the library at our school.

"Where's our first stop?" Honor asked me when I stopped texting.

"She might still be at her school library so that's where we're goin'." I answered him as I pulled out of the driveway.

"Where the fuck you been at nigga?" I asked him.

"Shit nigga, that's a long ass fuckin' story for another day," Honor said.

"Man, we almost got a twenty-minute drive, so you might as well tell me where you been." Honor started to tell me what happened between him and that stripper.

"So, you let a bitch get the drop on you?" I chuckled, a nigga couldn't believe that shit he was spitting.

"Man, if anything, you let her ass get the drop on me because you found her ass. But nah nigga, she everything I needed, she got that bitch Nicki to tell the truth. Nicki baby not even mine or my Dad's, that fuck nigga paid her ass to tell the hood that shit," Honor said.

"I know Nicki posted a picture on all her social media pages wit' her daughter and daughter's dad together. Talkin' 'bout some, her daughter got the best dad in the world. She said, if she had that maybe she wouldn't have made some of the decisions she did growing up or some shit like that." I had seen the post a few hours before when I was scrolling through social media waiting on Truly.

"She said he paid her to say that Truth had slept with her too, because there were rumors that he was gay. I ain't neva heard no shit like that," Honor said and the car instantly became silent.

"Patch, nigga tell me what you know." Honor looked at me and said, as I tried not to look at him or answer him.

"Check this, I use to see your brother hangin' with this nigga and I thought they were just boys. Until a couple of times I seen them holdin' hands and shit when they thought no one was lookin'. I thought you knew and I ain't say shit to no one else, 'cause that wasn't my business." I told him. Truth and Honor were close, so I thought he already knew and just didn't want to speak on his brother's life.

"Why didn't he tell me?" Honor asked but I don't think he was asking me.

****

When we got to Truly school, we found out she had passed out and hit her head. I had to tell them I was her husband and show them my identification to get the information I needed. One of the security officers told us the name of the hospital Truly was taken to.

"Why wasn't I invited to the wedding?" Honor asked. As we waited for a nurse to take us to Truly's room after talkin' to the doctor and finding out she was okay.

"We're not really married, Truly just changed her last name a few years back. Truvon started askin' questions 'bout why he had my last name and his mama didn't if I was his daddy. It was not time, if it ever is going to be, to tell Truvon how he was made and why he got my name. So Truly changed her name to Jackson, and he stopped asking questions and plus she wanted to change it. She found out the man her mom is married to isn't her real dad and is just her step-dad. Since he was the one that kicked her out afta that shit went down she didn't want his last name anyway." I told him, and it was silent until the nurse came to get us two minutes later.

She had a cast on her right hand, her lips were swollen, scrapes and bruises covered her entire body. Seeing her like that crushed a nigga to the core, because I let that shit happen. I keep swearing to myself that she would never feel pain again and then something like this happens. It was like I kept failing her, repeatedly.

"Whatsup nigga?" Honor looked over at me and asked.

"Seeing her like that just fucks me up inside. It makes me feel like I should make anybody that ever even looked at her wrong feel pain. "I told him as I took her hand in mine.

"You think you feel like that because you love her. Instead of just love her like a friend or sister." Honor looked at me.

"Shit, I ain't never say I wasn't in love her. I just want to be with her as husband and wife when I get all my shit together and not out here living wild. I don't want to hurt her to the point that she turns to harming herself.

"My mother use to be in recovery for a long time. She'd find a man she wanted to be with, then that man would hurt her somehow and she relapsed," I told him.

"One thing bro, Truly ain't your mother and she's stronger than her." Honor said, and it started making a nigga really think.

"Patch, I didn't get on drugs because I was raped. I got on drugs because a man I thought loved me laced my shit. The drugs numbed me and made it where I didn't have to deal with the pain, but Truly is not like that, Son. She has people to turn to when it gets too much for her and we're all in this room." My mother said after she came into the room.

"I just keep failing her, Ma. You taught me that a man loves and protects his family. I just feel like I'mma do something to fuck it up. Truly the type of person that will leave a nigga in the dust with one screw up, and I can't take that." I told her.

"Paevon, Truly didn't love those boys that she left at a drop of a dime. She been comparing them to you just as you been comparing women to her. The two of you get with people that you know is not going to work. Y'all belong to each other. It was just that the two of you needed other life experiences in order to build together. Don't be like me and miss something that can be the best thing in your life." My mama said as she pulled out a bottle of Hennessy and handed it to me.

"What do you mean by that last shit you just said?" I asked her as I twisted the cap off the bottle.

"I had a man that wanted to be there for me just like you do with Truly and Truvon. He was only three years older than me and I didn't want to tie him down. I just felt damaged beyond measure. He did check on us throughout the years and bring money whenever we were down on our luck. I always regretted not saying 'yes'. But I think if I said 'yes' I would have ruined us because I wasn't ready to start healing. I let that man who took my innocence reign over my life for decades, before I took my power back." My mom said. The room filled with silence for several minutes.

"Mom where Truvon at, and how you get here?" I asked her.

"Oh, I paid the twins lil sister to watch him at my house, I had to come check on my baby. I caught an Uber," she told me.

"The doctor said she not going to be up until the morning, they gave her something for the pain. Honor gon' take you home and stay with y'all just in case y'all needa get here quick," I told her.

"Oh, so you're kicking us out?" my mom asked as she snatched her bottle back.

"Nah only one person can be in here, and they bouta come check on her again soon. I'm not tryna start no shit in here with these people and get us all kicked out; when they come in here sayin it's too many people in here." I told my mom.

"Okay baby but let me know if she wakes up before then." My mama hugged me, and Honor dapped me up before they left out of the room.

I sat there and contemplated everything my mom said, and knew she was right. There wasn't a doubt in me that even if I got out of the streets, I would still have to ride around with a full clip on me. When you tried to turn your life around, that's when niggas thought you went soft and really tried you. And I knew Truly would ride it out with a nigga even with knowing that I would have to always do that. I guess I just don't want her to have to. I couldn't see myself with no one else or Truly with no one else. She made me want to strive for the better, and make my life and the man I am better. When I needed it, she gave me that shove, when everybody else gave me a push. She knows exactly what I need and when even when I don't.

The first time she cried on my shoulder it woke a nigga heart up and had him caring for someone else, other than the woman who birthed me. I knew as long as I had Truly by my side a nigga would never fall off, and if I did, she would be right there helping me get back up. Truly was gentle when a nigga needed it and a Pitt when I was fucking up, and she had to get on me.

When I thought she was gone it made me finally realize that I felt like I didn't need a woman, because Truly was already that to me. As soon as Truly woke up I was telling her that we are doing what we had been avoiding for years, being together fully. Shit, if we thought about it, we been together for years just without sex. And I couldn't live anymore without consuming everything she had to give me.

When she wakes up I'mma tell her, I just didn't make that move years back because I knew that before now; it would have been broken promises. The streets would've been my excuse for everything. I didn't want to lie to her about me cheating and shit, because I wasn't ready to be everything she needed if we crossed that line too soon. And I couldn't take her crying over something I did to her; she was already broken too many times. A nigga couldn't do that to the woman I loved beyond measure. But now it was time to stop running scared and be with my girl on all levels, we were just gone have to figure it all out.

I took off my clothes except for my boxers and put them in the dresser next to Truly's hospital bed and placed my phone on top of it. I slid my gun under the pillow I was going to be laying on and got into the bed with Truly. My right hand automatically reached for her and pulled her head on my chest, then went for her ass.

Honor

"We're sorry, the number you have called has been disconnected. Please hang up and try your call again." I hung up the phone and redialed green hair number, only to get the same message again. For the past week her phone had been going straight to voicemail when I called her. Now it's playing the recording saying it's disconnected.

A nigga even tried to stalk her ass on every social media site I could think of, but I couldn't find nobody that looked like her. Even though she didn't give me her name our city was hella small. I knew somebody I knew, knew her. So, I went through my friends list of girls from my city and looked at their friend's list for people with the letter H in their name. One time when we were talking, she told me her first name started with a H, but no matter how much I looked through the pages I couldn't find her or her name. Until one day I found one of the strippers that had came through with Patch had posted a picture on social media. She had one picture with green hair girl in it and the only H name that was in the caption of the picture was Haven. I started looking through every social media site I had for the name Haven. I don't think she was on social media or Haven was just a fake name she gave them.

I tried to call once more and got the same me message. I looked down at my phone then tossed it against the wall and watched it break. I had been listening to her voice on her voicemail, and now a nigga had nothing of her.

I hadn't heard from or seen Haven, since I got that call from Patch about Truly missing two weeks ago. When the ringing from Patch's call woke me, I realized I was in bed alone and her side was cool to the touch. She had been gone hours before I got the call, but at the time I didn't have time to think. I jumped up and went to help my nigga look for his girl and didn't give Haven being missing a second thought. Later that morning when I called her to have her come through, the phone went straight to voicemail. A couple of minutes later I got a text message saying, 'I'm sorry' from an unknown number and when I texted back asking for what, I got no response. I called the number only for the call to go straight to voicemail. I didn't know if it was Haven texting me or somebody texting the person who had the number before me.

I leaned back on my black leather sofa and uncapped the bottle of Hennessy that was laying on the couch beside me. It was just starting to sink in that Haven had disappeared on a nigga. After I let her ass in and let her see both sides of a nigga she became ghost. She pretended she could feel where I was coming from, and said I didn't have to pick and choose which side of me I had to be around her.

I was split in two when it came to that Haven shit, and how I should feel and move when it came to her leaving. The educated calm gentleman part of me was like, she's going through something and her leaving don't have nothing to do with you. Maybe she thought you couldn't handle it or wanted to do it on her own and she'll be back.

The hood gangsta side of me that felt like a person I trusted crossed me, thought something totally different. It had me thinking that the bitch took my heart and killed that shit without a second thought. Fuck her stupid ass, just go find a better bitch and fuck the shit out of her. And when you see that bitch, choke the hell out of her until she passes out then tie her ass to a chair. Fuck the shit out of a bitch in front of her and make her watch the whole thing. I wanted her to hurt like she did me. That was the way the treacherous side of me thought. I would break her. She broke something in me and I needed to break something in her. Hell, it was gonna be an eye for an eye situation going on. Only the strongest was going to survive.

I was split with which way to go when it came to Haven. Once again, I was separating one side of myself from the other and trying to decide which side to go with. I couldn't help but to remember when Haven said, I shouldn't have to be one side of me or the other. She said I should always be true to both sides of me at the same time. When I let my thoughts move like that, it changed my whole perspective.

When both sides of me came together my thoughts changed, but not that drastically. It made me feel as though yeah, my heart was breaking now, but that I shouldn't let that shit turn me into one of those bitch niggas. Yeah, she could have called to let me know what was up, but I don't know what she's going through. I needed to take it as a lesson learned and get my shit together. Hell, I don't have my shit all the way together to even be tryna wife up somebody. I needed to get on my shit and boss up my life. It needed to be fuck the dumb shit at that point.

Shit I was renting one of the apartments next door from Patch moms now. I had just a couch in the living room that I was sleeping on. I still hadn't got a bed and the only other thing I had was my big screen TV and clothes. I didn't even have shit to eat off and had to eat all my meals at Patch moms house. And I didn't want to touch the money Patch had made us over the years because I wanted that to be specifically for us buying up businesses and flipping some houses. It was time for me to only focus on getting on my shit; by getting it how I lived on the streets and in the corporate world, to make niggas feel me in both of my worlds.

I got up and went to my briefcase that I hadn't touched since I left Haven's house. I unzipped the bag and pulled my computer out, so I can start making business moves. I opened my laptop when I sat back down on the couch, and there on my keyboard was a letter with my name on it. I opened the letter and contemplated reading it, before I started to read it.

I'm sorry I had to leave you, but my world is in turmoil right now. I don't know which way is up or down. Right now, I can't tell you what is going on, but I will eventually. Don't try to find me because once you find out what I did, you're going to wish you never met me. Find someone that is not broken and give them your all and if they can't accept both sides of you, keep looking until you find someone that does.

I didn't say goodbye in person because it was too hard for me. I didn't want to leave you, but I had to for both of our sakes.

Honor, use your law degree to make business moves to wash up the money you and Patch make on the streets. That way you're not splitting both sides of who you are again.

I will always love you, Haven.

Reading that made a nigga think different about her, and see that she was still who I thought she was. I wanted to go find her ass and drag her back to me but I couldn't. I wasn't giving up on me and her. She had to figure some shit out and so did a nigga, maybe we would find each other once we got ourselves together.

****

"Damn nigga, your ass hella folded," Patch said as he walked into my apartment a couple of hours later.

"So, check this shit nigga, you know how earlier afta I told you 'bout findin' the letter from Haven and her phone being off. You told me to ride by her house, so I did. Nigga, there's a for sale sign up." I told him, and I could hear the slur in my voice.

"Aye, I think this the first time you ever took my advice and a nigga proud of that. But let's google the address and since it is for sale, maybe her new number would pop up." I tried to do what Patch said but I was too out of it, so he did it instead.

"Damn this shit say the house was for sale when she had you there. It's a new type of home they are trying out, one that turned a regular room into a panic room that is larger than the average panic room. I need to buy this shit for me and my family or get one built like it, you need to tell me how that room was."

"Man, get your stupid ass out of here with that shit. You not buying me and Haven house, nigga. Go find your own damn house," I told him and all he did was laugh at a nigga.

"I'mma leave you to your hangover and the stalking of Haven, nigga." Patch said as he got up off my couch.

"Nah I'm not stalking her any more nigga, she changed her number on me, a nigga 'bouta move on." That was the last thing I said before I passed out and I meant my last words.

Honor

One year later...

"Baby where are you, the guests are showing up," my fiancée said as soon as I answered the phone. I met Layne two months after I found that letter from Haven. Layne's father owned one of the businesses that Patch and I became silent partners in. She was the opposite of what I always went for.

"Honor, don't do this to me, you promised." Layne said when I didn't respond to her. I couldn't respond. I was staring at an envelope with familiar handwriting on it. All the envelope had on it was my name and address, nothing more. I knew whatever it was, it was from Haven and I didn't know if I should open it or not.

"I'mma be there in a second. I was just about to walk out the door and get in my car," I told Layne.

"Honor, my family is starting to talk; the only person from your family that's here is your father. Your mother was here, but when she saw your father, she disappeared. I think she left."

"Layne, I didn't invite my dad so how is that nigga even there."

"Well, I sort of invited him when I saw him a few weeks back and must've forgotten to tell you," Layne said. I knew she was bullshitting about that last part.

"Layne, I have never introduced you to my dad, and you know I don't fuck with that nigga like that."

"When you talk about your dad, I can tell you have this contempt for him, so I never told you him and my father are friends. I don't know why you feel that way about your dad; when he's around me and my father he is one of the nicest men I know," Layne answered.

"So, you hid the fact that you knew my dad from me, then turned around and invited that nigga to my shit?" Layne knew what she was doing by inviting him. One of the things I hated about Layne was that she did shit she wasn't supposed to but didn't own up to her shit when she got caught up.

"See, you need to open up more to me and stop only giving me a part of you. If you would just let me in fully, I would've known not to invite your dad even if I had good intentions." Shit like that made me want to leave her ass at times.

"Man, just hit me up when that nigga leave, then I'll be there," I told Layne and hung up before she could say anything more than 'but'.

Her dumbass must've been in the car already on her way here, I thought when I heard Layne trying to open the door to my house a few minutes later. She had hella keys on her ring, so it always took her awhile to find the one to my door.

I was shocked to see Patch, his moms, Truly and the kids walk in my house instead of Layne.

"Why y'all here instead of at my engagement party?" I asked them.

"Shit, we not stupid enough to go there knowing your ass not really 'bouta marry her ass," Patch said as he sat down on the couch across from me.

"We goin' to the game room until y'all ready," Truvon said; they walked their lil asses to my game room like it was their house.

"What y'all do, pull up to get moms then seen my car out front still?" I asked them, referring to Patch's mother.

"Nah, we all just knew, more than likely, you was going to find an excuse not to show up," Truly replied.

"I was 'bouta go, but then I checked my mailbox and found this letter from Haven. I came back in the house to decide if I should read it or not." I told them and lifted the envelope, so they could see it.

"Read it, nigga. If you don't I'mma take it and let Truly read that shit," Patch said.

I ripped the letter open then started reading it.

Dear Honor,

As time goes by, I feel as though I need to tell you everything that I have been hiding from you. I knew your brother Truth, he was my brother Savon's boyfriend. Your dad read Truth's journal and found out Truth was gay, and he didn't like that. Your dad beat Truth so bad that he had to be taken to the hospital, because he told him he wasn't going to leave Savon. Your mom was scared that your dad would do it again, so your brother spent a month at my house recovering. I believe they told you that Truth was at a summer internship or something like that, so you wouldn't look for him. Truth made sure to call you almost every single day. After that day, Truth left his journal at our house and only wrote in it when he came over. I have Truth's journal and I read it again a couple of weeks back. I think this is something you should read too. Stop the letter here and look in the envelope. I sent you a copy of something I think you should see from Truth's journal. Don't look at the pictures yet. Just read the other paper.

Dear, Honor & Haven   Marqua'lla

I read the copy of a page from Truth's journal, then handed it to Truly. One day, Truth was running errands with our father and they ran into Truly's mother. She made our father give her money or she would tell our mother Truly was his daughter. Truth found out Truly was our father's daughter and Richy tried to hide it. I continued reading the letter...

I saw her name tagged in a picture on your page and thought the two of you should know. So anyway, back to what I was saying about our brothers. Your dad came to my house the day before Truth's funeral and told my brother he couldn't come. He told Savon that he would have his men at the front doors of the church to kill him if he showed up. The morning of Truth's funeral I found my brother hanging from a banister in his room. On the day of my brother's funeral, your dad was at his burial with one of his boys. My dad and his patna beat their asses, and a few weeks later, I found my parents dead in a pool of blood on the kitchen floor. I wanted revenge for my family and wanted to hurt your father like he hurt me. So, I made it my business to find out everything about the two of you. That's how I learned about the party Patch was throwing you. I kidnapped you to torture and kill you, but the more time I spent with you the harder it became. The night I left, I stood over you with a gun in my hand and tears in my eyes, going back and forth about killing you or letting you live. I couldn't do it because the love I had for you was stronger than the hate I had for your father. And I knew our brothers would be disappointed in me if I took your life to hurt that fuck nigga. So, I left to get my head on straight and heal from the pain of my loved ones' deaths. I almost became your father by taking the life of someone who didn't have nothing to do with anything.

I'm sorry for all the pain I caused you, but maybe what I'm about to show and tell you next will heal that in time. A month after I left you, I found out I was pregnant; it happened that first night in the hotel. We have a beautiful, five-month-old baby girl who is the spitting image of you; every time I look at her all I see is you. I named her Sayvonna Truthly after our brothers. Right now, me and Say are not in California, but we will be soon, and I will bring her to see you. Until then, I sent a few pictures of her with this letter, and I will send more soon.

Love, Haven and Sayvonna

I handed Truly the letter and sat back on the couch as I took out the pictures. I flipped through the pictures; Sayvonna looked like my baby pictures. She had Truth and our mother's nose. Behind the last picture was another piece from Truth's journal, but the page wasn't a copy, it was ripped straight from his journal.

I can't hide who I am from the world anymore, so I'm 'bouta come out to everyone. If you're reading this and I'm dead, my father murdered me because I was not who he wanted me to be. I also know a lot of his secrets. They don't call me Truth for nothing. My father was having an affair with his brother's wife, but she didn't want to leave Rocko. My father retaliated by sending his goons to kill Rocko's family. Fuck that nigga and his secrets! Tell Rocko his brother is a snake!

There were rumors in the hood about my brother's murder being a hit. In that moment I made up my mind that Rocko didn't have to do that nigga dirty. *I'm going to slowly kill his ass and take everything he got!*

Part 2

Dear, Haven

SOUL Publications

Truly

I looked over at Patch and couldn't help but to be mesmerized by him despite everything that was going on around us. Patch had smooth, dark chocolate skin, a strong jawline and dreads that fell just past his shoulders. I had just re-twisted them. He only had one tattoo and it was of the globe with Truvon's and Paevon Jr.'s names written in the middle.

Whenever his onyx, hooded, deep-set eyes stared deeply into mine, I shivered. Patch had a scar that went from the center of his left eyebrow down to his chin. He was handsome and rugged at the same time. He had an athletic body that he joked was from running from the police and Miss Brenda's shoe all his life.

I was so caught up in admiring his body that I tuned the conversation he was having with Honor out. I didn't snap back until they said they were heading out.

I ran out of the house after Honor and Patch; I still had the last letter Honor handed to me in my hand.

"Go back in a house, Truly," Patch said to me.

"Hell no; if I let you two go alone, y'all will end up in jail with murder charges," I said to Patch as I climbed in the backseat of Honor's car.

"Matter of fact, Honor, get out the driver's seat; I'm driving," I said to him as I started climbing over the seat. If it was up to him and Patch, they would probably be out there in an accident or in handcuffs, because neither of them could control their tempers at the moment.

Honor looked back at me and said, "yeah, I'mma let you drive, because it'll be easier for me to jump out the car that way." Honor got out of the front seat and climbed into the back. As I was adjusting the driver's seat, I could've sworn I saw the curtains at the house across the street moving as if someone was trying to discreetly watch us.

"Where we going?" I asked Honor as I started the car.

"To my engagement party since that nigga is there. He 'bouta regret ever showing up to that shit, like he not a snake ass nigga," Honor said as we pulled off.

I didn't even have time to process what I read and what it meant to me. When I looked at those words I was shocked; all those lies my mother told me were better than the truth. After discovering what I just had, believe it or not, I preferred being ignorant to the truth. Because of all the things I heard about Richy on the streets, I knew I would've been better off not knowing he was my father.

Twenty minutes later, we pulled up to a two story brick building where Honor's engagement party was being held.

The parking lot was packed making it hard to find a parking spot, so I parked directly in front of the entrance.

"Stay right here and leave the car goin'; we'll be right back," Patch said.

I wanted so badly to say no, to get out of the car and stop the situation from getting too bad, but I knew from the looks in their eyes that nothing I said would stop them. It was best for me to stay in the car and make sure we had a smooth getaway.

"If y'all not out of there in five, I'm coming in," I told them as they got out of the car.

They weren't in the building for more than three minutes before they came running out. I could hear Layne calling Honor's name, yelling for him to come back as he and Patch made a beeline for the car. They left the car doors open so all they had to do was jump inside. Layne was almost to Honor's door when he slammed the car door in her face, and I pulled off.

"What happened?" I asked as we exited the parking lot. I pretended like I didn't see Layne running behind the car calling after Honor.

"The nigga wasn't there; he left a few hot seconds before we got there," Patch said.

"Drive around a few corners to see if we can spot that nigga," Honor said from the backseat as he silenced his phone. We all knew it was Layne calling to cry and beg him to come back. She did that shit a lot and would even go as far as blowing up his phone and mine. I blocked her and cussed her ass out a few months back, after she did that one too many times. If she couldn't get a hold of Honor, she would call anybody whose number she had until she talked to him. I didn't know what that girl's problem was. Patch's mom, Brenda, called her a fatal attraction waiting to happen.

I hit a few corners as Patch and Honor looked out of the window for any signs of Richy. The thought of him being my dad popped into my mind, but I quickly dismissed it. There was no way I was ready to acknowledge the fact that I was related to that nigga Richy.

"I need to call Rocko and let him know Richy was the one who did that shit," Honor said.

"I don't know if you should do that right now since he stuck in there and can't do shit about it yet. That might just make him go crazy in there and end up doing something he'll regret. We don't need him doing any more time or making it where he'll never get out," I said.

"You're right, but what if I tell him what's up when he gets out, and he's pissed because I waited to tell him?" Honor replied.

"How 'bout we tell him about Truly being his niece and see what he says. Then tell him we got some fucked up news that can make his stay harder. He can tell us if he wants to wait," Patch said.

"I'll tell him that when he hits me up tomorrow, but for now, drop me off at the nearest hotel. I can't deal with Layne's ass right now," Honor said.

I picked up my phone when I stopped at a red light and found the closest hotel from Patch's house on MapQuest. At the red light, I clicked on the one with almost five-stars and booked the room for Honor.

"We'll be at Patch's house, just call or text one of us if you need us for something," I told Honor after pulling up at the hotel fifteen minutes later.

"Nah, I'll just get what I need from that Target across the street. I'mma just need for one of y'all to come get me tomorrow or the next day," Honor said.

"Don't go get your ass kidnapped like the last time I left you in a hotel alone," Patch laughed.

"That shit not even funny no more, nigga," Honor said as he got out the car. He shut the door and jogged into the entrance of the hotel. Patch and I sat and watched him get his key and get on the elevator before we pulled off.

****

Patch and I picked up the kids from Brenda's and headed to Patch's house. As soon as we got into the house, I had to make sure the kids showered, ate and were in the bed before I went to take my own shower.

A couple of minutes into my shower, Patch climbed in. He pushed me behind him, soaped up his towel and body, then washed off and climbed out within five minutes. I wanted to smack the hell out of him for stealing my hot water, but the news I had learned earlier had drained me both mentally and physically. So I just let that slide as I walked up to the showerhead and let the hot water cascade down my body. The hot water felt so good, and it was helping to keep the crazy thoughts out of my head. Once the water turned warm, I washed the soap off and got out. I dried off and moisturized my body before brushing my teeth for the night.

My mouth practically fell open when I walked into the bedroom. Patch had a glass of wine and one of my favorite ice creams on the nightstand next to my side of the bed. It felt like he was testing me because he didn't allow food or drinks, besides water, in his bed.

"I'm only making an exception to my rule because of the shit you found out today; but let me find one crumb in the bed and I'mma knock your head off," Patch said.

"Nigga please, you'd kill yourself before you'd lay your hands on me," I told him.

"Suicide is a sin, and you know damn well a nigga don't commit sins," he joked. Well he'd better be joking because he knew damn well he had committed every sin in the book more than once.

"Patch please, you'd kill a nigga or bitch for just lookin' at me or the boys for too long. You commit a sin just by waking up in the morning." He smirked at me.

"Man, get in the bed and watch this movie with me, and you should've came out here and let me put that lotion on you," he said. I climbed into the bed then grabbed my wine.

"You wanna talk 'bout that shit you heard a couple of hours ago?" Patch moved closer to me and wrapped his arms around me before he asked.

"Not yet; I just want to watch this movie with you and stay in your arms all night. I can't deal with speaking that shit out loud yet. I'll let you know when I'm ready to speak on that fuck shit," I told him and gulped the rest of the wine down. I set the wine glass on the nightstand and picked up the ice cream. Patch watched me out the corner of his eye the whole time I ate the ice cream, making sure I didn't drop not one crumb. Soon as I was finished, he took my trash and the glass to the kitchen.

At times he could be a neat freak. I think it was because when he was younger one of the places he and Brenda lived had roaches in it. I think he was scared that the roaches would come back, and in his mind, he had to keep his place spotless even though he wasn't living in that apartment anymore. He came back into the bedroom a few minutes later, got into bed and pulled me into his arms.

He sparked up his blunt, and I felt bad that, for the first time in a long time, I hadn't been the one to roll it. When he handed me the blunt, I took my four puffs before I gave it back to him. He finished it off and we fell asleep like we did every night that we were in the same bed.

Haven

My eyes rolled to the top of my head as I read the text message from my fiancé Jace. He texted and told me not to wait up for him because a work emergency had come up. I didn't believe that because he didn't have a job; the nigga nickel and dime hustled for my best friend's brother. Jace wasn't important enough to call because of an emergency.

Jace and I had been together off and on since we started high school nine years ago. When I put my plan into motion to kidnap Honor, it was during one of our off periods. That night I left Honor I didn't know where I was going; all I knew was I couldn't stay in the same city as him. I was contemplating my next move when out of the blue, Jace texted me saying he needed me, and he would pay for my plane ticket to move with him in Vegas.

It was like a sign to me so I texted him back quickly letting him know I could be at the airport in under an hour. He found a plane ticket that would be leaving Oakland in two hours. Almost four hours later, I was getting off the plane in Vegas and hadn't looked back since.

5 Months Ago

"Man, hurry the fuck up and get in this car," Jace looked over at me and said. He was acting like he didn't

care or see me struggling to climb my pregnant ass in the car. I knew my baby wasn't his, but he promised to treat us as if she was his.

"Aww, what the fuck! You could've waited until I climbed the rest of the way in." I rubbed the small part of my head, which had slightly hit where the roof and car door met, when he pulled me the rest of the way inside.

"What the fuck is always taking your ass so long to come up out of that bitch?" I didn't respond at first because I wasn't in the mood for an argument. But I couldn't hold my tongue for too long because I was eight months pregnant, still working my ass off and my emotions were all over the place.

"Man whatever, you could've waited until I climbed all the way into the car," I told him as I slammed the door; he had pissed me off. I had just worked a long shift.

When a job to work in the oncology part of a medical center, became available I hurried to apply. I thought being a hospital foodservice deliverer would be easy, but that was further from the truth than I thought. I had a big, tender heart and seeing the kids and adults suffering from cancer hurt me to the core. I just wanted to help them, and it hurt me that I couldn't do anything.

"Nah, I couldn't wait. I been out here for almost thirty minutes waiting, and I got shit to do. I'm losing a lot of money by stopping what I was doing to come get your ass. If you would've caught a ride, it wouldn't be none of this." Jace was acting like picking me up was an inconvenience to him although he was in my car. Whenever he got like this, I wondered if I had made a big mistake by getting back with him.

"Well if you wasn't in my car then you wouldn't have had to stop whatever you was doing to come get me," I snapped.

"Somebody must be pumping your head up or some shit again. You must be starting shit with me because you want to be with one of them niggas from your job." Jace was stupid as hell; nobody was paying attention to my pregnant self. Suddenly, Jace started swerving a bit too much for my liking; it was as if he couldn't keep control of the car.

"What the fuck, are you drunk? Pull over right now so I can drive."

"Shut the fuck up, sit back and ride before I crash this bitch on purpose," Jace said. I didn't open my mouth to say anything else, but I wanted to. Sometimes he acted like one of those weak niggas by threatening to kill his damn self

whenever we broke up. In high school he had grabbed me by the collar in front of a crowd so,I left him. But not before I picked up the biggest thing around and knocked his ass upside the head. Ever since then, he knew not to try me with that. Sometimes I thought because I had already lost everybody in my family, I was scared of losing someone else close to me, so I went back to him continuously. There was something Jace was battling with, and I thought it might have something to do with what he did on the streets. Because one day he picked up and moved an eight-hour drive away. He would be the Jace I knew and loved for months, then get drunk and become the asshole that was next to me.

"Pull over and get the fuck out of my car!" if he thought he could come at me wrong while in my car, Jace had another thing coming.

"I'm so sorry, I swea'. I'mma get this shit together before baby girl comes; please forgive me for this," Jace professed, trying to calm me down.

"Tell me wha—" I didn't get to finish my sentence because a car swerved into our lane from the other side of the freeway. Jace tried to swerve to the next lane but there was a car coming up fast and it clipped the side of us. Our

car went tumbling across the freeway like a tumbleweed until we landed in a ditch.

When I came to, I was in the hospital. I learned that Jace didn't have not one scratch on his body nor did the person who hit us. I had to have an emergency C-section and that was how my daughter was born.

Sayvonna reached for my phone; when her finger touched the screen, she liked the picture of Honor. I felt embarrassed; my child had just given away the fact that I was stalking her father's social media page. Then I remember I was on my fake page and sighed from relief. To be honest, I stalked his page every day to see if he posted new pictures, but I told my best friend Amity it was only to show Say pictures of her father.

I had mailed Amity a letter to put in Honor's mailbox today, and I was anxious for him to get it.

Sayvonna grabbed for my phone again with her chubby hands and pulled the phone to her slobbery mouth. I watch as she brought the picture of Honor closer to her face. Say started talking in gibberish to the picture. It made me feel guilty, because the only way she saw her father was through the pictures I stole off his social media. I wanted Say to have a connection with her father, and I didn't want it to be hindered because of my actions. The fear of my actions encompassed me and prevented me from taking the next step. Which was the face to face meeting so Sayvonna and Honor could form a bond. Sending the letter first was my way of gauging whether or not there would be major backlash.

Truthfully, I couldn't tell him all the secrets I needed to face-to-face, and I wanted the letter to do it for me before I took Sayvonna to meet Honor.

Ring. Ring.

My phone started ringing in Sayvonna's hand; I prayed it was Amity but it was one of those damn telemarketers calling. I silenced my phone and closed my eyes as my heart thumped in my chest from the anxiousness I was feeling. I was on pins and needles waiting on that one call that would change my life for the good… or the bad.

I had the urge to bite my nails off; I was so nervous, and I didn't understand why because all Amity could tell me was that he got the letter, nothing more nothing less. I guess the majority of my nerves were from having a tug of war in my head centered around if he would forgive me for everything I did and hid from him or not.

Well it didn't really matter to me whether or not he forgave me as long as he didn't push my mistakes off on our daughter. But knowing Honor, my heart knew that wasn't even a possibility, but my head was still trying to prepare me for the worse.

My phone started to ring; I looked down and noticed it was Amity finally calling. I literally took a deep breath before I swiped to answer my phone. It had taken her so long to call that I was afraid Honor had caught her putting the letter in his mailbox and that he might be on the other side of the FaceTime. I breathed a sigh of relief when I answered, and it was just Amity's face looking back at me.

"What took you so long?" was the first thing I said to Amity; her face hadn't even fully popped up on my side of the screen.

"Bitch, you mean what took him so long to get the letter out of the mailbox and read it. And no, I don't know how he reacted to the letter because I don't have X-ray vision. Your ass already got me sittin' in a bitch-I-don't-even-like's house to see when he gets the letter, so don't ask for more. You could've just flew out here or called or texted him to tell him everything," Amity said as she rolled her eyes and looked at me as if I were stupid.

"Girl, you love your cousin, don't do too much," I joked, because that was whose house she was using to spy on Honor for me. "And I just can't find the words to tell him everything," I told her.

"Haven, you have never been one to shy away from anything. I think your feelings for him are deeper than you want to admit. You're always so sure and go straight after what you want and need without giving a damn what the next person thinks of you," Amity stated. Little did she know, I could only do that when it was a stranger, or I didn't think a person I had love for would be disappointed in me because of it.

"I know that, but that's just not me anymore, and I can't move without thinking like I use to. Everything I do has to be with my daughter in mind, and I'm not taking her out there if I think she'll be rejected. Me moving like that got me into the fucked-up situation I'm in now. The only way I would move like that again is if I felt like somebody disrespected me or my family. Don't get me wrong, I'm still that person it just takes more to get me there; some people don't even deserve a reaction from me now," I explained. In the last year, I had to evolve into a more mature persona of myself, but there was still that crazy person on the inside of me ready to explode if needed.

"Girl, I don't know if it's about the letter or not, but I just saw Honor and his friends run outside and hop into a car." Amity continued to inform me of their every move until she couldn't see them anymore.

"Get up and run out to your car so you can follow them before you lose them." The words slipped out of my mouth before I could stop myself from sounding like a stalker.

"Hell nawl, I'm not getting killed for your dumbass. What the hell I look like following the car with Patch's crazy ass in it?" Amity belted.

"I hear Jace coming in, I'll call you back later." I hung up the phone right before Jace walked in. Jace walked right by me like he didn't see me when he came into the house. He was probably mad because I hadn't responded to his text.

****

Jace was in the house for over an hour when he came storming down the hall.

"What the fuck is this?" Jace barked. When he got close to me, he tossed his phone at me. His phone hit me in my chest then tumbled onto my lap. I picked up the phone and looked at it. Honor had posted one of the pictures I sent to him of Sayvonna as his cover and profile picture.

"I don't get the fucking problem," I said to him and tossed his phone right back at him; the phone popped him square in his mouth. I was hoping to hear it crash to the ground as well, but he caught it in his hand before that could happen.

"Before you got in contact with this nigga, we should have had a discussion about it. You didn't say shit to me about him having your number or you telling him about her. After all the shit I do for y'all, you should've had enough respect for me to give a nigga a heads up. So I wouldn't be out in the streets looking stupid as fuck. We should've discussed this, but instead I had to be blindsided as soon as a nigga clicked on social media. The first thing I saw is that he switched his pictures out with ones of Sayvonna. When we discussed this before you even had her, I told your ass I didn't have a problem with her knowing her real father, but that I needed to be respected in the fucking process," Jace shouted.

"I didn't call him; I just sent him a letter about all the shit you said I should tell him. Nigga, that was your idea and while writing the letter I felt as though he needed to actually see his daughter as well. If you weren't out in them streets ignoring me, then I wouldn't have sent it without you knowing," I screamed and it made Say start crying.

"Man, I'm not finsta be arguing and screaming with your ass in front of her," he said as he picked up Sayvonna before I could reach my hands out to get her. Jace took Sayvonna to the kitchen and pulled out one of the bottles I pumped for her. I watched as he walked back to her room feeding her without even so much as a glance my way. Ten minutes after he put Sayvonna to sleep, Jace walked out of the house without saying a word to me.

I grabbed a bottle of my sweet pink wine and checked on Sayvonna before I headed to my bedroom. I sipped on my wine and dissected the last couple of hours of my life.

Truly

One month later…

I went and sat across from Patch and Honor and started streaming a movie on my phone. When they changed the channel to watch another Hockey game. I was okay with watching the first two games but when it came time to watch another, I was done with it.

A pop-up telling me I had a message on my social media interrupted my movie thirty minutes into it. My thumb accidentally clicked on the message and took me to my inbox.

_candies00flexable:

Tell me how my pussy tastes on your man's tongue…

I didn't even read the rest of the message I just stopped at the first sentence and stood up.

"What the fuck is this?" I asked Patch as I tossed my phone at him. Patch picked up my phone and read the message then chuckled as he handed my phone to Honor. Honor read the message and laughed too before handing my phone back to Patch. Patch started clicking some more and laughing but he never said anything to me or denied it.

"Ain't shit funny and instead of clicking on her page you need to be tellin' her to stay off my shit. While you still got my phone in your hand click on the message and put that bitch back in her place." Patch just looked at me then turned his attention back to the game.

"Instead of your attention being on that game, it needs to be on me, and you need to be setting shit straight about this message," I told Patch.

"If you stupid enough to think I would fuck that then that's on your stupid ass." Patch said as he waved me off.

"I need a drink," I said to no one in particular, as I snatched my phone out of Patch hand then walked off.

"I don't care how mad you are, don't be snatching shit from me." I heard Patch say but I ignored him just as he was doing my feelings. He was more pissed at me for snatching my phone back than he was about a stripper having the audacity to message me. The more I thought about it pissed me off.

I had every intention of going to the kitchen for a drink but instead, I just bypassed the kitchen and headed out the door. I got in my car and pulled off.

An hour later...

Despite the fear, I clicked to hear the voicemail Patch had sent me. I knew he wasn't sleeping with the chick who had sent me a message, but I was still pissed at him. Not because of the chick insinuating that he was cheating on me but because of how he responded. He basically waved me off and told me I shouldn't have any feelings about the woman being bold enough to step into my inbox since I knew he wasn't cheating. I just wanted him to acknowledge that she shouldn't have felt comfortable enough to do it in the first place, but he dismissed me.

"Hell nawl, I'm not letting her calm down from some shit I didn't even do." I heard him say as the voicemail played. "If she wanna calm down, her ass can do that shit while sitting next to me staring at one of the walls. Letting your girl disappear on your ass and waiting to look for her is how you got stuck engaged to a gold digger ass bitch you don't even really like. And now you can't find the person you want to be with.

"Truly, your ass just played right into that bitch's hands by getting mad and running the fuck off. But since you wanna play games, ready or not here I come." I listened to Patch's voicemail two more times and couldn't believe what he said to Honor.

I drove around trying to find a place where he wouldn't look for me, but I couldn't come up with one, so I just went home. When I pulled up, Patch was already in my driveway leaning against the trunk of his car. He walked over to my car and opened the driver's side door.

"Climb to the passenger side," was all he said.

"How did you know I was here?" I asked him as he pulled off.

"We we're at Honor's house, and the only other place you would go to was to my mothers. My mama would've cussed your ass out worse than me, though, once she found out why your ass was trippin'." I needed more friends besides him and Honor, because that's exactly where I would've gone. And he was right, Brenda would've cussed my ass out and made me feel worse than I already did for going off on Patch about a prostitute stripper.

"Where are we going?" I asked.

"To straighten this shit out since you wanna let a bitch I never even fucked, fuck with your head. Gettin' pissed off for nothing," Patch replied when he stopped at a stop sign. I rolled my eyes at him.

"Roll them motherfuckas again, and I'mma knock those bitches out your head, acting like one of them gullible bitches. Disrespect me again by raising your voice like that because a bitch tryna fuck with what we got, and you gonna regret that shit. And fix your fuckin' face," he ordered.

"I didn't say I believed the bitch. I just wanted you to be as pissed as me and for you to check the bitch. A bitch shouldn't be bold enough to even think she could step to me with the shit. You said you would make sure it didn't happen, but when it did, you was on mute and dismissed my feelings. So you damned right I cussed your ass the fuck out; just do what you said you would, and it won't be no problems," I told him, folding my arms and turning away from him. Patch pulled over and tugged my arms until they unfolded and turned me towards him.

"Look, on the real, though, before we were official, I went to the strip club and tossed a few dollars for a few lap dances. But what I didn't do was fuck none of those bitches like I had everyone thinking. There were two strippers that I fucked with; they're married to each other but not a lot of people know that. When I wanted to fuck it was either one or both of them. They called me for threesomes whenever they wanted to add dick in the mix, and I called whenever I needed my dick wet. A few weeks before we became a couple, they asked me to be their sperm donor because they wanted a baby, but I couldn't just have a child out there and pretend I didn't. Plus, I knew you wouldn't want me doing no shit like that. So, I stopped fuckin' with them and they know not to even look your fuckin' way on some bitter bitch shit. But they both hella cool; so if I find a nigga I think would fit with them, I'mma steer him towards them.

"I don't want you to ever think I'm dismissing your feelings. I just knew that shit you was seeing was faulty as hell. It pissed me off 'cause I thought you believed that shit and thought I would even step to a bitch like her on some other shit." Patch gripped my chin as he leaned over towards me. His eyes stared into mine; he kissed my lips and our eyes closed as our kissed turned deeper.

He pulled back off and twenty minutes later we were at the strip club. The twins, Cashae and Marshae, that worked for Patch were dragging the girl out of the back door by her hair. The girl already had a bloody nose and she was screaming.

"I'm sorry, just tell them to stop; someone paid me five hundred to do that and I got two kids. I ain't passing up no money," she stated.

"Nah, apologize to my woman first, and if it's not sincere enough I'm letting them back on you." Patch spoke nonchalantly as if the girl wasn't half dressed and pleading for mercy.

"I am so sorry for insinuating that your man was cheating on you with me, and I will never do it again. I just needed the money, a man came in here a couple of hours ago with a stack a money, asking me to imply that Patch cheated on you. He even wrote the message; he just paid me to use my account," she said. I asked her what the man looked like and she described him.

"I'mma kill your fuckin' dad," Patch told me.

"That ain't my daddy; he's a fuckin' sperm donor, nothin' more." I wanted to slap him for even calling that man my father.

"Aye and I heard you two fuckin' with Marco little brother and his best friend," Patch looked at the twins and said. The twins' parents died in a fire last year and Patch took on the big brother, protective role. Cashae and Marshae were identical so it was hard to tell them apart. The majority of people in the hood just called them Twins as their name.

"It's not like that with us; we just gettin' money with them," Cashae spoke up. Of the two, she was more vocal.

"Let me find out different, and I'mma show up embarrassing the two of you. Y'all got kids so you bet not be doing faulty shit that will come back on them," Patch warned them.

"We not; I promise," Marshae answered and Patch nodded.

"Let me find out different," he said as he tried to pay them, but they waved the money off.

"Meet us at The Round in an hour with the kids and bring those niggas," Patch told them before we got in the car.

We met the twins, their kids, Marco's lil brother Brendan and Brendan's best friend Oak along with the boys. For the first hour Patch interrogated the boys and threatened them until he felt he got his point across. Then the three of them took the kids to play games while the twins and I sat in the bar area drinking wine.

I loved how Patch made it his business to protect the people in our hood who didn't have no one in their corner. He made sure they knew they had someone to turn to, and that's one of the things I loved most about him.

Two days later...

"I just wish my father was someone else; maybe somebody that I could look up to. But when I heard who he really was, all I could think about was how others would treat me or even Truvon because of him." I blurted out to Patch as soon as he walked into the house after dropping the boys off to school.

"I get what you are saying; since I was a child people assumed my sperm donor's actions would be mine. One time, my mom told her friends they could leave their kids with me while they went stealing or whatever they were going to do. When my mom left out of the room, I heard her friends whispering that basically there was no way they would leave their sons and daughter with me because I was my father's child," Patch told me.

"And what did your crazy ass say to them?" I asked, knowing he cussed them out and made them feel stupid.

"I didn't say shit or tell my mama what they said. I just stepped out of the kitchen and stared at them until they looked back at me with regret and shame written all over their faces," Patch responded.

"Wait, you didn't tell your mama, is she still friends with them?" I had to know because as a mother I would have wanted to know and beat their asses. Well, I wanted to beat their asses on one hand, and on the other, as a parent, I was proud of them for being cautious.

"I didn't tell her because I knew how she would act towards them. But she did the same thing and wouldn't let me stay with those ladies' husbands alone or anybody else she didn't really know. It only pissed me off because they were judging me based on a motherfucka's actions that I wasn't raised by. It was the fact that they thought I was capable of some off-the-wall shit like that, and I guess it hurt more because they weren't strangers on the street," Patch said.

I could see that their words still bothered him. I understood that it was more so that the ladies knew who he was as a person and knew he hadn't even met his father. And yet they still thought he was capable of those actions. If it was strangers or someone who knew little of him, he would have just brushed those words off and not given a damn.

"That's what I'm afraid of; people who don't even know me judging me by the actions of someone else. But more so, that I don't want his enemies thinking they can use me or my son to get back at that nigga," I told him.

"The last part is something you don't have to worry 'bout; everybody knows harming you is like telling me they want me to kill them. And 'bout that other shit, fuck anybody that got some shit to say or feel 'bout it. You needa stop givin' a fuck 'bout what the next person thinks of you and your life; especially when they ain't doing shit for you," Patch said.

"Plus, all you got to go on is Truth thinkin' that he was your father. I can go ask your mom for you," Patch told me, looking into my eyes. His eyes told me everything he was thinking about when he mentioned talking to my mother.

"Nah, I don't need you talkin' to that lady, 'cause she gonna say somethin' that pisses you off and you're gonna react. Plus, with the way you looked when you said that, I already know you want to go there and put her in, what you believe is, her place. I don't need you over there cussin' that lady out so she can call the police on you. Hell, I don't even know why my step-dad is still with my mom in the first place.

"I remember one time they got into a bad argument and she called the police, so he left. When the police got there, she lied and told them he had punched her. What really happened was that she was pinching herself the whole time and banging her arm into a wall. When I told them the truth, she slapped me as soon as she closed the door behind them. She slapped me hard enough to leave a mark. My step-dad asked me about it, and I told him the truth; his ass still stayed," I told Patch.

"Shit you ever try to pull some shit like your mama on me, I'mma be the one to slap the shit out of your ass," Patch grunted.

"Whateva, I'mma go see them after I get out of class to ask her myself, and no you can't come," I told him. I stood from the couch and went to get my school bag from by the door.

"A'ight, just hit me when you get there and when you're leaving. I'mma go get that nigga Honor, and we gonna ride out for a lil min. Just remember to get the boys from my moms when you get done talkin' to your moms," Patch said, following me out of the house.

Patch walked me to my car and waited for me to get in before he headed to Honor's car.

Forty-five minutes later, I pulled into the parking lot of my school. It didn't hit me until I got there that it would be my last time going to school until my graduation next year. Since I was graduating in the Fall I had to wait until Spring since that was the only time my school had their graduation ceremony. I just had to turn in one last paper and sit through one last lecture, and I was finally done with school.

****

"Truly, come in; Victor is in his office," the lady I had been staring at for the pass thirty seconds finally said. When the woman opened my parents' door after I knocked, I couldn't bring myself to say anything. It was a shock that someone other than my parents had answered the door. The woman opened the door wider and moved out of my way.

"Thank you," I told the woman while stepping into the house. I hadn't been there in years. Everything in the house looked and felt completely different then when I lived there.

"Alisha, why you knocking on the door? Just come in," Victor said when he heard my knocks on his office door. I twisted the doorknob then slowly pushed the door open and stood in the doorway. I watch as his face, which previously had a smile on it, formed a frown and then a scowl.

He never took his eyes off me as I walked further into his office. I don't think he even blinked. The expression on his face let me know he was pissed that I was there. If Victor had been light-skinned instead of chocolate, his face would have been red from the anger radiating from him.

My eyes watered as I noticed the small changes in Victor's appearance. He was no longer sporting dreads he had a curly afro instead that was mostly grey at the roots.

Victor had gained a bit of weight making his face a tad rounder than I remembered.

"Well look who finally decided to come home," Victor stated with a bit of anger in his voice. I was shocked by his response; after the way he and my mother treated me when I got pregnant with Truvon, he should have been happy I was there.

"You ran away to your biological father, because you didn't think I could protect you or had enough money, right?" I could hear the agony in his voice. I had no idea what he was talking about, but his anger let me know nothing had changed. I turned on my heels heading for the door.

"He didn't mean it," Alisha rushed to say. I turned to look at her and her expression begged me to talk to him.

"He's your father," she humbly added.

"Hmm, you mean he's the man who raised me, then kicked me out because my rapist got me pregnant and I wanted to keep the baby," I spat, turning to face her.

"What are you talking about, Truly?" I heard him yell from inside his office. Before he could come to the hallway, I was on my way back to his office.

"I didn't kick you out or know you were pregnant," Victor said to me as he walked around his desk. Confusion was etched all over his face.

"When I got back from school my clothes were packed in trash bags waiting for me by the door. Mom had found out I was pregnant and she said, you said I had to get rid of it or I couldn't stay here. I told her I couldn't do that and went to live with my grandparents, but I couldn't stay with them for long because their house was already sold and they were moving into a retirement place. I moved in with Paevon from school a few months before my son was born," I told him.

"When I got back from work that day your mom said you went to live with your father, because you believed he could protect you more than me, after what happened to you. I tried to call your phone, but it was turned off." Victor said. That day was slowly starting to make even more sense.

"When is mom coming home? I need to speak to her 'bout something else?" I asked him as I sat down in one of the chairs.

"I divorced your mother a few months after you were gone. I was only staying with her because of you. And since you were gone there was no point in me staying with her any longer. I met Alisha a few months later and we got married last year. I looked for you for a few years to tell you everything but couldn't find you," Victor told me as he sat back down.

"I wanted to ask my mom who my father was, because someone else just told me who he was. They also said my mom was extorting money from him to keep it a secret," I told him.

"Before we get to that, I wanna know why you had to move in with some dude from school. I had an account for you that I had been putting money in for college; your mama told me you took the debit card with you. You could've spent your money on getting a place to live and still went to college, instead of doing all that moving in with strangers shit," Victor said.

"I never even knew you had gotten me a bank account, let alone took the debit card for it," I replied.

"Fuck! That bitch lied to me, kicked you out and stole from the both of us. And here I am still having to give her alimony," Victor fumed.

"We wanted you to come to our wedding and tried to find you on Facebook but got nothing," Alisha remarked as she walked further into the room.

"My page is private; people can only find me by searching my email." I told him as she sat in the chair across from me and Victor.

"Where's your child?" Alisha asked.

"He should be at my boyfriend's mom's house by now," I answered.

"Do you think I can meet him?" Victor asked.

"After learning the truth about what happened, of course, but I need to find my mother so she can tell me who my biological father is," I answered him.

"She wouldn't tell me who he was, but I heard her call him Richy when she was talkin' to one of her friends." Victor gave me the answer I didn't want or need.

"Richy!" Alisha exclaimed, and the look on her face let me know she knew who he was firsthand.

"I was hoping when someone said he was my father that they didn't know what they were talkin' 'bout."

"You know him?" Victor asked Alisha.

"He stalked one of the girls who worked with me, and it got so scary that she had to transfer to another state," Alisha said. I wanted to change the subject from Richy when I heard that, so I started catching Victor up on my life. An hour later, I had to end the conversation.

"I have to go get my son, so Brenda can go to work," I told Victor and Alisha.

"How about you, your boyfriend and son come to dinner this weekend, so I can get to know them," Victor said.

"We'll come, just call me tomorrow sometime," I told Victor as I wrote my number down on a piece of paper. Victor and Alisha stood up and walked me to the door. They stood on the porch and waited until I got in the car before they walked back in the house and closed the door.

I pulled off with more information to process than before I arrived.

Haven

One months later...

"Mom!" I yelled out as I stormed into the house. I was scared because for the first time she had left me standing outside of the school for an hour. Ever since Savon's death my mother had been picking me up from school, and that was the only time she got out of bed for the day. I had to walk over a mile home right after running two miles in P.E.

I called my dad to come get me, but he wasn't answering his phone either. I went from my parents' room to the living room looking for them and didn't see either one of them. The next place I went to look was the kitchen, although my mother hadn't stepped foot in there in a little while.

"Mom! Dad!" I screamed as I ran further into the kitchen where both my mother and father's bodies were laid out.

I dropped down next to them on the ground and tried to shake them hard enough to come back to me, but it wasn't working.

The sound of my alarm going off woke me up out of my sleep. Thank god for the alarm I set to alert me to check my office email, because I didn't want to re-experience my parents' death again. When it got close to my parents' birthdays, I always had the same dream back to back until I woke up. I hated that, and I wished I knew who did it. I think I would have been able to grieve my parents properly if their killer or killers would have been found. My dad's friend was still trying to figure out who killed them. For a while after their death no one let their kids go outside because my dad's crew was picking up any and everybody for information on my parents' death no matter who they were. I just needed closure because these feelings running amuck inside of me were just too much to keep holding onto.

My chest ached and my nerves were shot. I wanted to roll a big fat blunt to calm my nerves but Sayvonna was home so I couldn't. My apartment wasn't properly insulated so smoke traveled into every room of my house, and I couldn't have that. Instead I got up and went into the kitchen to open a bottle of wine. I grabbed a glass so I wouldn't feel like a lush.

I sat on the couch staring at the door as I sipped on my last bottle of wine feeling dejected and alone. Despite my fiancé, and I used the term loosely, living with me I still felt alone, and I was struggling emotionally and financially. A couple of months after I moved to Vegas, he proposed to me and I said yes. My yes was based solely on how he was my rock in high school and nothing more. He wanted to get married at the court house right before Sayvonna was born, but for some reason I just couldn't.

Jace had become so cheap but only when it came to me, my daughter and our household. When it came to himself, he had no problem spending his last dime on material items. However, if I asked for rent or some daycare money, it was a problem. I was tired of his ass, but I was trying to hold on. I could still remember how he made me feel when I found Savon hanging from the ceiling in his room, and when I found my parents' bodies.

Back then when I was feeling hurt and all alone in the world, Jace was the one by my side helping me up when I wanted to give up.

I polished off my last glass of wine as Jace came stumbling into the house.

"Jace, you know the rent is due, right." He looked at me as if I was crazy before he answered.

"Man, can I get fully in the door before you start that shit?" he asked as he closed the door behind him. I couldn't even really hear what he had said because I was too focused on the five shopping bags he had in his hands.

"Where's your half of the rent?" I asked him for what felt like the hundredth time in the last couple of months. He started off paying his half of everything, but four months ago I started having to pay the full rent. My savings account was depleted because I had to pay all the bills alone. It was like Jace became materialistic and selfish; maybe he was always like that and didn't show his true colors until it was almost time for us to sign on the dotted line.

"Man, the rent out here is not even that much; that's why I moved out here. The rent is only like six hundred dollars. You can afford that shit on your own," he said like it wasn't a big deal.

"Actually, the rent went up to eight hundred and eighty-nine dollars a few months back, and it is going up another hundred in a few months. And no, I can't pay it by myself. I just paid for all the back backpay for Sayvonna's daycare you keep forgetting to pay. Since, all of a sudden, you started acting like you couldn't watch her for a couple of hours. So, you need to cough up some rent money." *I shouldn't have to ask him for the rent nor daycare money,* I thought to myself.

"Look Haven, I don't have that shit right now; hit me up in a few days," he answered nonchalantly.

"Take those new Jordans you got on your feet, those designer shirts, and that watch you bought last week back, and then you can pay the rent. Better yet, take that shit back that's in those bags in your hands."

Jace was so frustrating; all he cared about was looking good in the casinos. He didn't care if we had a roof over our heads as long as he had decent shoes on his feet.

"I ain't taking shit back. A nigga worked hard for this shit, and I'mma wear it." I wanted to punch his ass in the face. It was alright, though, because when he woke up he wasn't going to have shit.

"You got until the tenth to give me your half of the bills for this month and the last couple you missed or else you have to get out," I told him. In my mind I wouldn't back down no matter what he said. He had talked me out of kicking his ass out plenty of times but not anymore.

"Yeah, yeah what did you make for dinner?" Like always he ignored everything I said.

"Nothing for you; I only cook dinner for adults who pay bills and children," I told him. He gave me a funny look like he was ready to cuss me out, but his phone started ringing and interrupted him. He looked at me one last time before he answered it and walked towards our bedroom, leaving me wondering how we got to this point in our lives and why I was even with him. I still couldn't believe I was with someone that resembled Michael Ealy, if he was fat with brown eyes and a round face.

It had been becoming increasingly clear that something had to give in my life. Jace stayed out all hours of the night, and I knew it wasn't because he was hustling. He had to be fooling around on me with other women, but I didn't have any proof. Whenever I went through his phone there was never any text messages or calls from other women. But something deep inside of me was telling me that he was creeping. Still, a part of me felt as though he had been there for me more than anyone else in the past. So I couldn't leave him when there wasn't any proof, just a gut feeling.

Ideas formed in my head as I headed to the sink with my empty glass in hand. Once I put my glass in the sink and the bottle in the recycle bin, I had a full-blown plan in my mind. I was going to get me and my baby up early in the morning and take everything Jace had bought back to the stores. Then I would pay my light, phone and water bill with that money. His dumb ass always left the receipts in the bags until he wore his clothes. I was going to make sure he regretted trying to skip out on the bills for material items.

A couple of hours later, I realized I was somehow in my own bed when I knew I fell asleep on the couch. My eyes weren't even all the way open, and I was still in between sleep and consciousness. Jace thought he was slick; I pretended to still be asleep as I felt him spread my legs wide and press my thighs into the mattress.

If he thought a little head was going to make me forget he didn't have his half of the rent, yet again, his ass had another thing coming. Usually I would've stopped him, but I hadn't had a proper licking nor sucking down there in a while. And I knew he would give me superb head because he was trying to get me to forget all his fuck ups.

Fuck this feels so fucking goddamn good, I thought as his tongue did a tentative swipe of my clit. I felt his tongue swirl around my pussy teasing my clit. I was about to slap him in the back of the head, but he finally sucked my clit gently but firmly into his mouth

He slipped one finger, then two inside of my tight passage, moving slowly at first, then a bit faster as he sucked harder and harder driving me insane. He rotated his fingers around in a fast motion while alternating between sucking and licking on my clit.

The friction from him sucking on my clit while he twirled his fingers around inside of me, caused a gush of my cream to coat his hand, mouth and the inside of my thigh.

My eyes shut tightly as I bucked my hips down towards him while groaning, "right there," repeatedly.

He pumped his fingers in and out as his mouth alternated between sucking and nipping on my clit. It was as if my legs had a mind of their own and before I knew it, they were spread wider, giving him better access.

"Damn, a nigga almost forgot how you taste; you taste so good." Jace said as he pulled back and bit the sides of my thighs right before he dove back into my pussy. His mouth seized my clit and sucked harder as I reached for my fully erect nipples and pinched them at the same time. I squeezed harder and harder trying to match his every suck, lick, and thrust.

I cried out, gripped his head and pulled him deeper into my pussy. I could feel my juices as they flowed freely onto his tongue. He never let up as he quickly took me from one orgasm to the next. He didn't stop until I smacked him on the forehead a few times.

I was exhausted. I think I passed out for a second because the next thing I remembered was Jace wiping my pussy and thighs with a warm cloth then drying me off with another. I turned over once he was finished, curled up in a ball and fell asleep.

When I woke up the next morning and looked at Jace's spot, he was gone. The bags he had brought in with him were empty except for the shoe bag and the one that held his coat. I got myself and Sayvonna dressed and we headed straight to the mall to take the items back.

I took back the jacket and shoes he had purchased and treated me and Say to breakfast.

After breakfast I paid Sayvonna's daycare for the upcoming week since that was all the money could pay for. I couldn't believe his punk ass had told me he didn't have money for bills but had spent over two-fifty on shoes. Especially when he knew we barely had groceries in the house and the lights were a few days from being cut off.

Seeing everything I had to do just to keep a roof over our heads confirmed that there was no point in being in Vegas or staying with Jace. I just had to get up enough money to get us back home. Once I did, I wasn't looking back.

Truly

I prayed my mother didn't see me as I walked the boys towards the barbershop; she was headed to the nail shop next door. A sense of relief washed over me when we made it to the door without her noticing me; on the other hand, it was sad to me that my mother didn't recognize me or her grandson. Although she hurt me with words and physical abuse so many times, there was still a part of me that craved a mother-daughter relationship with her. When I was a kid, I was desperate for her love and affection.

"Where's dad?" PJ asked. He looked through the window at the barbershop and didn't see Patch.

"He's on his way here," I answered him, opening the door to the barbershop.

"Truly, is that you?" I heard my mother's voice. My breath hitched in my throat and I couldn't breathe for a second.

"Mom, who's that?" Truvon asked as he looked over at my mother. He probably asked because I look so much like her; only some of my features came from the paternal side.

"That's a shame; he doesn't even know his grandma." My mother Jennifer had the nerve to say as if I was keeping him from her.

"And whose fault is that?" I quickly shot back. There was no way I wasn't going to respond after she tried to put the blame on me. She never took accountability for the things she did to me. Instead, my mother would create a whole different scenario to make it seem like she did no wrong, and it was all my fault. At first everyone would believe her lies about me, because she was my parent and what parent would lie on their child. But one day my mother didn't know my grandmother was in the house. She slapped me because I told her I was hungry in front of our family. She said I was trying to embarrass her in front of them so they'd think she wasn't feeding me. Then she marched outside where the family was and told them that I had hit and yelled at her.

"Here we go with you lying on me again," was the only thing she said. She was trying to repeat the toxic cycle that had been our relationship for so long, but I was older and there was no way I was jumping back into that cycle. Growing up, she would say degrading things about me whenever we were around other people. She would wait until people were around to ask if I had showered that day or put on deodorant and she'd say she was only asking because I smelled. It would make me feel so self-conscious that I would sniff myself. But when I did that, I never smelled anything nor did anyone else. My mother would never apologize, and I would pretend it didn't happen until the next time it did. Whenever my grandmother would ask me if I wanted to live with her I would say no because I was desperate to have that same mother-daughter relationship I noticed all my friends at school had.

"What's going on out here?" Brenda asked as she walked out of the 711 with the boys' snacks.

"Who the hell are you?" Jennifer asked Brenda.

"Her mother; who the fuck are you, bitch?" Brenda replied.

"You can't be her mother because I gave birth to that lil' bitch right there, and I have the fucked-up stomach to prove it," Jennifer said as she walked closer.

"Boys, take the snacks from grandma and walk inside with Mr. T," I told them. I had to tap Brenda for her to hand them the snacks. She was too busy staring my mother up and down and daring her to jump bad with her eyes.

"What if grandma need help?" Truvon asked.

"I don't need your help, baby," Jennifer told Truvon, assuming he was speaking about her.

"You're not my grandmother; she is," Truvon told my mother as he pointed to Brenda. That pissed my mother off.

"Boy, grandma is good; now listen to your mother." For the first time Brenda took her eyes off my mother and cut them at Truvon.

"A'ight Grams, just call me if you need help. My Pa-Pa said I'm the man and need to protect my ladies whenever Patch is not around," Truvon said as he took PJ's hand before walking into the barber shop. I was going to have to give my grandfather another talk about telling Truvon that stuff. I knew he was just going to ignore me and give Truvon what he called man-to-boy advice. He said he was preparing Truvon to be the man his father had taught him to be.

"Now, that my grandchildren aren't around I can give you this ass whopping for tryna fuck up my daughter's life and self-esteem. Selfish, insecure bitches like you try to break their children down because you don't want your children surpassing you. I know all 'bout the fucked-up shit you said and did to her growing up, and I've been wanting to fuck you up for a long fucking time," Brenda said as she started taking off her earrings. Brenda tied her dreads up into a bun quickly. People tended to dismiss Brenda because she was five foot nothing with a bit of curves on her. Patch had got his eyes, coloring, and facial features from her.

"I don't got time for this ghetto shit, and Truly ain't nothing but a fuckin' liar tryna make me seem like a bad fuckin' parent," my mother said, trying to place the blame on me again.

"Nah, your mama told me all the shit she caught you sayin' and doin' to Truly that you tried to lie 'bout," Brenda told her as she kicked off her flip flops.

"Look, I ain't got time for this ghetto ass shit when I need to be getting pampered," Jennifer said. She liked to pick on people that she knew wouldn't challenge her. That included kids and men who didn't believe in hitting women.

"Not in the nail shop Truly and my son just bought, you won't," Brenda told her.

"Nah, Ma we don't discriminate when it comes to money; she can go in there and we'll get our pampering done in one of the VIP rooms in the back," I told Brenda.

"I'mma still kick your ass, just not when my grandkids or anybody that will stop me from fucking your ass up is around," Brenda snapped.

"Bitch, I don't take too well to threats," Jennifer finally said as she took another step towards Brenda. She had courage now because she noticed a crowd was forming.

"What the fuck is going on here?" Patch asked as he walked up.

"We ran into my mother, and now Mom is ready to beat her ass," I told Patch.

"Oh, that's your mom? The lady that kicked you out and stole your college money?" When we went to dinner with Victor last month, he and Patch had a private chat. Victor must've told Patch about the money because all I told him was that my mom lied when she said Victor had kicked me out.

"Mom, beat her ass," Patch chimed in.

"Patch, stop that! The boys are here and there are too many people around," I told him, gesturing for him to stop his mother as she ran up on mine and started swinging.

"Oh, y'all gonna pay for this, especially your lying ass!" my mother shouted before she stormed to her car holding her bloody nose.

"She must not know who she fuckin' with, thinkin' she can threaten my family," Patch said making me wish my mother had never spotted me. Although she had done me wrong, there was still a part of me that wanted to have that connection with her. I knew from her threat that Patch nor Brenda would let her get away with it. It kind of made me feel as though it was all my fault.

"I'm just gonna go home," I told Patch and Brenda after my mother sped out of the parking lot. My heart felt as though it was being squished in my chest and those feelings from my childhood started to resurface.

"A'ight, I'mma hit you up to see what you want to eat when me and the boys get done here," Patch said as he walked me to my car.

When I left I had every intention of going to my house or Patch's, but I ended up in front of my childhood home. I was going to pull off but when I looked at the house one last time, Victor and Alisha were standing on the porch looking at me and waiting. I got out the car and headed towards them contemplating why I was there.

"You seen her, huh?" Victor asked with his arms stretched out for me; I walked straight into them as I nodded my head.

"We'll order your favorite ice cream and watch your favorite movie. Come in; you can shower while you wait, some of your pajamas are still here." I knew Victor was trying to suggest a shower because by then I had dried up tears and probably snot on my face. I was out in my car sobbing for a minute before I looked up and noticed Victor and Alisha.

"I have to run into work for a couple of hours for an emergency, but I'll bring dinner back," Alisha said, as her phone started beeping back to back. Without another word, she left the house.

"We came to the door almost twenty minutes ago, so Alisha could go put out the emergencies popping up at her job. That's when we saw you crying. Alisha wanted to go comfort you but I know how much you hated that when you was younger," Victor said.

"Thanks, Dad, and get me some caramel on the side for my ice cream," I told him before I headed upstairs to my old bedroom.

Thirty minutes later I came down the stairs fresh out of the shower in my pajamas. Victor was at the door getting the ice cream that had just been delivered. Just like old times, I sat on the couch next to Victor with my ice cream in my hand and watched my favorite move *Love and Basketball.* I laid my head on Victor's shoulder. This movie always gave me comfort and had me believing in imperfect fairytales.

I woke up on the couch a few hours later and was happy to see that Patch and the kids were there. Patch and I decided to stay the night at Victor's house with the boys, and for the first time in a while I felt like I had everything I needed to survive life.

Three days later...

"Who the hell you texting on my phone?" I asked Patch when I walked out of the bathroom and into the bedroom.

"Some nigga that just texted back sayin' he's your dad, but I'm 'bouta call that nigga," Patch said.

"That's Victor you texting, dumbass." I told him when I looked over and saw the number he was texting on my phone.

"You just tried to lie to me like I ain't got that nigga's number in my phone," Patch said.

"He called my mom to tell her she had to pay me back the money she stole from me and forgot to block his number. She stared callin' his phone non-stop so he changed his number. He texted you too in our group message to give you the new number," I told him.

"Oh, I silenced that group chat; y'all motherfuckas text too damn much 'bout nothin'," Patch said.

"Wait, so do you be putting me on silent when you think I'm texting you too much?" I asked him.

"Hell yeah, I even put your ass on the block list when you be mad and be texting those long ass paragraphs. When people start callin' my phone too much, I put my phone on do-not-disturb too. But don't trip you're in my favorites so your calls come through." I wanted to punch his dumbass, but that shit didn't faze Patch; as long as I didn't hit him in the face, he was cool.

He was about to say something else when there was a knock on my door. I went to my front door and opened it, standing before me was a woman I had never seen before.

"Truly Jackson?" the woman asked.

"Who's asking?" Patch asked as he walked up and stood behind me.

"You've been served," the woman said, tossing a yellow envelop at me before she ran off.

I picked up the envelope and opened it knowing it had something to do with my mother's ass. As my eyes scanned the paper my heart started to pound in my chest, my hands started to shake and my tears made my vision blurry.

"His mother is filing for grandparent rights!" my voice trembled as I shouted. The same woman who spit in my face and told me I should've been a woman and spread my legs for her son, and he wouldn't have taken it, had the nerve to want rights to my fucking son. After she called him a bastard that would never amount to shit and that I should've gotten rid of him.

"Oh, that bitch and his whole family 'bouta die!" Patch barked.

Haven

"My assistant said you had a question or two for me." Mrs. Clark, my new boss, said as she walked up to my desk. I worked as a receptionist at a realty firm. The hospital I worked at let me go a month or so after I had Sayvonna because they needed to downsize.

"I wanted to know if there were any position at the California office and if so how do I start the process to transfer?"

"I believe one or two of the realtors are looking for assistance; I can contact them to set up an interview for you," Mrs. Clark said to me.

I was about to thank her when a loud commotion near the entrance caught my attention. I turned my head around to look and I noticed it was Jace storming in with Sayvonna in his arms. He had a pissed off look on his face. I jumped up to go get my baby from him praying he wouldn't do anything stupid.

I tried out to grab Sayvonna out of his arms, but the next thing I knew Jace's free hand was wrapped around my neck.

"Bitch, you got me out here lookin' stupid with my family and think my family 'bouta keep watchin' a kid that's not mine!" Jace's cousin owned a daycare and I paid just like everyone else for Sayvonna to go there. I didn't know what the hell he was going on about.

I started to claw at his hands trying to get him to stop as I struggled to take a breath.

"Let her go! I'm calling security and the police right now!" Mrs. Clark shouted. Her words must've snapped Jace out of it, because he pushed me to the ground.

"And take your baby with you, dumb bitch," Jace said as he damn near tossed Sayvonna into my arms.

"Miss Pane, I can't have altercations of this sort in front of clients; you're fired and don't bother with trying to apply at the California office," Mrs. Clark said as she watched me struggle to get off the ground with my baby.

When I finally managed to catch my breath and get up, Mrs. Clark was standing there with my purse and phone in her hand. I snatched my shit and stormed out to my car only to notice it wasn't in the parking lot.

"Where's my car?" I asked the parking lot security guard.

"A man and woman took it a few minutes ago." I knew it had to have been Jace and whatever woman he was cheating on me with.

Fuck! That nigga left me stranded at work with my baby. I FaceTimed the only person who I had left in my corner and prayed she didn't give me her I-told-you-so speech.

"Bitch, what the fuck happened to your neck?" Amity asked seconds after our FaceTime connected.

"Jace bitch ass," I told her as I swiped tears from my eyes.

"Where he at?" Amity asked as she pulled her hammer from her purse. Ever since one of the dancers at the club where she worked got robbed, Amity carried either a hammer or kitchen knife in her purse. I understood the kitchen knife being in her purse, but I didn't get why she carried the hammer.

"So you gon' bust him in the head from over 500 miles away?" I questioned her.

"Hell yeah, fuck that bitch ass nigga! Or I'll just call my brother to do it," Amity spat; she couldn't stand Jace.

"I know, I know. I don't know why I stayed with him," I replied, because I had no clue what else to say.

"Haven, I'm sorry to say this but I feel as though you were trying too hard to walk the same path your parents did. Your mother went hard for your father, and I get that you want that relationship with Jace, but you're ignoring the warning signs. Your parents might have been perfect for each other but that is not the case with you and Jace.

"I seriously think you're holding on because you want to marry a man your parents met. You're so focused on stayin' with the person who took your virginity that you runaway from everything that could make you happy pass you by. All that matters is making sure you and Say are happy. Say hardly knows Jace and he lives with y'all. Plus, she has a whole father waitin' to meet her." When Amity said that I wanted to tell her she was wrong, but I couldn't. My parents had always told me that you stick by your husband no matter what, and I took that advice to heart. I thought Jace had to be my husband, because he had been there for me and they knew him. My mother went against her family to be with my father because she loved him, not because he was the person they thought she should be with.

What I didn't realize was that in trying to honor my parents, I was doing nothing but making me and my child's life miserable. I kidnapped Honor to make him pay for what his father did, because that was what my father would have wanted me to do.

I had to stop thinking like that and start focusing on what I wanted. The first thing I wanted was to leave Jace and for his ass to stay the hell away from me.

"I know and I have nothing holding me back here anymore since he made me lose my job. As soon as I get paid next week I'mma buy a plane ticket to come home," I told her.

"I'll send you the money so that you can come home today," Amity said.

"Okay and I'll pay you back next week when I get my check. I'll call you when I get to the house so we can get my ticket," I told her before I hung up.

"Miss Pane, that's your cab pulling up now," the parking lot security guard said, walking up to me. He apologized for letting Jace take my car without confirming it with me and gave me the money for my cab ride. I thanked him for the money and got into the cab.

Fifteen minutes later, the cab dropped me off in the parking lot of my apartment building. When I got in front of my door, there was another eviction notice on the door. I had just given them a check to pay for the two payments of rent I had missed so I was all caught up.

I didn't understand what was going on and felt defeated; my baby started crying in my arms, and I couldn't do nothing but cry with her.

Haven

After I read the eviction notice on the door, I tried to stick my key in the lock but nothing happened. I marched to the office only to learn that my check had bounced. Confused, I used my banking app on my phone to check my account. I was at a negative three thousand dollars; I noticed he started using my debit card a few weeks ago and ran through my shit.

A couple of days after I took Jace's jacket and shoes, he finally came home and was pissed about what I did. He threatened to do the same thing to all my clothes before he left the apartment and never come back whenever I was home. A couple of days after he left, I had to figure out a way to pay everything on my own. So, I hid my debit card from myself because I didn't want to spend unnecessary money; I started using checks to pay the bills instead. Jace, must have found my debit card and he started using it without my knowledge.

The office clerk said I had to pay them at least half of last month's rent in order to get inside the apartment to get as much stuff as I could. I paid my next-door neighbor to watch Sayvonna with the last of my lunch money and went to find Jace. That 'find my phone' option came in handy when you were really in a pinch and needed to find a punk ass nigga. I called a cab and headed to where his phone said he was.

"Pull over right here," I told the cab driver when I spotted Jace's ass surrounded by a bunch of niggas.

"Do you need me to stay ma'am?" The driver asked as he looked over at the men standing on the corner in front of some run down apartments.

"Nah, I'll be fine, sir," I told him as I handed him the money for the ride before I got out.

"Man, what the fuck your ass doing here?" Jace questioned when he spotted me walking towards him.

"What am I doing here, nigga? I wouldn't be here if you didn't steal and start using my debit card. Bitch, you ran through my money and got me and Sayvonna kicked out. On top of that, you practically threw my fucking child at me, choked me, and stole the car I just paid off! I'm here to get my fuckin' car and the money you took so I can go back home!" I shouted.

"Oh so that's what this is about? Bitch, you just keep tryna play me like I'm some type of punk ass nigga. You thought I didn't hear you on the phone with Amity's bitch ass, planning to go back to Cali to be a family with the next

225

Dear, Honor & Haven   Marqua'lla

nigga? You got me fucked up. I'm not one of those sucka ass niggas you can walk all over; miss me with that bullshit. Me taking that money was back pay for all the bills I paid a couple of months ago. The only reason I didn't kick you out in the dead of the night behind this shit is because of your daughter. I left you enough money in your account for you to feed Say and pay the rent that's it!" Jace spat.

"Sayvonna's daddy is getting married; I wasn't going back to be with him, nigga. I was going so she could meet her daddy. You would have known that if you ever answered my calls or stayed at home long enough for us to fuckin' talk, but nah that's too much like right. And my account is over three thousand dollars in the fucking negative, so you spent way more than you said!" I shouted back at him ass.

"Man, you lying; I left that shit upstairs in my room at my homegirl place," Jace replied.

"Oh, you don't believe me? Look at this, nigga, and while I'm pulling it up start getting your money ready because you owe me over four thousand dollars," I told him as I tapped on my banking app.

"He ain't make your account be overdrawn that was me, bitch, because you tried to play my nigga." Some girl said as she climbed out of my car.

"So come run me my motherfuckin' money, bitch, and give me the keys to my car or get fucked up."

"You ain't gon' do shit you, bitch," the woman said.

Everything in my head was telling me not to whoop her ass, but my heart was saying, *she took from your child. KILL HER!* I hopped on that bitch; we went tumbling to the ground. I gripped her hair tightly in my hands then rammed her head into the cement. I started punching that bitch in the face repeatedly. I wanted her to feel all the pain me and my daughter felt.

"Get the fuck off her," Jace said as he tried to pull me off.

"Jace, you got two seconds to let her the fuck go, my nigga." I heard Amity's brother, Amir, say as he walked up on the scene.

"Haven, get the fuck up off that bitch and get in my car. I should slap your ass for being out here fightin' over a cheating fuck nigga," Amir barked.

"I'm not fighting because he fuckin' that bitch. This nigga choked me, stole my debit card and my car that I paid for. Then he let this bitch use my debit card, and now I owe the bank over three thousand dollars. And 'cause of that, the check for my rent check bounced and now me and my daughter can't get our shit or get home." I told Amir. Suddenly, Jace was flying into the side of the building because Amir two-pieced him.

"Don't ever come out here again acting a fool over no nigga about some money even if it's your husband. You know I got you and Say like I got Amity," Amir told me as he pulled me towards him.

"Amir, I didn't know you knew her," the woman said, then hurriedly handed me my keys.

"Run my sister her money now," Amir barked at her.

"All I got is this," she pulled out a bunch of ones and twenties and gave them to him. Amir motioned for me to take the money from him and count it.

"It's only enough for me to drive home, not to pay off the debt her ass put me in," I reported to Amir.

"Jace, since you the reason why she was able to steal from my sis, come up off them four stacks," Amir said.

"Hell nawl, I'm not 'bouta let your ass punk me; whatever happened with the debit card is between Haven and Chantel," Jace insisted, trying to discreetly reach for his gun. Two of the men Jace was just chopping it up with pulled out their guns and pointed them at him.

"Mace, run through that nigga's pockets and give my sister everything he got," Amir told one of his workers.

"Thanks bro." I kissed Amir on the cheek and walked off to my car after Mace gave me the money from Jace's pockets.

"Go back home and don't let me find out you went back to this bitch ass nigga." I heard Amir call out to me before I got in my car and pulled off.

Two hours later, me and Sayvonna were headed home, a place I shouldn't have left in the first place.

Truly

I was in the kitchen marinating some of the meat for a bar-b-que Patch and Honor had planned for Rocko in a few days. He had gotten out of prison a couple of days ago.

I heard the emergency alert blaring from the TV, and my nosey ass almost broke my neck trying to get to the living room to see what happened.

"Breaking news," a news anchor said, "coming live from SK State Prison. The manhunt is on for an inmate who escaped from the prison a couple of hours ago. Damaria Jones, was a model inmate, but during a special cleanup assignment the inmate disappeared." As soon as I heard the name fear instantly took over my body, and I couldn't move—I was speechless. The person who took my innocence was out, and the only thing I could think about was that he was coming for us.

Boom! Boom! Boom! Boom!

My heart began beating out of my chest when someone started pounding on the side of my house. I heard glass shattering somewhere in the house. Fear halted me until my fight or flight instincts kicked in; needless to say flight was the option that came natural. My body went into autopilot and before my thoughts could register, I was hiding in the pantry with a knife in my hand.

I don't know how long I was in the pantry before I heard someone walking around my house.

If he comes in here, you better stab his ass until you can't stab no more.

"Truly! Where the fuck you at, girl." For a second my body froze until the voice registered.

"Patch! Damaria escaped and was just here; we gotta go get Truvon before he finds him," I screamed to Patch as I ran towards him.

"Man, that punk ass nigga not gon' do shit to neither one of y'all, so calm your ass down." I was damn near hyperventilating in his arms and that was the only thing he thought to say to me.

"Nigga, yes he is; he was just here!" the panic in my voice was evident.

"No, he wasn't. That nigga is at the warehouse being guarded by Honor and Rocko," Patch replied.

"Well who the hell was that banging up against the house?"

"Man, it was probably the tree being blown against the house again. Your ass hella scary; you keep letting that same tree scare the fuck out of you," Patch said nonchalantly.

"I don't believe your ass; you're just tryna make me not scared. You tryna to tell me y'all found a man before the News even reported he had escaped?"

"Mannnn, one of Damaria's victims, cousin is a CO; she didn't get a chance to speak out because she committed suicide before he got locked up. The CO and Rocko came up with the plan to help Damaria escape. Damaria's dumbass believed he was lucky when he walked away without anybody seeing him. We were waiting right there in a van. Shit, we had him locked away in the warehouse an hour before they realized he was gone," Patch replied.

"I came here 'cause your uncle thought it should be your choice on whether you wanted to watch him get killed or not," Patch told me.

"What do you think?" I asked him, because I was on the fence on whether or not I should be there. On one hand, I believed seeing it might make my nightmares go away. But at the same time, I was scared that it would backfire and make them worse.

"Honor don't think you should be there, but Rocko thinks you should.I think you need to be the one that kills that nigga because knowing you, you're not gonna really believe he's dead unless you do it. Just know you took your control back, even if you have nightmares," Patch told me, and he was right. If someone else did it my mind I wouldn't have my control back.

"I'mma come but I don't know if I can kill him. If I don't, I need it to be you," I told him, and he agreed.

"Get a jacket; it's freezing out there, and let's go," Patch told me as he looked down at the emergency alert on his phone and smiled.

"Okay, put the meat in the fridge for me while I get my jacket," I replied. After I put on my jacket, Patch and I left the house heading for the warehouse.

On the thirty-minute drive, Patch told me how he had been planning to kill Damaria ever since he sent his cousin to my house last year. He went as far as to find a couple of lookalikes so Damaria could be spotted in different places for a few days after he was dead. Patch had settled on it only being one lookalike at the last minute because he didn't want a lot of people knowing what was really going on. Patch had given the one he picked the jumpsuit Damaria had on from the jail, and a car that would be reported stolen in a few hours. Patch even stole one of Damaria's mom's credit cards and gave it to the lookalike to make some purchases before he disappeared to another state.

"How do you know dude won't snitch?" I asked Patch as we pulled up to the warehouse.

"Noah is my brother from Arizona our mothers were best friends and they were raped by the same man a few days apart. Because everyone hid what happened to my mom, he was able to do the same thing to my brother's mom. When Noah's mom found out she was pregnant, her parents moved her to another state." Patch never said the person who raped his mom name out loud because it used to send his mom in a downward spiral.

I was shocked he was in touch with one of his siblings from that man. He didn't talk to none of his other siblings, but maybe that was because he had something in common with Noah. The other siblings all had the same mom and she knew what their sperm donor did to Noah's and Patch's mother's but she still married and had kids by him.

"Why didn't you tell me 'bout him?" I asked as we got out his car.

"Shit me and Noah don't even talk like that, just here and there. We mostly keep up with each other by looking at one another's social media."

"Let's go get this over with," Patch told me. He noticed me hesitating and wrapped his arm around my waist. I took a deep breath, then took it one step at a time until we were standing a few feet away from Damaria. He was tied to a chair, Honor and Rocko were standing on either side of the chair and there was a man standing in the shadows.

Demaria was dark-brown with blemishes on his face that looked as though he picked at his skin. His lips were pink with dark spots and his beady eyes creeped me out. He was tall and skinny with a small 'fro he reminded me of J.J. off *Good Times*.

"Man, you really brought her?" Honor questioned; I could tell he was pissed.

"Yeah; why the hell you got a problem with it?" Patch asked him.

"You know how bad seeing someone get killed can fuck with you? she don't need that on top of everything else," Honor answered.

"Man, you don't be there when she wakes up in the middle of the night from nightmares of that fuck nigga escaping and coming after her. Or her waking up in a cold sweat 'cause she remember when he raped. I'd rather her wake up dreaming 'bout this instead," Patch responded and Rocko agreed with him.

Patch motion and the big husky man in the shadows started walking closer to Damaria.

"If it's somethin' you don't wanna see, turn around, and if it gets too bad go wait in the car," Patch insisted. He waited until I gave him confirmation that I understood. Seconds later Patch was on Damaria beating his ass.

"Untie him so he can fight back," Patch said, stepping back as Rocko and Honor did as he instructed.

"Get up and fight back." At first Damaria and the others just stared at Patch as if he was crazy.

"I don't feel right whopping a nigga's ass that can't fight back; hell, I'll even give you a chance for a cheap shot." Damaria quickly stood up on wobbly legs. When his legs were steady, he swung and hit Patch in the jaw; that pissed me off but all Patch did was smirk.

"I'mma give you one more shot but make it count," Patch told Damaria.

"Don't do it," Honor warned Damaria, but he didn't listen. Patch caught his punch mid-swing and twisted Damaria's hand until it popped. It was my first time hearing the sound of bones breaking and I didn't want to hear it again. Still, Damaria's screams were quite satisfying because everyone was ignoring his pleads for help… just like he did mine.

I watched captivated as Patch landed punch after punch; maybe it was strange to some, but I was turned on watching Patch get revenge for me.

"I'm done with his ass, get him up and sit him back in the chair." Patch motioned for the big man standing off to the side to come forward as Damaria bitch ass cowered on the ground.

"When niggas like him are around real men they cower on the inside, because they know their weaknesses are noticeable," Rocko said as he watched Damaria cry while holding his broken wrist.

"Just please take me to the hospital; I'll gladly go back to jail, please," Damaria started to plead, and it took me back to when I was pleading for him to stop.

"Pleaseeeee." Demaria begged.

It took me back to when I was pleading for him to stop.

"Make him shut up!" I screamed as tears poured down my face. The big dude punched Damaria in the face and then it was all quiet.

"If you want to go out to the car, I'll finish it up," Patch told me, wrapping his arms around me.

"No, I need to do this." Something deep inside of me made me feel as though I would regret it if I didn't follow through.

"A'ight, let me know how you want to do this, and I'll make it happen," Rocko said.

"I need him woke so he can see that I'm the one who's taking his life. And I want, no, need a hammer and a gun," I said to Rocko as I wiped my tears. It was time for me to take back everything he took from me.

You can do this!

"Take off his pants," I told the large man standing behind the chair Damaria was in. He did as I told him.

Damaria was still passed out; everything they did to make him come to didn't work. I lifted the hammer above my head and brought it down on his dick. He woke up howling with tears in his eyes, and I couldn't help the smile that spread on my face.

The way he made my skin crawl when his hands were all over my body, and the way he smelled made me want to throw up. It made me swing harder as I tried to make the smell and feel of his hands dissipate from my mind.

My eyes closed and my mind blocked everything around me out. My swings got harsher after every connection and pretty soon his screams were nonexistent.

"Baby, he's gone." Patch's words sounded like they were far away, and my mind didn't fully register what he said at first. When it finally clicked, I dropped the hammer. My eyes finally opened and all I could see was the blood seeping from Damaria's wounds. His face was beaten beyond recognition. For some reason a sense of pride took over me while looking at what I had done to him.

"Drink this," Rocko told me, handing me a fifth of Hennessey. I took the bottle from him, gave Damaria's body one last look, then headed to the car to wait on Patch.

It was like all my adrenaline had run out of my body, and all that was left was nervous energy. It took my shaking hand a second to uncap the bottle, and I started drinking until I felt a little relaxed.

Thirty minutes later, Patch finally made it to the car and the bottle was a few big gulps from being half gone.

"You good?" Patch looked over at me, and I could see the concern in his eyes.

"Yeah; that was kind of therapeutic. There was a lot of emotions taking over me at one time but I'm fine now," I answered truthfully.

He stared me in my eyes for a long second, and I could feel his love and understanding. Whenever I was with him, I knew I would always be okay. He took his shirt off to clean the blood from my face. Next, he rolled down the window and tossed the shirt to Honor and Rocko.

Patch took the bottle from me and started drinking from it as he stared out of the window. He pulled out a wad of money when a hearse pulled in and parked next to us. A tall man with dreads got out and walked over to Patch side of the window.

"Make sure everything is incinerated," Patch told him, trying to hand him the money.

"Nah keep that, she's family; this one is free," he said to Patch.

"I gotta pay you somethin'." Patch didn't like to feel as though he owed somebody and I didn't either.

"Truly, gets the family discount from my son!" Rocko shouted.

"Dad, tell 'em," the dude shouted back.

"Give that to your sister then, Eagle," Patch said as he gave him half of the money.

"Let's get you home so you can get that shit off you," Patch said, starting the car. He pulled back as Rocko, Eagle and Honor walked back into the warehouse.

As Patch and I pulled away from the warehouse, a peaceful feeling washed over me for the first time in years. I didn't have to look over my shoulders in fear of Damaria getting out and assaulting me again.

Forty-five minutes later, I stood under the showerhead letting the hot water cleanse my body of Damaria's blood. I jumped a tad as a cool breeze hit my back. Patch had opened the shower door and climbed into the shower behind me.

"Damn your crazy ass got that nigga's blood everywhere," Patch said as he began to wash my back. When my backside was clean, he turned me around and as the water cascaded down my back taking the soap with it. Patch started to clean the front of my body making sure to take extra care of the parts that needed a bit more attention.

My eyes closed as he turned my body around and pulled my back to his chest. I moaned as one of his hands gripped my right breast and the other one went for my pussy. Patch's fingers slid between my folds; a groan slipped from me as he pinched my clit. The pressure he applied to my clit sent my nerve endings into a pleasurable overdrive. My hips bucked as Patch's fingers drew figure eights around my clit with the right amount of pressure.

"Faster," I moaned when I felt myself about to come. Patch flicked his fingers faster across my clit until I couldn't hold back anymore.

"Fuck!" My shouts echoed throughout the shower while pleasure took over my entire body. Patch held my body up with his until I could finally stand on my own without crumbling to the floor.

I turned around quickly and pushed him back until he sat on the bench in the shower. I leaned forward, grabbed the base of his dick in my hand and squeezed as I took his tip between my lips and started to suckle. I pulled my lips back just enough so my tongue could twirl around his swollen head before I slid Patch's whole length in my mouth. A string of pre-cum dangled from the tip of his shaft, I stared into his eyes as I flicked up his nut making it disappear down my throat.

Patch tightly gripped the back of my head; I could feel the tip of his dick probing at my mouth for it to open. I waited until I could hear his groans of frustration before my mouth opened wide enough for him to slip his dick in my mouth. Patch thrust his dick in and out of my mouth.

"Fuck, keep doing that," Patch groaned.

I took his dick deeper in my mouth and moaned as I sucked him off because my pussy was on fire waiting for her turn. I could tell he was close when he started to pump his dick into my mouth faster and faster. His body stiffened, and his load shot to the back of my throat.

"That's from seeing you kill that nigga; it turned me the fuck on," Patch said when he noticed the shocked look I had on my face. When he pulled his dick out of my mouth, I noticed it was still hard.

"Your turn," he told me. He practically slammed me against the wall, snatched up my legs and let them rest in the crooks of his arms. I felt his hands on my ass pushing me up until my pussy was directly in front of his mouth.

His tongue snaked out of his mouth and swiped up my juices as he slid two fingers into me. He moved his finger in and out of me as he licked my clit vigorously. A moan escaped from my lips as my hips started to buck up and down. My juices gushed freely into his mouth when he sucked my clit between his teeth. I grabbed a hold of his dreads to slow him down as my pussy clamped down around his fingers and my legs began to shake beyond control. Before I knew it, a tidal wave of my juices poured into his mouth and the pleasure of coming took over my body.

My legs were still shaking when Patch sat me on the bench in the shower. He bent my legs back so they were pressed on either side of the shower wall and his tip pressed against my fleshy entrance. My pussy quivered and dripped with anticipation. I cried out in pure ecstasy when I felt his dick pierce through my opening. I bit my lip as he pushed more of his thickness through my tight opening.

"More," I screamed. I needed him to go deeper with long, hard strokes until I felt like I couldn't take anymore.

He teased me, thrashing in and out of me good and hard before he switched to slow, steady strokes. Just as my body got use to one rhythm, he switched back to the other; driving me mad with desire. My fingernails dug into his arms and my hips bucked beneath him as he pounded harder and faster inside of me.

"That's right, fuck your dick back," Patch groaned out as my fingernails dug into his arms. I threw my hips up and down and in a figure eight trying to match his speed.

"Daaammmmnnnn!" I screamed as Patch hammered inside of me. I came and my juices gush onto his dick. He was buried so deep inside of me, my legs started to tremble. I closed my eyes tight and held onto his arms as he filled me up with everything he had. Patch collapsed against the wall while still inside of me.

We stayed like that for a minute, neither of us able to move.

"Let's take this to the bedroom before we have to go get the boys," Patch said as he lifted me into his arms and carried me out of the shower.

Haven

My thumb hovered over the 'add friend' button as my
heart pounded in my chest. All the what ifs ran through my
mind. Looking at his picture was intimidating and made me
fear what would happen when we finally came face-to-face.
Maybe I felt that way because I was hours away from being
in the same city as him.

I chickened out and began to scroll down his timeline
instead. The first thing I noticed was his fiancée tagging
him in picture after picture of their engagement party, but
he wasn't in any of the pictures. My heart wanted me to
stop scrolling and click out of his page, but my head
wouldn't let me. Honor hardly ever posted; the majority of
his posts were him being tagged by others. In my head
there were screams telling me to continue scrolling to see if
he even mentioned the engagement party. My heart was
actually agreeing with my head. It was telling me if he
hadn't mentioned anything about the engagement then he
didn't really love her.

*Stop that! You're only going there to give your
daughter the family she needs and become the best co-
parent there is. You stay out of Honor and his fiancée's*

shit, unless she fucks with your child. Then and only then can you bury that bitch alive. Now stop being a punk ass bitch and do what you came here to do. I checked myself and gave myself a pep talk in my head at the same time.

I was scared to add him as a friend.

You're a Pane act like it. I thought to myself as I took a deep breath and clicked back onto my fake page. I signed out then reactivated my real page, went into the settings and changed my name to **Haven SayvonnaTruthly'sMommy Pane** then added hella pictures of me and Sayvonna.

As my thumb hovered over the 'add friend' button once more on Honor's page, I just couldn't do it. When my eyes landed on my sleeping baby, I knew something had to give. I scrolled down Honor's page like the stalker I was until I came upon the tag, I was looking for then I clicked on the name.

My thumb hovered over the 'add friend' button for a few seconds before I clicked it and quickly signed out of my account. There was a fear that the person wouldn't accept me because of the letters I sent. If I stayed signed in, I would have been checking every few seconds to see if they accepted or rejected me. Instead of agonizing over it, I curled up next to my baby and prepared to go to sleep although it was only seven in the evening. I had to be up before two am so I wouldn't have to drive in traffic on Highway 5 all the way to Richmond.

Sayvonna gave a little snore whistle that reminded me of her dad and put a smile on my face right before I went to sleep.

Layne

2 days later…

I scrolled through the comments under the picture of Honor and me from our engagement party as I sat in my car outside of his house trying to calm down.

Jaylona James:

Roderick James Jr look bro…this bitch broke off your engagement to pop her pussy for the next nigga. Now the only picture she got of him at their engagement party is the back of his head walking out the party that she had to sneak to take.

Then she proceeded to tag her mama and a few of their family and friends that never liked me. When Honor and I met I was engaged to Rod, and we were a few months away from our wedding. Rod had put almost all his money, that wasn't going towards our wedding, into a business with his cousin, who had just gotten out of jail. I knew he was going to be broke soon. Honor screamed money, and a woman like me needed security. After seeing Honor on the side for a few months, I called off the engagement a month before our wedding.

I deleted Rod's whole family except his sister, Jaylona, because she always mumbled some off-the-wall mess about me under her breath. I knew it was her childish ass that had put candy in my gas tank and took a bat to almost every part of my car. So it was only right that she saw my new car a couple of days later all up and down her timeline.

April James:

Jaylona and Roderick I clicked on her fine ass fiancé's page and that nigga posted pictures of a baby the night of the engagement party. That's what happens to bitches that think they're better than everybody and their shit don't stink. They get humbled eventually.

April was Rod's cousin, and she was the only person in their family that actually gave me a real chance, but now she didn't like me. Rod didn't comment on his sister's post, but I knew he had seen it. He didn't comment on posts like that because he said shit like that was for females. When he needed female stuff done, he left that to his sister.

I quickly deleted the picture hoping a lot of people didn't see their comments under the picture. My best friend told me I was stupid for dumping Rod, then she called me even stupider for posting the picture of the back of Honor's head.

I clicked on Honor's page and there was a new picture of his daughter. Despite my intuition telling me not to, my thumb had a mind of its own and it clicked on the comments. My heart said, "don't do it", but the dumb part of me said, "do it", so I started reading the comments and they pissed me off. People were asking Honor was the baby with his fiancée and there was Honor's mama, Patch and Miss Brenda in the comments saying hell no in all caps.

It was hard to admit but I was a bit on the hurt side; and when I was hurt, I wanted everyone to feel exactly how I felt. That, plus everything I had just read pissed me off. I got out my car, slammed my door then stormed towards Honor's house.

I went around destroying everything I knew Honor felt some kind of connection to. At the end, as I sat on the couch drinking a glass of the old expensive Scotch Honor was saving, a bitch felt kind of good.

I was on my second glass of the Scotch when I heard Honor's keys in the door. When he walked into the house, he was so busy on the phone that he hadn't noticed me or the mess.

"Yeah, my realtor said that the house is mine, and that she found a couple more rental properties thirty minutes away that I can buy right now. Then I'mma rent them bitches out and those will pay for the mortgage of that house I been looking at for over a year now," he said, more than likely, to Patch.

"Nah, I'm good, brah. I hadn't touched that insurance money from Truth's death. It's just been sitting in this IRA account my mama put it in when she got the payout. My realtor said winter is the best time to buy houses, and if I find the right ones, I'll be set. But I'mma buy up a few storefronts too." When he said "brah" there wasn't a question in my mind on whether or not he was on the phone with Patch.

"Aye yo, Patch, let me call you back," Honor said when he finally noticed me and the mess.

"You know what, I'm not even 'bouta go there with you. Just know this time you're cleaning up and replacing all of this shit," Honor said as he tried to walk pass me.

Whenever me and Honor were in an argument it was like I was arguing with myself. He was so nonchalant during the arguments and it made me feel as though he didn't care. I could be screaming at the top of my lungs at him, and he would just stare right through me and reply calmly with an answer that made sense. Me being me I just wanted him to react, and he finally did when I broke everything in his apartment.

So when I wanted a reaction from him, I started to trash his home. Then and only then would he start yelling back at me and get in my face like I needed him to when we were arguing. Now it felt like I was losing him because breaking his stuff apparently wasn't getting a rise out of him anymore.

"I see you posted a new picture of your daughter." I tried a different tactic. He just raised his eyebrow slightly. Honor looked at me like he was daring me to say something else about his daughter.

"As your fiancée and your daughter's stepmom, I'mma need to be there during the conversation and exchange when you get in touch with our baby mama," I told him.

He laughed out loud. "My baby mama would kill you and me both if she ever heard you saying some shit like that."

"Whateva, why would she kill us if you said y'all don't fuck with each other like that?" I really wanted to know the answer to that.

"Nah she gon' beat your ass 'cause for one, she ain't gonna want you to be calling yourself Sayvonna's step mother since we ain't married. Even then, she wouldn't until she's able to feel like you ain't tryna be funny with the shit. On top of that, I know you and you're gonna be the one acting like the bitter baby mama during the meeting not her, and that's gonna set off her crazy fuel. You throw temper tantrums and want all the attention on you, but Haven throws murder parties," Honor said and walked away.

Normally I would have stormed after him cursing him out and trying to smack him in the back of the head. But I knew I was skating on thin ice. I needed to be the girl I pretended to be when we first got together.

I turned on the music on my phone, put my ear phones in my ear, and grabbed the garbage bags and broom. In between cleaning the different rooms, I ordered some groceries. By the time I got finished cleaning, two hours later, the groceries had arrived. I put a roast in the oven and started ordering replacements for the stuff I broke before making the sides.

A couple of hours later as Honor was eating his roast, cabbage and cornbread, I slid under then table, pulled his dick out and sucked the hell out of his dick. I stayed under the table until I swallowed every drop of him. then I left his house without a word.

Let the manipulating games begin. I thought to myself as I walked to my car knowing I was about to reel him back in.

The Next Day

When I walked into Honor's house, I noticed he was sitting on the couch. When he noticed me; the expression on his face changed to anger. He motioned for me to sit across from him on the couch.

"So you been stealing from me," Honor leaned forward and accused me.

"No, I haven't been stealing from you; we're about to be married," I answered.

"So getting a credit card in my name, is not stealing because you *were* my fiancée? Taking my checks out my mailbox yesterday then writing yourself a ten-thousand-dollar check, ain't stealing either? Soon as they called saying a woman tried to cash the check but left before they could do anything, I knew it was your dumb ass. Then your stupid ass came straight here after."

The credit union Honor banked at had to buzz people in and out, and the security was always standing outside the door. After the teller said she was going to the back so the manager could add the amount into their system for tomorrow, because they needed a twenty-four-hour advanced notice for that amount, I knew I had to get out of there. When another teller buzzed someone else in, I turned around and left out of the building. Thank God the security guard was making his rounds around the parking lot when I walked out, because by the time I pulled off he was running around the building to the front.

"Look, I'm sorry, I just wanted to pay for the wedding dress I saw yesterday," I lied.

"Your dad was buying your dress so try again," he demanded.

"Look I'm sorry; we can work this out; we're getting married at the end of next year," I pleaded.

"We're not engaged anymore nor are we getting married. You better hurry up and leave my place before Truly and Mama Brenda get here. I already called them and told them what you did, and they are on their way to beat your ass," he said to me as if I was just a stranger off the street. I wanted to go off on him, but the way he looked at me let me know my rants and pleads wouldn't faze him.

"Oh and give me that credit card and my checkbook," Honor demanded when I got up from the couch to leave his house. I took the credit card and checkbook out of my wallet and tossed them on the couch next to him.

"I'll be back when you've had time to calm down and fully process everything," I told him before I walked out the door. If he thought we weren't engaged because of a misunderstanding, he was sadly mistaken.

I gave Honor a full twenty-four hours to get over our little mishap, but he wasn't answering any of my calls or replying to my text messages. So now I was sitting in front of his house waiting for the U-Haul truck to move out of my way. When it was gone, I climbed out of my car and headed to Honor's door. My eyes scanned my surroundings the whole time I walked to the door; Miss Brenda's place was too close to Honor's for my comfort. When I tried my key in the lock it wouldn't budge; maybe I had the wrong key. I quickly realized after trying five different keys that the locks had been changed on me. If he thought changing the locks would deter me, he was sadly mistaken. I looked around to find a rock; I busted out his front window and climbed in.

The living room was empty not a piece of furniture or anything else was in there. I ran to his bedroom and that too was empty, so was the kitchen. I could excuse the living room as being empty because he needed new furniture after I busted it all up the other day. But everything was empty including all the cabinets and drawers in the kitchen.

Climbing back out of the window, my hand snagged on some glass, slicing my palm. I felt stupid because I could have just walked out the door, but I wasn't thinking straight. The gash ran from the bottom of my palm to the bottom of my middle finger. Tears pooled in my eyes as I clutched my hand to my chest and ran to my car. Inside my car, I took off my shirt and wrapped it around my right hand and drove to my best friend's house. My best friend was a veterinary and kept some supplies at her house for an animal emergency.

She cussed me out when I walked into her house before pulling me into the bathroom. She numbed my hand, cleaned it, then started the stitches. I couldn't look at the needle, so I started to scan through my social media and that was when I saw it.

Haven

I closed my eyes and took a few deep breaths before I knocked on the door. My heart throbbed in my chest; it felt like a rock was lodged in my throat. Anxiousness. Fear. Excitement. Shame. Those were all the feelings bubbling up inside of me as I waited for him to open the door. The longer it took for the door to be opened, the more powerful those feelings became.

My breath hitched when I heard the door being unlocked as fear of rejection bubbled up inside of me.

The door swung open and there was Honor standing on the other side of it. He was about to say something to me until I adjusted Sayvonna in my arms and his eyes landed on her. He just stared at her with a blank expression on his face that I didn't know how to read. After a couple of seconds Sayvonna started staring back at him, and it made me feel out of place. Like I was intruding on a private moment between the two of them.

Honor was 6'1" with a lean, muscular build and broad shoulders. He was dark-brown with almond shaped, chestnut colored eyes; they looked hazel when the sun hit them. Honor had a strong jawline that made me want to run my fingertips across his face. He was now sporting a beard that I could tell he kept groomed to perfection. From the front he looked like a typical pretty boy, but when he turned around with his shirt off displaying his street tattoos, it told a different story. His back was a tattooed masterpiece.

"Daddy was having a bad day but seeing you just made all that shit irrelevant." Honor snapped out of the staring contest and reached for her. When she was in his arms, Honor turned around and walked further into his house.

He left the door open behind him, so I guess that was my invitation to come in. I walked in and closed and locked the door behind me. Honor's living room was bare; all it had was a long black leather couch and a TV mounted on the wall that had to be at least sixty inches.

"How'd you get this address?" he asked, confused. "I just moved in today," he added as I sat on the opposite end of the couch.

"Truly. I added her on social media a couple of days ago. We've been messaging back and forth. She tried to get me to bring her to a BBQ you guys are having tomorrow, but I wanted your first time seeing her to be private. I promised her that I would show up at your house today so they could see Sayvonna tomorrow," I rambled as my voice cracked.

"Nervous?" Honor smirked, zeroing in on my nervous rambling. "Take the garage opener out the drawer in the kitchen next to the dishwasher and pull your car into the garage. You can go out through the garage door in the kitchen," Honor insisted.

I followed his instructions. My imagination was running away from me as the garage door lifted. All I could picture in my head was walking back into an empty house. In my twisted thoughts it would be only right that he disappeared with Sayvonna since it took me so long to bring her to him. Those thoughts made me rush out to my car and pull it into the garage quickly. I walked back into Honor's townhouse in less than five minutes.

When I entered the living room there were toys everywhere and a pink sparkly kid's car. Honor was lying on the floor with a black barbie in his hand and Sayvonna was sitting in front of him with one in her hand.

Honor was making his voice mimic a girl's tone, causing Sayvonna to giggle. He made the doll hop over to a Barbie mall that was right next to him.

"When did you get all of this?" I asked him as I stepped over some blocks on my way to the couch.

"I got it all a month after I got that letter from you, and a few days after I bought this townhouse and the one next door. When I found out I had a child, I knew I couldn't keep staying in the townhouse Miss Brenda bought. She even got her own room upstairs," he told me, never looking up from playing with Sayvonna.

My eyes scanned the living room from, and I became a bit overwhelmed. Watching my daughter with her father made me realize what she had been missing from her life. My dad never did the things I was witnessing Honor do with Sayvonna.

"You don't like that shit in your hair, huh," Honor questioned as Sayvonna tugged on her ponytails. He reached over and took all the ponytail holders out of Sayvonna's hair and ruffled her hair a bit.

"Do you know how long it took me to get those parts perfect and you just messed it up."

"She don't like that shit in her hair, just put some oil on it," he answered.

"If I do that everybody's gonna be talking 'bout me as a parent 'cause her hair not done and mine is."

"So? Fuck them bald-headed motherfuckas; that's why they don't got hair now. Hell, if you want something in her head just put a headband on and call it a day." Honor dictated as if he knew anything about a girl's hair.

Honor and Sayvonna sat on the floor playing for another hour before we ordered pizza. We sat on the floor eating pizza with Sayvonna sitting in the middle of us eating crust and watching a Mickey movie. I couldn't believe she would be turning eight months in a couple of weeks.

"Do you gotta crib in her room?" I asked him when I noticed Sayvonna start to pull her ear.

"Yeah; why?" Honor responded.

"She's getting sleepy," I replied. "Just tell me where her room is, and I'll breastfeed her then put her to bed," I added as Sayvonna started trying to pull my shirt down.

"Upstairs; the first door on the right. It's some diapers and wipes in the closet. Come back to the living room once she's sleeping," Honor responded.

I took my time changing, breastfeeding and putting her to sleep in an effort to avoid the conversation I knew he wanted to have with me.

"Why?" he asked as soon as I got back down stairs.

"Why what?" I asked him, but instead of answering he picked up the pizza box and took it to the kitchen. I went and sat on the couch and waited for his answer.

"Did you wait so long to tell me 'bout her," he finally answered as he walked back in the living room and sat on the opposite end of the couch.

"I guess I was scared that you would reject or deny her when you found out why I did everything. Or maybe I thought you would take the last family I had from me once you found out everything," I answered him truthfully.

"My dad used to do shit like that to my mama; I would never do that to you or her. Me taking her away from you would hurt her, and I'd never want to do that," Honor replied.

"Deep down I knew that; I think I just didn't know how to tell you. There were times when I'd type out a message to you then chicken out. Then I'd put off telling you until the next day or week, telling you about our child just turned into something I wasn't anticipating it to. Every time I tried, I just couldn't form the words to tell you until my friend suggested for me to write a letter to you." When I wrote that letter everything just began to pour out, even stuff that I never wanted to tell him. It made me feel so free as I wrote it all, so I kept going.

"Where y'all staying?" Honor asked after a few minutes of silence.

"At the moment we're staying in a hotel room, but tomorrow we'll be moving into my friend's spare room." I honestly didn't want to move in with Amity because her new boyfriend had a staring problem and he was creepy.

"Nah, y'all not 'cause I need to be in the same house as my daughter; I'm not letting her out of my sight for a minute. Y'all can either stay here, it is three rooms, or y'all can stay in the townhouse next door, but I'mma stay there too." Honor gave me two options and honestly they were better than any of the other ones I had.

"How 'bout I stay in the place next door and Say can stay in her room. We can leave the garage doors unlocked and when I need to check on her, I can just come through the garage. I'll even start paying you rent when I find a job," I suggested. There was no way I could live in the same place as him for a long period of time, my feelings needed to be kept under lock.

"I need to find a job that will let me get back to decorating parties and properties on the side," I said, more to myself.

"A'ight, but no rent, just cook and help me decorate the properties I'm about to put up for rent. I wanna rent them out fully furnished, and you're gonna have to stay here for a few days because that place next door is unfurnished."

"Wait, why are you being so nice to me? I know I'd be pissed if I was you," I stated.

"Shit, I am pissed at you, but this right here is 'bout doing what's best for our daughter. I'm putting my feelings in check right now; shit, in a few days or weeks I might go off on your ass a time or two. But for right now, I'm just happy she's here, especially when hella shit for me is fucked." I didn't ask him what had gone bad in his life, because I knew I didn't deserve to know. But there was just one thing missing from the equation that we hadn't discussed but needed to.

"Will your fiancée be okay with me stayin' next door and walkin' into y'all place?" I asked not wanting to step on the next woman's toes.

"That bitch ain't my fiancée anymore, and even if she was, what goes on with my daughter wouldn't be her concern. My daughter's well-being comes before anybody else's and that means making sure you're straight as well." I could tell she had hurt him from the look in his eyes, and I wanted to hurt her because of it. But my actions had hurt him too, so I couldn't beat the next bitch's ass for making him feel the same way I had.

"So can you help me bring in some of my clothes out of the car?" I asked him, changing the subject.

"Just tell me where they are and I'll get them," Honor stated as he stood from the couch.

Honor followed me out to the garage and took out all the bags I pointed to. He carried them up the stairs to the guest room next to Sayvonna's bedroom. The guest room had more furniture in it then his living room did. There was a queen-sized bed, a dresser and television in the room.

"My room and office are down stairs and there is a bathroom next to Say's room," Honor said when he came in and dropped my last bag on the bedroom floor.

"Okay, I'mma put some of the stuff up then go to bed. That girl be up at five-thirty in the morning ready to eat," I told him as I searched through the bags for my pajamas.

"I'mma be up in the morning at that time anyway, so I'll get her; you can sleep in," Honor volunteered.

"Okay, I'll leave some of her baby food on the counter, and I'll pump a bottle and leave it in the fridge before I go to sleep," I told him.

"Just leave the bottle in the fridge. I got some baby food in the cabinets already. Is she allergic to anything?"

"No, but she doesn't like bananas," I told him then he left.

I put half of my clothes away, pumped her a bottle, took it to the fridge then passed out. For the first time in a long time I got some real sleep because I knew Sayvonna and I would be safe with her dad in the house.

Haven

I woke up feeling as though I missed something. My phone vibrated on the dresser next to me alerting me that there was a text message waiting for me. My phone was riddled with calls and texts from Amity worried about me not showing up or calling her.

Me:

I'm fine. I was sleep and I found a place to stay. I texted Amity as I got out of the bed. My mind was so focused on the text that I almost tripped over my own two feet.

Amity:

I was 'bouta call the police but my boo talked me into waiting twenty-four hours and that was almost up. And bitch where the fuck you stayin'? Amity texted back and her text looked like a mini paragraph; she always texted semi long paragraphs.

Me:

Say's dad had a vacant place next to his, I'mma move in there. I texted back as I made my way across the hall to Sayvonna's bedroom, but she wasn't there. Panic started to set in until I heard her giggles waft up the stairs; for a second I thought he had taken off with my daughter.

Amity sent back three paragraphs worth of eggplant emojis, the lady dancing in the red dress and the family emojis. Amity had put so many of the emojis that I got three separate text messages from her.

Me:

I'm not 'bout to play with you but I'm bouta shower and shit so hit you later, bitch. I texted her back with one hand while searching through my bags for clothes. I had to find something that made people think *damn* in their heads when they saw me. But I just thought "F" it and pulled out a midi green dress instead. It was my go-to dress since I had Sayvonna because the dress made it easier to breastfeed. I grabbed my underclothes and headed to the bathroom. When I walked into the bathroom, I noticed Honor had left a washcloth, a towel and an unopened bar of soap on the sink for me.

As I waited for the shower water to warm up, I sat on the edge of the tub, naked, thinking about where my life was. A mother with no job and depending on my child's father to provide me with somewhere to stay. I made a mental checklist of everything I needed to do in order to elevate myself and not be dependent on anyone. My resume needed to be redone and I needed to go back to freelance decorating.

"Haven! Hurry up in there; we need to leave in thirty." Honor banged on the door then yelled out. "That's right, baby, tell her to hurry her ass up." I heard Honor say after Sayvonna finished yelling gibberish through the door. It was a good thing my hair was braided into a ponytail; otherwise, I would've been assed out with that timeframe.

Twenty minutes later, I walked out of the bathroom dressed and ready to go. When I got to the top of the stairs the sound of Sayvonna whining penetrate my ears. At the bottom of the stairs, I could see her tugging on her ears. Honor was pacing the living room bouncing her up and down trying to get her to calm down. I smiled when I saw that he had on some dark pants with a turquoise and black plaid shirt and Sayvonna had on a dress with the same colors. They both had on some black Nikes with a turquoise Nike sign.

"I tried everything and it's not working," Honor said when he turned around and noticed me.

"She just wants me to breastfeed her, and she needs a nap," I answered. He handed Sayvonna to me and I prepared to feed her.

"When we get over there, go in the house and do that. Don't be whipping your breast out, like you just did, in front of my uncle, cousin and brother," he chastised. I rolled my eyes at him.

"Psshhh, if Say hungry she gonna eat wherever we're at just like everybody else," I told him.

"Try that shit and get your head knocked off."

I ignored his rant and continued to feed my baby. I watched as she tugged on her little ear until she fell asleep.

"We can take my car since her car seat is in there," I told Honor as he took a sleeping Sayvonna out of my arms.

"I bought one already, and this morning me and Say watched YouTube and put the car seat in my car. I got that one that turns into a stroller once you pull this bottom piece. That shit is deep," Honor responded.

"When you go get her diaper bag out of her room get a sweater out of yours," Honor demanded.

"A sweater for what? It's warm out and the wind not blowing all like that," I replied with a puzzled look on my face.

"One of your nipples is poking out of your dress, and the other one is semi poking out. You not finsta be around my niggas like that." Honor was tripping, I had on a bra and the dress wasn't that thin.

"Ain't nothing wrong with my dress, and I'm not putting on a coat because you want me to." He had me messed up; we weren't together, so I didn't know why he thought he had a say.

"We gonna stay here until you put on one, and when they ask why we were late I'mma just point to your ass," Honor responded as he leaned against the wall with Sayvonna's head on his chest as she slept.

"Then I'm just not gonna go, but you two can," I smirked at him.

"Shit, then all three of us are staying here. Say don't like drinking out of that bottle shit; I had to pour it in one of those baby cups and that shit got everywhere. The spill might have been my fault though since I didn't put the top on right but she still doesn't like that shit. When Mama Brenda calls to cuss me out for not coming I'mma hand your ass the phone and tell her it's your fault." Instead of answering him I just headed for the stairs.

I headed straight for my makeup bag. I was gonna put on a jacket, but I was going to make him regret even asking me to by beating the hell out of my face.

Truly

Three hours after the bar-b-que winded down I sat at my vanity. I was still at Patch's house because him and Miss Brenda decided that we were having professional pictures taken, in an hour, since the whole family was at Patch house. I had my robe on after the shower, and Haven was doing my makeup while Miss Brenda was curling my hair.

"Since you're finished with her makeup, go to the downstairs bathroom and change into the dress hanging behind the bathroom door," Miss Brenda told Haven after she sprayed my face with something she pulled out of her purse.

"I told you I don't think me being in the pictures is a good idea," Haven replied.

"You had a baby by my second baby so you're family now, sweetie. And I want my whole family in these pictures. Do you know I snuck into your room to get your dress size early this morning? Then I went to buy you and the baby a dress to match the theme, so you're gonna be in these pictures," Brenda said in her stern motherly voice. She did this thing where her eyes would get wide and take on a sad look that made it impossible to say, "no" to her.

"Okay, I'll give in just this one time," Haven responded.

"Take this and put everything on in the bag." Brenda handed Haven a bag before Haven turned and left out of the door.

"I just need to paint your toes, then head out to meet the camera man." Miss Brenda pulled a nail polish out of her bag then went to painting my nails.

"Why can't I see your dress?" I asked her because an hour ago she disappeared while we were cleaning, and now she had on a robe and her hair was done. She wouldn't let me see her dress for some reason and I was starting to become suspicious.

"Don't worry, you'll see it before the pictures. I just gotta add something to it before I show it off," Brenda answered.

Thirty minutes later, Brenda gave me instructions on what shoes to wear and where to find my dress. I headed straight for the closet and unzipped the garment bag my dress was in. The dress was white and stopped just above the knees, with a sweetheart neckline, turquoise beading and lace along the bust. The back of the dress was open with turquoise lace and embellishments going down both sides of my torso. When I slipped on the dress, I realized I couldn't zip it up. I decided to put on the turquoise shoes instead of worrying about that. When I pulled out the stuff from the bag Miss Brenda had given me, I had to blink back the tears. I couldn't understand why my eyes were watering as I put the white, lace choker with a white pearl on it and the pearl earrings.

I had just pulled out a pearl hair clip and was trying to figure out how to put it in when someone knocked on the room door. "Come in!" I called out.

I opened the bathroom door to see Haven walking in with Sayvonna in her arms. Haven had on an illusion neckline dress that stop mid-thigh. The dress was turquoise with black, lace embellishments from the neckline down to her waist. Sayvonna had on the same dress but the bottom of her dress flared out and she had a black bow in her hair.

"We were sent up to zip you up and hurry you up so the pictures can be taken during the sunset," they helped me get ready.

"Before I forget, Miss Brenda said put on this garter," I didn't know why I had to put it on for the pictures since it wasn't going to be seen but I knew she would trip if I didn't. I followed Haven and Sayvonna out of the room, down the stairs and into the kitchen.

The blinds to the sliding backdoor that led to the backyard were closed, and Honor was standing in the kitchen waiting on us. He had on black linen pants with a turquoise button up and a black tie.

"They want to do a reveal of what they did to the backyard for the pictures so y'all gotta put on these blindfolds," Honor blindfolded me then he wrapped his arm around my arm before he led me outside.

"We're. Getting. Married. Today!" Patch shouted out once the blindfold was halfway removed from my eyes, and I was standing in the backyard.

Patch was standing under a wedding arch, and Victor was standing behind him. I watched from the top of the porch as my grandpa walked my grandma to her seat. Then Eagle walked Miss Brenda and Victor's wife down the aisle with one on either of his arms. Miss Brenda had on a silk, turquoise dress and Victor's wife had on a similar one in black. My boys walked down the aisle together each with a pillow in their hands. They were wearing white linen pants with a white button up and a turquoise sweater and a tie, just like their dad. Haven and Sayvonna walked down next, they tossed flowers down the white carpet that rolled from the porch steps to the wedding arch.

Uncle Rocko and Eagle started singing "Must be Nice" by Lyfe Jennings. "He said to tell you to listen close to the words because when he met you, he finally understood the words and emotions behind this song," Honor whispered in my ear. Where there were pronouns in the song, they replaced them with our names in the perspective places.

Someone started playing Etta James "At Last" as Honor and I started walking down the stairs. I couldn't believe Patch remembered that I said, if I ever got married, I wanted it to play when I was walking down the aisle. Because when I watched my grandparents' wedding video, my grandmother walked down the aisle to it.

I could see a tear in Patch's eye when I reached the altar. "Who gives this woman away?" Victor asked.

"We do," everyone around me said at the same time.

"Surprised?" Patch asked when he took my hand from Honor's. I couldn't speak; all I could do was nod my head.

I just stared in Patch's eyes, and my heart felt everything he was trying to tell me. A tear slipped from my eyes and Patch reached up to wipe it away. We mouthed 'I love you' to each other at the same time. The whole ceremony went by in a blur; I didn't even remember when I said I do or repeated my vows. But I would forever remember that kiss because it had so much passion behind it that my chest felt like it would burst open with love.

"You better stop callin' me Miss Brenda now. All I better here come out your mouth is mama," Brenda said, and the crowd laughed. Everyone came over to join us by the arch.

"I need to fix your makeup before the pictures." Haven ran in the house to get the makeup. She came back and fixed the parts of my makeup that tears had messed up.

We took pictures just as the sun was setting behind us, and I couldn't believe everything that had just happened. On the right side of the archway was a long table with a black table cloth and a turquoise runner going across it. There was a black throne chair that was big enough for me, Patch and the boys to sit at and chairs on either side of the throne for everyone else.

"Everyone take your seats. The caterer just texted; they are about to come in with the food and serve," Brenda said as she waved for everyone to sit down. Patch and I sat in the middle of the long throne chair with PJ sitting beside me and Truvon on the other side of Patch. As soon as everyone was seated the caterer came in and set the food on the picnic tables, a couple of tables away from us.

SOUL Publications

After we finished eating and our dishes were collected, the wait staff left. A cake company pulled up with a three-tier cake with pearls embellished on the cake. The baker set the cake on the table in front of me and Patch.

"Don't forget the top tier gets frozen, and you eat it on your one-year anniversary." The lady who delivered the cake said as Brenda put a silver knife in front of us. Brenda called the photographer over as me and Patch stood to cut the cake. He put his hands over mine, and we cut the first slice of cake to share. The entire event felt surreal.

When the night started to wind down, Patch whispered in my ear that he had a wedding present for me. I followed him to the porch and before I could walk into the house, he picked me up and carried me into the house and upstairs to the bedroom. Patch sat me on the bed and told me to close my eyes; the anticipation of what it could be was getting the best of me. When I felt his hand on mine it made me want to peek, but I didn't want to ruin the surprise.

"Truly, you have always seen me for who I was, even as kids, when others didn't. Hell, adults would cross the street when they saw me coming, but you would smile and wave when you saw me. I still remember the time in middle school when I had to fight those two boys from high school, and all the adults just stood by and watched. But you, the shy person, ran to get my mom and helped her fight them off. And back then you only knew of me in passing from school. I think even back then I had fallen in love with you a little bit. Even when I didn't really know what love was. When that happened to you, I seriously felt as though I failed in protecting you. And it hurt knowing I wasn't there as you were for me the few times I needed you. I vowed from then on to protect you from everything even if it was from myself. That's why it took so long for me to take our relationship from a friendship to a romantic relationship, because I knew I wasn't ready to settle fully.

"Last year when I couldn't find you, I knew then that I just couldn't live without you. I realized what love was because of you. I love you despite your flaws; at times, those are what I love most about you. Open your eyes," he finally instructed. When I opened them, he was on one knee with a diamond ring that was perfect for me. I already had tears in my eyes, but I practically sobbed when I saw that.

"Despite already being married, I wanted you to experience a proposal and have an engagement ring," Patch said as he slipped the ring on my finger. I leaned forward, wrapped my arms around his neck and kissed him.

The kiss quickly turned from a peck to a frantic one with a lot of passion. I could faintly hear his zipper coming down as he deepened our kiss. Patch pushed me back on the bed, and I bit my lip as he lifted my dress up. I kicked off my heels as he slid his tongue in my mouth

Patch moved my panties to the side and slipped his finger into my hot, wet opening. I sucked on his tongue as he slipped another finger inside of me and begin to pump them in and out. I sucked his tongue deeper into my mouth as I bucked my hips searching for my release.

My moans were shut off by his kiss as my pleasure peaked. I was still in the throes of coming when Patch pushed his dick inside of me. I was caught off guard and my mouth made a big "O" as I felt his girth stretching me to capacity. I didn't even have time to lower my hips, so it felt like a new level of ecstasy as he entered me inch by inch.

"Fuck," he groaned as he pushed in and pull out of me. His arms slid under my legs and he grabbed my hips, gripping them tightly as he grinded deep inside me repeatedly.

"How you want it, babe?" Patch asked.

"Right now, fuck the shit out of me hard and fast; tonight, we'll make love all night," I moaned. I was so hot from the words he spoke that I needed him to give it to me hard, fast and rough.

Patch pinned my legs down and pounded into my pussy. My eyes shut tight as he pistoled in and out of me hitting my spot every time.

"God-damn that pussy is sucking the life out of my dick," Patch groaned as my body lifted slightly off the bed and I gripped the covers on both sides of me. He grunted and drove faster and faster inside of me as he fisted my hair until we both came. Patch slowed down, pumping slowly inside of me as my pussy gripped his dick tighter and tighter until he finished coming and collapsed on top of me.

"Now that right there was our baby," Patch whispered in my ear and I could feel the smile on his face. I wrapped my arms around him as his head laid on my chest until we started to hear a big commotion in the backyard.

"Go get cleaned up, then come out; I got this." Patch kissed me deeply before he stood up and headed out the door.

Haven

I was on top of Honor's fiancée, or ex-fiancée, whatever the hell she was to him, punching that bitch's lights out. She was screaming and trying to cover her face with her hands, but I didn't care I wanted that bitch to get the message. Eagle finally pulled me off her and held me tightly so I couldn't get to her.

We had been cleaning up the backyard while Patch and Truly were in the house. Somebody started screaming like a banshee before they even made their way to the backyard. Within minutes of Layne walking through the gate, she crossed a line she shouldn't have. My heart dropped in my chest when Layne had charged at Honor while he was holding Sayvonna in his arms. It pissed me off that she didn't even consider the fact that my daughter was in his arms before she put her hands on him. What if she had hit my daughter or made her fall out of his arms?

"You really just put your hands on me because I got the nigga now, just a jealous, hating ass bitch," Layne screamed.

"Bitch, y'all could be fucking in the same room as me and I wouldn't give it another thought. But when you put your fucking hands on him when my baby is in his arms, you best believe I'm taking off on your ass," I told her.

"Bitch, fuck you and your ugly ass baby, wasn't nobody gonna touch that lil bitch," Layne said as she tried to get up. I was going to leave her ass alone, but she just had to bring my baby into shit again. I tried to take a deep breath and count to ten before reacting but that just wasn't happening, so I kicked the bitch in her face. When my foot collided with her nose, she screamed and collapsed to the ground holding it in her hands.

"Haven, there are kids out here; don't go too far," Honor spoke just as I was about to stomp her ass in the face.

"Y'all are so disrespectful to me, inviting this bitch here and letting my man be around her without me. Damn, y'all could have at least invited me instead of me having to find out through social media," Layne said, looking at Patch while pointing to me.

"Bitch, this my house and my wedding; I invite whoever the hell I want over here. And you know damn well I don't like you so why would your ass even think you could come to my shit?" Patch said as he walked into the backyard.

"Patch, stop walking," Miss Brenda told him as she tried to tug him back towards the house. Layne looked like she loved negative attention.

"Nah fuck that, this bitch think it's all good to fuck up our day. She wasn't even invited. Like her ass didn't try to steal ten thousand from Honor or have a credit card in his name and didn't pay the bill," Patch barked, and then turned his attention to Honor. "She owe for that window she broke at my mom's place yesterday too."

"So you ain't got shit to say to me, nigga!" Layne jumped up and screamed at Honor as she tried to charge at him again.

"Hell nawl bitch, don't you ever run up on that nigga when he got my daughter in his arms." I palmed that bitch to stop her, then grabbed her by the neck and body slammed her. Everything fell out of the purse she had around her shoulders. I picked up her wallet and grabbed all the money out of it. I tossed the wallet back on her purse as Eagle helped her up. She grabbed her purse and he helped her to her car.

By the time Truly came back down, the backyard had calmed down and we were back to cleaning everything up.

"What happened?" Truly asked me as we all sat at the picnic tables watching the people take away the tables, chairs and throne that was rented. Her and Patch both listened intently as I told them what happened from the beginning.

"To make up for me having to whoop someone's ass at your wedding, shopping spree tomorrow on that bitch." I told Truly as I lifted up the cash from Layne.

"Damn I like her," Patch boasted about me.

Honor was quiet the rest of the time we were there and on the car ride to his place. When we got back to his place, he went to put a sleeping Sayvonna in her crib before he came back down stairs. When I turned around from placing a frozen bag of peas on my right hand, I saw him standing in the doorway of the kitchen watching me.

"Why the fuck would you do some stupid shit like that!" Honor snapped.

"What, are you mad that I beat your bitch's ass?" I asked him.

"Hell nawl, I'm pissed that you did some stupid shit without thinking about our daughter. Your dumb ass could of went to jail for assault for doing some dumb shit like that. Me and you both know Layne is not made for the street shit; she's a snitch. You should of thought about our daughter before making a move."

"I was thin-" I didn't even get to finish what I was about to say.

"Nah, I'm not done with you and the stupid shit you've been doing lately yet. Because of you I don't even know how to read my daughter's cries to know what the fuck she wants and needs. Do you know how fuckin' bad that makes me feel as a father; all because your stupid ass wanted to be selfish and hide? You should've told me 'bout her when you first found out and not a second after. Me and my daughter are fuckin' strangers because all you think 'bout is self! Fuck how your ass feel, and if you keep my daughter from me again, I'll body your ass."

I was stuck as Honor finally exploded on me; I knew I couldn't even defend myself because everything he said was true. After he finished yelling at me, he left the kitchen. His words made me feel like a selfish mother, something I never wanted to be. When he was yelling at me, I could see the pain in his eyes.

I headed up stairs and went straight for the bathroom. When I passed Sayvonna's bedroom, I could see Honor lying on the couch in her room. I quickly showered then got in bed with a lot of regrets and thoughts about how I could make up for them.

Layne

I stood in front of my bathroom mirror examining my face. My lip was busted, and my right eye was swollen shut and starting to turn black. There were scratches riddled all over my face; it looked like I had it out with a cat. Honor's baby mama had grabbed my face with her nails a few times as she screeched at me. Just looking at my face made me want to go back in time and at least pinch that damn baby or maybe even slap her in the face.

I wanted to go to my best friend's house or my dad's for them to help me, but I didn't want to hear either of them call me stupid. They both told me to stay the hell away from Honor after they found out what I did to him. But me being me, I just couldn't let him go behind petty stuff.

A couple of hours ago I was just thinking about him, and since I couldn't get in touch with him, I decided to surf his social media. During my searching, I found picture after picture of him next to his baby mama at a wedding that should have been ours. The only difference was if it was my wedding it would have been on a grander scale and had more people. I mean like, who in their right mind would have a wedding in a backyard of all places? I could see the beach, but a fucking backyard?

I winced as I pressed the alcohol soaked cotton ball into the scratches on my face getting pissed off all over again. If Honor and his baby mama thought I was just going to go away quietly and let this slide they had another thing coming. Their lives were about to feel like a nightmare with no way to escape the pain being brought on them.

And I knew just the person to help me get revenge on all of them bitches.

****

Nine days later, I sat across from the private investigator I hired. No one would tell me where Honor moved to, and it seemed like Patch and Truly no longer lived at their house. Two days after the incident I sat in front of Patch and Truly's house and no one came in or out of the place.

"I'll be right back; I have to get the file out of my office." I watched as the private investigator left the conference room. He knew what time I was coming today, so I didn't understand how he didn't have the file in here.

My nails tapped on the table in rhythm as the time slowly went by. His office was only across the hall, but he still wasn't back after five minutes and boredom was starting to strike. Pulling up my social media was on the forefront of my mind but seeing my man with a child that wasn't ours just did something to me. Each time I logged in there was a picture of Honor and his baby or just the baby on his page.

"Got your file." Another voice I didn't recognize said while tossing the file on the table. I reached for the file, but a large hand slapped down on the other end of the file preventing me from pulling it towards my side.

"Word of advice, when hiring a private investigator make sure it's one that doesn't work for the people you're trying to have him investigate." I looked up and into the eyes of one of the older men that was in Patch's backyard during the wedding.

"I was just tryna make sure that woman that says she's his baby mama wasn't trying to steal from him or set him up. Her ass just pops up out of the blue with a baby then he dumps me? Nah something's not right with that picture," I told him.

"You mean lie and steal from my nephew like you did?" the man replied. Honor only had one uncle so the man in front of me had to be his uncle Rocko.

"That was just a misunderstanding on his part, and I just need to make him see that." Honor must have gone around blabbing our business to everyone, just telling them *his* truth. Hell we were to be married in a few months so that money was mine too.

"Fuck all that, just stay away from my family and your family won't find your head on their porch one day," Rocko said. He started rattling off my father's and best friend's addresses, then mine before he stood from the table and walked out.

I reached for the file he left behind and opened it, but it was blank. I was just going to have to turn their lives inside out in other ways until I found out where they all lived.

Haven

I hurried down the stairs after reading the text from Truly telling me that she was around the corner.

I thought I had started getting ready early enough to have Sayvonna and me ready to go when Truly showed up. When I looked at the time on my phone, I realized Truly was almost twenty minutes early. I had to hurry up and get Sayvonna's car seat out of my car and make sure there was enough snacks in her bag.

"Go put on something your size; it looks like you're suffocating your legs or some shit." My mouth dropped when Honor said that as I walked in the living room.

"You just mad my legs look juicy as fuck in this, and somebody gonna want to take a bite out of me. My jeans aren't even too small; they hug my curves just right, hater," I replied.

"If you say so, but I'mma take Say with me to see my mom; we'll be gone for a few hours," Honor announced as I set Sayvonna's diaper bag on the couch. The two of them were sitting on the couch watching a cartoon.

"Why didn't your mom come to the wedding?" I asked, then regretted it. I promised myself I would only talk to him regarding Sayvonna and work after he blew up on me that night

"Ever since she escaped my dad, she doesn't come out this way. She's scared he'll pull her back in somehow, so she stays far away from anywhere he could be," Honor replied.

"But on to business," he said. "I picked up the keys to one of the spots today. I wanna have it rented within the month, so I need you to buy the furniture to stage the house today. I added you as an authorized user on my credit card for the furniture place. They said all you need is my card for their store and your ID to buy the stuff. I emailed you a 3D floorplan of the house, pictures of the new flooring and color scheme. Tell Truly to put their living room furniture on my card too as a wedding present."

Honor also told me to buy stuff to stage the townhouses because the renovations on his house would be finished in a few weeks. I was making a mental note of having a few weeks to find a place, but he told me I could move into the mother-in-law suite in the backyard of his new place. Saying no was on the tip of my tongue, but when I looked at him and Sayvonna it felt like I owed them that time. And, at the moment, I just couldn't see myself being far from my daughter for too long; even if she was just with her dad.

"Truly's outside I have to go," I told him before I bent down and kissed Sayvonna all over her face.

"Take the garage opener, I'll leave the door in the kitchen unlocked," Honor handed me the garage opener and his card. He promised to have me a key made to both places when I got back.

"She just needs her baby snacks for her diaper bag," I told him before I left.

"Where's Sayvonna?" Truly asked when I got in her car.

"Stayin' with her dad; they're going to see his mother," I answered while putting on my seatbelt.

"I thought we were going to have a girls' day of shopping for furniture and a spa day after." Truly was excited to have a little girl around and someone to do girly stuff with.

"Yeah that would be a no for Sayvonna; she doesn't like to sit in the same place for too long. The nail shop would ban us because she likes to throw shit when she can't get down and crawl around. But how was your honeymoon?" I asked her.

"It was nice! You have to come back to that private island with us when we take the kids in a few months. I loved the private heated pool at the house Uncle Rocko rented for us; it was so nice and relaxing. I spent so many hours on that swim out bench in the pool that the chlorine or something else in the water chipped away at the polish on my feet and nails." I agreed to go with her because I needed a relaxing vacation badly, but I was only going if my decorating business picked up and I made enough money.

"Um, can you block calls from coming through when someone calls you through social media?" I changed the subject as Truly pulled onto the freeway.

"I don't know, why?" she asked.

"Somebody keeps callin' me from fake pages. At first I didn't answer but they kept callin' over and over again until I finally answered. Then they just breathed on the phone for a few seconds before sayin', 'I'm coming for you bitch' and hanging up in my face." The calls were getting so persistent, I had to delete Messenger. But I needed it back on my phone for business purposes.

My hand gripped the door handle, and I shut my eyes tight as Truly slammed on the brakes. She rolled down her window and switched lanes. Truly picked up her milkshake and tossed it out the window at the lady that cut us off seconds go. If Truly hadn't slammed on the breaks, we would've rammed into the back of the lady.

"It's probably that bitch Layne callin' you, get my phone out of the cupholder and go to my Messenger. Click on the message from her," Truly told me as if nothing was happening.

My heart was still pounding in my chest as Truly followed behind the lady on the freeway. She got off the same exit as the woman and kept riding the woman's ass until the lady pulled into the police station.

"I been trying to curb my temper, but it seems like that won't be happening being around y'all crazies." Truly laughed as if my words were a joke. I could just picture myself in a cell waiting for someone to bail me out because of something her or her husband started.

I clicked on Truly's Messenger as she pulled back on the freeway.

Layne Ashby

Truly, you're a funny acting bitch, smiling all in my face then two days later in the next bitch's face. You could have called and told me about your wedding instead of letting me see it on social media. But not only did you do that, you invited that bitch who fucked my man and her baby. You ain't no friend of mine, now you're my enemy and can get it just like that bitch...

I didn't even get to finish reading the message because 'New Message' popped up at the top of the screen. I scrolled down and read the new message from Layne to Truly.

Layne Ashby

Oh so you can see my message and not respond like a scary bitch. Must be hanging with that stupid bitch now, but you gonna get my car detailed. Some of that milkshake went into my car and I'm filing a police report, bitch.

"Me and that bitch didn't even call each other on no personal shit so how could we be friends? She's delusional. She only called me when she was looking for Honor's ass. Hell, I hardly said hi to her when I saw her ass, so I don't know why she thinks we were friends," Truly responded as we pulled off the exit for the furniture store.

"She's a self-absorbed bitch; you could just simply wave at her and that'll give her the green light to start talkin' 'bout herself," Truly said as she pulled into the parking lot of the furniture place.

We went into a sandwich shop and ate before we headed into the furniture store next door. While we were eating, Truly informed me that she and Patch wanted to hire me to decorate their place. We chatted about their personalities and different designs they liked; it helped me gain prospective on how to merge their styles with certain furniture.

It took me four hours to pick out the right furniture for Patch and Truly's new place and the three properties Honor hired me to decorate.

It felt good to be working for myself again instead of making someone else rich. I couldn't wait to add the pictures to my website and business social media page after I got everything decorated. I wanted to leave my daughter a business and wealth that she could build on if she wanted to.

Truly

I sat on one of the couches in the far corner as Haven paid for everything she picked out. I had already paid for the furniture she picked out for Patch and me, well, everything except for the stuff for our living room. Patch had surprised me with a six-bedroom, four-bathroom house the day after our surprise wedding. It had a pool in the backyard and one of those pool houses. I was trying to talk him into making the pool heated and adding a bar.

It was like I had been getting one surprise after another ever since my wedding. My uncle Rocko surprised Patch and me with a five-day honeymoon, and Patch paid for an extra three days.

My phone rang as Haven and I were walking out of the furniture store; it was my neighbor Miss Patricia and she never called me.

"Hello," I answered while climbing into my truck.

"Truly, I need you to stop by my house as soon as you can; it's an emergency," Miss Patricia responded.

"What's the emergency?" I asked her. If it was something minor it could wait until after the nail shop.

"PJ is at my house," she responded.

"I'll be there in twenty minutes." I couldn't understand why PJ was at her house. His mother didn't even speak to Miss Patricia so he shouldn't have been there. But his mother had been slipping ever since she got with that married man, so PJ being with Miss Patricia kind of scared me.

Haven asked me what happened as I zoomed out of the parking lot of the furniture store. I explained what I knew as we got on the freeway and headed back towards my old place.

Thirty-five minutes later, I pulled into the driveway of my old house. I noticed the driveway to PJ's mama's house was empty. Which was unusual because on Sunday evenings she was always at home so I could pick-up PJ. Sunday through Thursday afternoon was Patch's time, and she got PJ the other days. I think she spent the days Patch had PJ with that married man, so she was always rushing PJ over to my car before I could get out.

"Is that garbage bags on your porch?" Haven asked.

"Where?" My eyes zeroed in on my porch, and there were three big garbage bags on the porch. Seventy-year-old Miss Patricia walked out of her house holding PJ's hand.

"What's going on?" I asked as I got out of the car and walked towards them.

"Two days ago, my granddaughter came outside and seen him laying on top of some garbage bags. She took some pictures of him with my phone in case you needed them," Miss Patricia explained,

"What happened?" In my mind something had to happen to his mother for her to just leave him out there.

"Sweetie, how about your friend take him inside the car or house first, and then I'll tell you the story," Miss Patricia said to me.

I picked up PJ and took him to the car where Haven was waiting. I gave him a snack and went to listen to what Miss Patricia had to say.

"I heard his mother and that man arguing really loud, but I stayed in the house. They got so loud that my nosey granddaughter went outside to listen. My granddaughter told me she heard the man yelling about how he didn't want any little kids around anymore as his kids were all almost adults, and that if she wanted him to leave his wife, she had to get rid of her son." Miss Patricia shook her head as she told me everything her granddaughter heard.

"It was all quiet then they both came outside with garbage bags in their hands and tossed them onto your porch. Then she brought the child outside and set him on top of the bags and just walked off without so much as a word to him. Then I heard the man tell her they needed to go get his clothes from his wife's house, so he could move in with her and then they left.

I knew you and your husband were on your honeymoon, so I brought him in and one of his bags of clothes. I waited until my granddaughter said you posted that you two were back before I called you. And his mother and her man friend just left to do something over an hour ago." When the old woman told me that, all that ran through my mind was beating the shit out of that bitch.

"Can you call me when they pull back up if I'm not here?" I asked her because both of them needed their asses beat.

"If you're coming back to beat her ass, I'll even hold her down while you beat her ass, sweetie. My mother did the same thing to me because my step-father only wanted his own kids living with them and she agreed." The older woman said, and I could see tears misting in her eyes.

I thanked her, then got in the car so I could take PJ to Victor's house where Truvon was. I knew better than to take him to Brenda's house because I knew she would call Patch and tell him everything. Then she would want to come with me to fuck Keisha and that nigga up. But I wanted to handle her ass before the two of them got their hands on her.

****

"I just want to be waitin' in her living room when she gets home, then boom my hands are wrapped around that bitch's neck. The bitch needs to sleep on the streets with that fuck nigga," I said to Alisha and Haven as we sat at the table in the home Alisha shared with Victor. The boys were in the backyard watching Victor put together the swing and slide set he had bought for them. Victor was taking the grandfather thing seriously and making up for the time he didn't get to spend with either of the boys.

"I get your anger, but you have to think about the long term. If you don't go through the proper channels, PJ's mom can come back and get custody of him. If you beat her, she might even claim that you threatened her and made her give up PJ. My sister works with parents that are trying to get custody or sign over their rights. She tells me stories about that happening all the time; a parent comes back years later out of the blue and gets custody back. I can call my sister and have her help you through all the proper steps, so you can make sure he doesn't go back to that woman. Then you can do whatever the hell you want," Alisha said being the voice of reason I didn't want at the moment but needed. She got up from the table and went into the other room to call her sister.

"If you still want her to hurt, I can make sure she regrets doing what she did to PJ and not leave any visible marks on her," Haven said after she made sure Alisha was completely out of the room.

"I wasn't letting her get away with that scot-free no matter what Alisha says or thinks," I replied.

"Plans are swarming through my head, right, and I can just picture making that bitch scream. I hate when a woman puts a man before her kids and leaves them behind some dick." Haven stopped talking when Alisha walked back into the kitchen.

"My sister said Patch should file for full custody first; then after a year of PJ's mother not seeing him, the two of you can terminate his mother's parental rights, and you can adopt him," Alisha said as she walked back into the kitchen while still on the phone with her sister.

"Patch got full custody of PJ sometime last year when PJ's mother started dropping him off to me more than she already did," I told her; she relayed what I said to her sister on the phone.

"My sister said just wait a year if you want to adopt him and get a lawyer now. It will help the case if the mother doesn't get in contact regarding PJ for a year," Alisha told me. I started formulating how I could get her to stay away from him for an entire year.

"Can you tell my dad that I'll be back for the boys once I finish telling Patch and his mother what happened?" I asked Alisha after thanking her and her sister for the information.

"They can stay as long as you need them to; your dad turned your old room into their room. He bought two full beds and a lot of boy stuff for the room. If you ever need us to take them for a few hours or days just call or text one of us," Alisha said as she hugged me before Haven and I left.

"I can torture her and make her understand that she is not to have contact with y'all ever again," Haven said as we walked down the driveway towards my truck. She was starting to make me feel as though she just wanted to hurt anybody.

"Not today. I wanna do it when she's least expecting it…to make it seem like it didn't have anything to do with us." I waited until we were in my truck to respond to her.

The car ride was silent as I drowned in my thoughts. After I dropped Haven off, I headed straight for a bar close to Patch's house and took a few shots. I had to think of the best way to tell Patch that would prevent him from killing PJ's mama and her man.

Haven

My phone started beeping as I walked through the garage. When I saw who it was, I rolled my eyes and groaned.

Jace:

You see me callin' you, answer your fuckin phone, I'm sorry.

Jace:

I deposited some money in your account, come back home baby.

Jace:

There's this house with a backyard like you wanted for baby girl, I'm bout to get it for us.

Every time we broke up Jace wouldn't reach out to me for a few weeks. Then he'd blow my phone up and promise to give me everything I asked him for while we were together. I would always go back to him, and for a few months, he would buy and show me everything I had practically begged him for. Jace would go back to his ways when he thought I wasn't going anywhere.

Jace:

Fuck you bitch and watch your back hoe.

I knew that was coming when he noticed I was reading his messages but not responding. I closed the garage and blocked Jace from contacting me on everything.

"You got everything?" Honor asked me when I walked in. He was sifting through a pile of takeout menus. All he had in his fridge was baby food, breakfast food and some cereal. I had been meaning to go grocery shopping, but I had gotten caught up with getting my business off the ground.

"Yeah, I took pictures of everything on my tablet for you to see. They're going to call you next week to set up a delivery date," I answered him. I waved for him to follow me to the living room, so I could show him the pictures on my tablet. I was in the process of pulling up the pictures when my phone started ringing. I looked down and noticed it was a private number. I regretted answering when I heard someone breathing before they said, "I'm coming for you, bitch, and everybody close to you."

"How the fuck did she get my number," I grumbled.

"How did who get your number?" Honor asked as we sat down on the couch. I turned toward him and told him everything Layne had been doing to me and Truly.

"She's just acting out 'cause she doesn't like you, and she knows Truly never liked her. To Layne, you and Truly got everything she wants and needs so she hates the two of you," Honor responded after I told him everything.

"Why would she be mad at me; she doesn't even know me? Is it because I beat her ass at the wedding? I told her I wouldn't have touched her if my baby wasn't in your arms."

"Nah, she has a mouth on her and is used to that. She's mad because I called her your name when we were fuckin' a few times; she ain't liked you ever since then. Plus, she believed all you had to do was say the words and I'd leave her for you. So me callin' off our engagement around the time you got back in town has her gunning for you. Don't even trip off her ass, I got it," he told me and basically waved Layne off.

"She must not know you'd never fuck with me like that after everything that happened between us," I responded.

"Shit she's right, I might be pissed at everything you did but that doesn't mean I don't still love you. It's going to take some time for us to get to where we need to be. But our daughter is not growing up without her parents being together in the same home because the adults around her fucked up. I want her to have what I didn't have growing up, and I'll be damned if my father's actions fuck her life up like he did me and my brother's. I already forgave you for the kidnapping because if it was my brother, I would've done the same thing and more. But what I can't just let pass right now is you not telling me about Sayvonna sooner," Honor said to me. Even though I wasn't trying to feel anything by his words, they made my heart swell in my chest. I still loved Honor, but I was scared of what my actions had done to his feelings for me. I was scared to feel anything for him as well.

It seemed like everyone I loved deeply disappeared on me in one way or another. Honor made me feel things I didn't want to feel, because I couldn't lose another loved one again. Finding my brother's and parents' bodies did something to me, and it made me vulnerable in ways I didn't want to be. I craved to have somebody hold me and to be in my corner. What was holding me back was I didn't want to love Honor without any boundaries. That was a big reason why I left when I did a year ago; I didn't want to love anyone else because although love doesn't perish, the people I love do. And I was scared to fall completely in love with Honor only to experience that hurt again when something happened to him.

"I'll just prove to you with my actions that I'll be there to catch, support and protect you. And I'm not going anywhere anytime soon," Honor said to me after I spilled all of those feelings and thoughts to him.

Although his words touched me, only time would tell if I could finally let go or not.

****

"Hello," I answered my ringing phone. I didn't even bother to look at the caller ID; I just knew it was Truly calling to tell me she was outside waiting.

"I need you to let the lady at the door in and sign the paperwork she got." Honor didn't greet me or anything, he went right to business. I could hear Sayvonna blabbing in the background.

"Why, do I need to sign anything?" I asked him because I was confused.

"In case I'm not around, you can authorize some shit on my behalf for my business," he replied. I ran down the stairs to let the woman in. She was so short and top heavy that I thought she would fall over at any minute.

Honor told me he would call me back, because he had to take his mother somewhere and I should text him once everything was done. I hung up the phone and invited the woman inside.

"Sorry, I had to bring my girlfriend with me; Honor called at the last minute." The woman said as another woman followed her into the house.

"No problem. I was just told about this before I opened the door; we can take this to the kitchen." I pointed them towards the kitchen before closing and locking the door.

"How do you know Honor?" I asked the woman as I sat across from her at the kitchen table.

"I'm Salita, his lawyer. We met in a parking lot after we both finished taking our bar exam. A couple of months later I saw his page pop up as 'people I may know' and I added him. We got to talking and I told him my dad's firm was looking for people who had recently graduated. My dad and his partners liked Honor and now he works for my dad's firm part-time," she answered as she pulled papers from her briefcase.

"I highlighted all of the parts you need to sign, and as you're signing, I'll just give you a quick run down of what you're signing," Salita said as she slid the packet of papers and a pen across to me.

"That first small packet is papers to help you promote your business," Salita told me. I signed all the highlighted parts then slid the papers back to her. The next stack I signed was to give me the authority I would need to make decisions regarding his businesses if something happened to Honor, and he made me a silent partner in one of his businesses.

"Give this small stack to the man outside waiting for you, and I will go file these now," Salita told me. We stood to leave after she handed me the first stack of paperwork and put the other stack in her brief case. I couldn't find my keys to lock up the house, so I grabbed the garage opener out of the kitchen drawer.

Salita and her girlfriend followed behind me through the kitchen door, leading to the garage then out of the garage.

There were three cars in front of Honor's house, and a man was standing between two of them. One of the cars had a car cover covering it. I headed over to the man and handed him the paperwork. He stood in front of me flipping through the papers then he handed me the keys. I was about to ask him what was going on, but he walked over to the car and uncovered it.

The car had a custom vehicle vinyl lettering on it. Haven's Décor was written in big, red pretty letters. Underneath it in black was my tagline Beautifying One House and Party At A Time in smaller letters. Under the tagline was my social media business page and website. The decal was on both sides of the car.

Me:

Thanks for the car! I added the crying, excited and heart emojis.

Patch:

Yeah 'cause she needed it! That shit she had looked like it shaked when she tried to go over sixty.

Damn, I had accidently texted our group chat instead of Honor individually, like I tried to do. I forgot the group chat was the last place he and I had texted each other.

Truly:

Shut the fuck up Patch! Haven come get me…we need to be at the nail shop in thirty.

Me:

I'm on my way Truly.

I texted Truly back as I got into the Limited Jeep Renegade that I had been wanting for over a year. My phone went off once more, right before I was about to pull off. When I looked down, I noticed Honor had responded back to me but not in the group chat.

Honor:

I told you I'll show you with actions. Go have fun with my sister…me and Say will be back tomorrow.

I smiled at the message as if he could see me before I pulled off. I drove towards Miss Brenda's house where Truly and her family were staying until they moved into their new house.

Haven

December 5ᵗʰ

11:00 am

"Vanessa, put these at the front and pass these out to the VIP customers," Truly said walking up to one of the nail technicians and handing her my business cards. Which she found a couple of minutes ago when she went to put her wallet in my glove box. Not only did Honor get me a car, he had some business cards made too.

"Truly, you can't just walk into this nail shop and force them to display my business cards without asking first." I loved how she took the initiative, but I didn't want the people to think we were rude.

"She's the owner," Vanessa replied to me as she pointed at Truly.

"Oh, I must've forgot to tell you we were coming to me and Patch's spot," Truly said as she shrugged her shoulders.

"So, you really do own this place," a woman walked up to Truly and said.

"Yes, Mom, I told you that already." Truly rolled her eyes.

"See, and you questioned why I said what I said to you or had to smack you here and there. I was making sure you wouldn't think you were any better than you really were, like your father does. Without me, you would be out there like his ass, but I made sure your ass stayed in your place unlike him," Truly's mom said. I didn't like the look on Truly's face behind her mother's words.

"Out." Vanessa looked at Truly's mom and pointed at the door.

"I don't have to leave I'm a payin' customer," Truly's mom stated.

"I'll call Mr. and Miss Jackson right now for you, Mrs. Jackson, if she don't leave. And I'll call the police the next time you try to come in," Vanessa said.

"Call them," Truly's mom challenged Vanessa.

"I swear you married into some ghetto trash. I thought I taught you better than that."

"You keep speaking a bunch of bullshit. I wasn't gonna say shit because I didn't want to disrespect Truly's mother. But bitch, you ain't a mother and the only ghetto trash is your ass. Be honest, you only said and did what you said to Truly because you knew she would be and have more than you ever did, and you couldn't stand it. So you thought you would fuck up her self-esteem so she wouldn't surpass you and she still did. And that ghetto trash you talking about stuck by her and helped her become the woman she is today, something you couldn't do. Truly didn't become a success because of you, she became one despite you." I couldn't hold me tongue any longer.

"Mom, I just want you to know what you think of me and your words can't hurt me anymore. If you 'bouta spend money in here, sit down and shut up; otherwise, get the fuck out," Truly finally spoke up.

"Who the hell you think you're talkin' out the side of your neck to?" Truly's mother said as she tried to walk up in Truly's face, but I blocked her. I grabbed Truly's mom by her arm, dragged her to the door and pushed her out of it, and Vanessa tossed her purse at her.

"Thanks," Truly spoke as we walked to the back where two nail technicians were waiting for us.

Truly and I took off our sandals and rolled up our pants after we sat in the chair. The nail techs turned on the chairs to massage our backs after we placed our feet in the water. Vanessa walked in with two glasses of champagne for us.

"Where did your parents come up with your name?" Truly asked as our feet soaked in the water.

"My dad named me after the only foster mother he liked; she died when he was sixteen," I answered her then took a sip of my champagne.

We continued our small talk about me and Honor, my décor business, and more as we got our toes and nails done. Vivi gave us a facial as we waited for our polish to dry before we left.

I dropped Truly off at Miss Brenda's with the promise that we'd make the nail shop a monthly girls' trip.

2 am…

I just had to have some ice cream in the middle of the night and went to the twenty-four-hour grocery store. What was supposed to be a quick in and out grocery run turned into a two-hour grocery shopping trip.

The hairs on the back of my neck stood as I walked out of the grocery store. It felt like someone was watching me, but when I looked around the, now practically empty, parking lot I didn't see anyone. When I got there all the stalls in the tiny parking lot were filled so I had to park at a distance from the door.

Since I had to park so far away, I made sure to park under one of the lights. When my eyes looked towards my car, all the lights in the parking lot near my car were no longer working. That alone amped up my paranoia as my eyes scanned the parking lot for a threat. I didn't see anyone, but I still felt like someone was there, so I took my gun out of my purse.

I was in middle school when my brother told my father about the grown men staring me down and making comments about my body. One man even went as far as to stop my brother one morning before we walked in the donut shop to ask him if I was his woman. When Savon told him no, he started to try to hit on me even after my brother told him I was only twelve. The man snatched me by the arm and tried to pull me towards him, and Savon and the man got into a fight. Thankfully Truth was there and they whooped that grown man's ass. That was the first day we met Truth, he had been listening to the conversation and felt disgusted by what happened and wanted to help.

After that incident my dad bought me and Savon both guns and told us to carry them everywhere. My father put me in martial arts and had me at the gun range with him When I went to high school, he upgraded the gun he bought me, and I still had it.

I placed my head through the strap of my purse then let the cart go as I started running towards my car. Behind me

I could hear someone faintly curse before footsteps started pounding the pavement. I cried out when my body hit the ground as someone tackled me from the back and my gun slid out of my hand. The air was whooshed out of my lungs, but I managed to still jerk my elbow back a few times elbowing my attacker wherever my elbow landed. All I could think about was fighting to save my life and getting back to my baby.

He gripped my hair in his hand and yanked me towards him causing me to yelp.

"Bitch, don't move!" he yelled in my ear while placing a knife at my neck and applying pressure. I was scared to breathe as he pressed the knife deeper into my throat harder and harder drawing blood.

"I'mma slice your throat then take the pussy as you slowly bleed out and leave your body on that nigga's porch." My attacker growled in my ear then licked the side of my face.

"Aye, I'm not paying you to play with her, either kidnap or kill the bitch." I heard Layne's voice call out.

"Bitch do-" The man pulled the knife away from my throat as he turned towards the sound of Layne's voice. I knew that would be my only chance, so I used the distraction to my advantage.

"Fuck," my attacker yelled as my elbow connected with his dick He tossed me to the ground and started stalking towards me with a look that could kill on his face. I started crawling backwards to get away from him until I was able to grasp my gun. I took the safety off and pointed the gun at his head in one fluid motion.

"Bitch, you don't even know how to use that gun put it down," he said as he moved for the gun. I pulled the trigger just as his fingers were a millisecond from grabbing the gun. He grunted then fell on top of me; it took a few tries before I was able to push him off me.

I noticed Layne and an older man running towards me when my attacker's body was off mine. I started shooting at them; they ducked before they turned around and ran towards their car. Before I could get off the ground, their car came barreling towards me. I had to quickly roll out of the way, but I wasn't quick enough because the tire had bumped my foot.

From pure adrenaline alone, I was able to stand and run to the car as they turned around and started heading back towards me. I managed to press the button to pop the locks and start the car before they reached me. I jumped in the car and pulled off just as they tapped the back of Honor's car.

I felt stupid for not waiting until Honor and Sayvonna got back in the morning to go to the grocery store like he told me to. Because of that I was being chased by his ex. I couldn't call him for help because he was so far away, so I called the next best thing.

"Who the fuck is this?" Patch barked into the phone.

"Haven! I almost got kidnapped; now they chasing behind me!" I screamed into the phone as they rammed into the back of me again. I looked up in the rear-view mirror and noticed that there were two men in the car as well.

"Tell me where you're at; I'm already out." The way he said that sent chills through me, but I told him where I was anyway. He told me to come towards his direction, so he could get to me faster.

"Hurry, I'm out of bullets," I yelled out as I took a sharp right turn. Layne and her accomplices took the turn with me. After a few more turns I could see headlights a few feet ahead of me and knew it was Patch. The car Layne's was in turned around quickly when they saw the lights ahead.

"It was Layne and three men. I had to leave my groceries and kill a man," I said all in one breath. We had both pulled over and Patch had approached my car.

Dear, Honor & Haven   Marqua'lla

"A'ight, get in the passenger seat, Eagle will drive my car to the grocery store and get the body. But your baby daddy is buying me a new car," Patch said as he walked away.

I moved to get out of the car, but a sharp pain moved through my stomach as I tried to move.

"Patch!" I called out after checking my body. "I've been stabbed!" I yelled. I pressed my hand on the wound, but the pain was too much, so I released the pressure. When I looked at my hand it was soaked in my blood; I passed out.

I woke up to shooting pain in my side as Patch ran with me in his arms. All I could do was close my eyes tight and pray the pain shooting through me would be over soon.

"You know the drill lay her on the bed in the second room to the right." I heard a male voice say to Patch.

"She was passed out the whole way here, Doc Stephens," Patch told the man as he laid me on a hospital bed.

"Did you hit your head?" Dr. Stephens asked as he flashed a light in my eyes.

"No, I just have a thing with seeing my own blood. Oh and my foot was hit by the tire of the car. I can still feel it throbbing," I answered through the pain as Dr. Stephens pulled out a needle. My eyes shut tight as Dr. Stephens gave me a shot near my knife wound before he started to clean then stitch my wound up.

I gripped the bedrail tightly as he took off my shoe then wrapped my foot. I swear my foot hurt more than the damn stab wound.

"Take one of each in the morning and at night," Dr. Stephens specified as he handed me two pill bottles and gave me further instructions for my stitches and sprain.

"I added a donation for the clinic," Patch said to Dr. Stephens as he pulled out a stack of money and paid him.

"Your generosity will go to helping a lot of patients at the free clinic," Dr. Stephens praised Patch as he handed him a bag of supplies to clean and dress my wound.

Dr. Stephens helped me off the bed and into a wheelchair. He wheeled me to Honor's car as Patch followed behind him, then they both helped me inside.

"Eagle and Rocko gonna meet us at Honor's place, and they'll stay with you until Honor gets back," Patch said as we pulled off from the free clinic.

"You told Honor?" I asked him.

"Hell yeah, I know your ass didn't think you would be able to hide this from him," Patch answered.

"He's gonna be pissed; he told me not to go to the store that late and look what happened."

"That nigga just happy you not the one in the body bag," Patch said; his words made me realize just how close I was to being dead.

My eyes started to fill heavy and I couldn't hold them open anymore. When I finally opened them again, I was in Honor's bed with him lying next to me and Sayvonna was sleeping on his chest.

I tried to reach over to move Sayvonna's hair out of her face, but my arm movement was restricted. As my eyes scanned around, I realized my feet were chained together and my wrists were cuffed to bed.

"Paybacks a bitch ain't it? And you should've listened to me," Honor mumbled without opening his eyes.

I couldn't help but to agree with his words in my head.

Truly

It had been two weeks since the incident with Haven, and I still hadn't seen her. Honor told me I could only text her for right now, but for some reason he wouldn't let me come over to his place. I wanted to say forget what Honor was saying and go over there, but Patch told me to mind my business. They wouldn't even let me FaceTime her; even when I texted her, most of her responses were sent back with only emojis. When I told Patch he just laughed and shrugged his shoulders.

"What's going on in here?" PJ's mom, Keisha, screeched as she walked in the house and noticed all the people packing her stuff.

When PJ was an infant his mom's house went into foreclosure and she was about to get kicked out of the house by the bank. Honor bought the house and put it in his name instead of keeping it in Keisha's name. When Patch learned what she did to PJ, he said it was time to give her and that nigga a taste of their own medicine.

"Y'all can't do that; this is my house!" Keisha yelled as tears ran down her face.

"Nah this my shit, bitch," Patch said with a calmness that gave me shivers.

"We gonna call the police for an illegal eviction," Keisha's boyfriend Mark had the nerve to finally speak up.

"Gon' head and watch y'all be in there for child endangerment; we got witnesses and pictures," I replied, and he shut right up.

"Y'all got five minutes to pack whatever you're taking with you; everything else getting donated," Patch barked at Mark causing the man to jump back a bit.

"You left your son out in the cold for someone else's husband who can't even protect or provide for your ass." I got up and slapped Keisha so hard my hand started to sting; she fell back into her boyfriend. I promised myself that I wouldn't touch Keisha but Miss Patricia had just sent me the pictures of PJ lying on those garbage bags crying. I should've had her send them to Patch's phone. Seeing what he looked like on those clothes, and how scared he looked pissed me off. It made me want to kill the bitch. I didn't think I could let her live after seeing his pain, Keisha needed to feel that same hopeless pain she made PJ feel.

"Where are we going to go?" Keisha asked Mark as they both walked into the living room with a garbage bag.

"I'm going back to my wife; I don't know where your ass going," Mark replied.

"I gave my son up for you! But soon as we don't have a place to sleep, you saying fuck me and tryna go back to your wife? The jokes on you, she moved her second baby daddy into the house as soon as he got out." Keisha dropped her bag and started hitting him.

"You're lying; she wouldn't go back to that hoodlum," Mark said as he blocked her hits.

"That's why none of her kids are yours; she told one of the other ladies at church all about it. She was sleeping with that man almost y'all whole relationship," Keisha hissed.

"Oh, thank God, son, your mother must've sent you to come get me right on time," Mark said as Eagle walked through the door.

"Call me son one more time, and I'mma knock your ass the fuck out. How many times I gotta tell your ass not to disrespected me or my father by callin' me son," Eagle barked.

"Your daddy ain't never been around; I raised you since you were in middle school."

"My daddy wasn't in my life when you met my mom because my mama didn't tell him about me. All those times my mama had you think we were with my grandma we were with my dad. Hell, we spent months at a time with him out of the state or the country, and your dumb ass didn't even know." Eagle stated as he walked towards the man with his fist balled, daring him to say more.

"So that was it, he just wanted to keep y'all a secret?" Mark said.

"Yeah, he wanted to keep us a secret because of what happened to his wife and their kids. Now that he knows who did it, him and my mom are together raising my sisters," Eagle replied.

"That thug is not about to be living in my house," Mark mumbled.

"My dad been moved my mama and sisters out of there; before you even moved out with Keisha. You're gullible as fuck, you really believed my mom been taking care of my grandmother for over a year and that you could only see her at church. Because my grandmother didn't want you in her house, just a stupid ass nigga." When Eagle said that, Mark stormed out of the house with Keisha running behind him.

Four hours after all of the commotion, we had the house cleaned up and the stuff sitting on the curb with a 'Free' sign in front of it. People were stopping by and tossing the stuff in their cars. Half of the items were gone by the time we walked out of the house.

****

"Man, cuz, we finished now, right?" Eagle asked me as he maneuvered bags around in my trunk so the new ones could fit. Since Layne paid someone to try and kidnap Haven, I couldn't go anywhere without someone from my family. I had to finish Christmas shopping for my kids and Sayvonna since Haven couldn't. Eagle came with me because he had to get his sisters and mom something for Christmas.

"Nope, we just need to run in and get a couple more things then we can go," I told Eagle as he smashed down my trunk closed.

"This the last time I'm going shopping with your ass; you ain't even let a nigga stop to get food or nothin'," Eagle grumbled as he followed behind me towards the mall entrance.

I ignored him as I texted Haven to tell her I found everything she wanted to get Sayvonna for Christmas. I was putting my phone back in my pocket when someone wrapped their arms around my body and lifted me off the ground. Out of my peripheral vision I could see a Toyota coming straight at me, I started wiggling in the person's arms.

"Truly, stop moving!" Eagle shouted. Eagle turned so my body was facing the opposite way of the car. Before the car could hit us, he dove onto his back on the car next to us. The Toyota ended up slamming into the Honda we had landed on. The impact from it jarred my body out of Eagle's arms and into the window of the Honda we landed on.

"When I say run, hop down and run into the mall," Eagle told me as he reached for his gun. The car was about to run back into the car we were on, but instead pulled off when people started coming out of the mall.

"You okay?" Eagle asked as we got off the trunk of the car.

"No, I need to go to the hospital," I answered as Eagle helped me to my car. The left side of my body started to throb with intense pain, and I knew it would only get worse. Eagle helped me into the passenger's seat of my car then walked around to the other side. When he climbed in, he was on the phone with someone more than likely Patch.

"Patch said to take you to the clinic so there won't be any questions," Eagle told me before he handed me his phone.

"I'm okay." I answered what I knew would be his first question before he could even ask it.

"I'm a couple of hours away, but I'mma be there soon," Patch said. Then all I heard was him honking at people and cursing them out.

"Calm down, I'm fine I don't need you speeding and getting into an accident before you can get back." I didn't think he heard me because I could still hear him yelling out the window at people.

"Man, I'mma be a'ight," Patch replied and went back to cussing somebody out in another car. I hung up the phone in his face, hearing him yelling was starting to give me a headache.

"Aye, didn't you hit your head? Your ass bet not go to sleep," Eagle said as he reached over and shook my body.

"Why?" I asked, confused.

"Hell, if I know; I just hear that shit on those TV shows," Eagle replied as we pulled in front of the clinic. Dr. Stephens was already waiting outside for us with one of his nurses. When Dr. Stephens wanted to open the clinic in the hood, he couldn't get a loan to save a life. So he started a crowdfunding account. When Patch learned what was going on, he donated to the clinic and ever since then he donated to make sure the place was supplied. Whenever Patch needed a doctor with no questions asked, Dr. Stephens was there opening the door to his clinic no matter the time of day or night.

Dr. Stephens helped me out of the car, into the wheelchair and wheeled me into the clinic.

An hour and a half later, Patch walked into the room and laid down across the bottom of the bed.

"What's that noise?" Patch asked.

"It's…" I didn't get to finish answering him because seeing all the machines in the room and me in the bed must've triggered something in him.

"Fuck! They could've killed you; that bitch wanted a war now she got it." Patch moved to stand up, but I grabbed his arm and pulled him towards me.

"Christmas is in a few days, just let it go until the day after. You can get them all before the new year," I pleaded with him, although I knew it wouldn't happen. I just wanted to have a nice Christmas and not have to worry that Patch could be locked up behind Layne's bullshit.

"A'ight, I'll have my lil niggas out lookin' for them, but I won't hit the streets lookin' for them until after Christmas," Patch said, then mumbled something under his breath.

When Layne tried to run me over, she didn't know the hell she was bringing to her and her families' doorsteps.

Haven

December 20th...

One day of not being able to move when I wanted to was more than enough to drive me insane. I felt like a prisoner, Honor kept my hands cuffed together even when I went to the bathroom, and the door always had to be kept open. Other than that, being chained to the bed wasn't as bad as I thought it would be because Honor catered to my every need.

Honor took off work to make sure I didn't have to move a muscle. Some of the stuff he did for me felt more intimate than sex for me and like a long foreplay. He carried me to the bathroom each morning for a shower and took his time methodically cleaning my body. Honor also cooked for me and took care of almost all of Sayvonna's needs. It was a serene experience, the first few days, but after a while it started to feel daunting. I was used to doing everything for myself and being busy from sun up to sun down, so sitting idle just didn't do it for me. It was Sayvonna's first Christmas and I wanted to be in the store shopping around for her gifts, but instead I had to do my shopping online and have Truly find the stuff I couldn't get shipped.

SOUL Publications

"Christmas is in a couple of days, and I still have to wrap everything," I said to Honor when he walked in with Sayvonna crawling behind him.

"Don't worry 'bout that shit; I'mma handle all that, man." Honor waved off my concerns.

"But I need her first holiday to be perfect, and I'm just tired of being stuck in this fuckin' house chained to this damn bed." The frustration I was feeling was apparent in my voice.

"You see how I felt now don't you and your ass had me chained to the bed way longer, you'll be good for a few more days," he had the nerve to say.

"At least I left you uncuffed for a while and you had a whole room to roam around," I replied.

"Man, you really buggin'; for real though, just trust the process."

"Wait, what process?" I asked him, confused.

"Dr. Stephens will be here tomorrow to see if the stitches can come out. Me and you both know if you weren't handcuffed to the bed by now your stitches would've been busted and your wound reopened, because your ass can't sit still." I hated that he knew me so well.

There were old clients I had decorated houses and parties for contacting me and I wanted to meet with them right away. But Honor scheduled the consultations with my clients for a week or two after the new year. I loved and hated that he checked my website and responded to the emails I got online. Every afternoon after lunch he laid beside me on the bed and showed me the response I was getting to opening my business back up.

I didn't even need Messenger like I thought, clients were clicking on my website and messaging or requesting appointments through there. It made me feel good that people liked my previous work so much that they were willing to wait a couple of weeks just to get a consultation.

"Well you can at least let me respond to the emails on my website myself." I just needed to do something to occupy my time.

"I put on longer cuffs so you could feed yourself after the first day. That gave you more leeway than you gave me the first week," Honor said as he watched Sayvonna use his pants as leverage to stand up.

"All lies, you only gave me longer cuffs 'cause you was tired of your food getting cold afta helping me and Say eat. And I uncuffed your ass then gave you free range of the panic room before the week was out, but your ass ruined your freedom." I told him as I watched him pick up Sayvonna.

"Fuck all that you speakin', we 'bouta have family movie night." He waved me off and Sayvonna copied him before they walked out of the bedroom. Honor kept dismissing my concerns and it pissed me the hell off to the point where I wanted to stab his ass. I now understood why he tried to break out of the panic room I locked him in over a year ago, and all the aggression and anger I saw him display while doing so. Whenever he left out of the room, I tried to break out of the cuffs or break one of the wooden poles on the bed to get out.

It pissed me off that another day had slowly gone by without me even seeing the light of day. Unless the little bit of light peeping through the window counted.

"Do I at least get to pick the movie?" I asked Honor as he walked back into the room. He had Sayvonna in one hand and soda, kettle corn, baby snacks and juice in the other.

"Nah, you picked the movies the whole time I was locked in that room; it's my turn." Honor replied while handing me my own bag of kettle corn and a soda. I watched Honor as him and Sayvonna laid down with their heads at the foot of the bed.

"We're watching *Avengers: Infinity War* because Patch got us kicked out of the movies the day we went," Honor stated as he purchased the movie.

"Do you need to go pee before we start the movie?" Honor asked, and I shook my head in reply.

"Since you said no if you gotta pee during the movie your ass betta shake that shit up. I'm not gettin' up to take you once I press play." Honor shrugged his shoulders.

"Pssshhh, you gonna let me go to the bathroom if I have to or fuck around and be cleaning piss stained sheets. And you're buying *Ant-Man and the Wasp* after we finish watchin' this."

Thirty minutes into the movie, Honor paused the TV to help me to the bathroom and he bought the movie I wanted. But I fell asleep halfway through *Ant-Man and the Wasp*.

The middle of the night...

"Ummm," I moaned in a sleepy haze when I felt an arousing sensation. I could feel something on my neck and stomach simultaneously that was making my pussy tremble with need.

When my eyes opened, Honor was kissing and biting the side of my neck as his hand cupped my mound. I bit my lip when he repeatedly pinched the hood of my clit then released it.

"Harder," I groaned. Honor chuckled against my neck sending shivers down my body as he gave me what I desired.

Honor grazed my clit with his finger then pulled away a few times teasing me.

I wanted to clobber his ass, but I couldn't move since my hands and feet were still cuffed to the bed. Honor flicked his finger across my clit then pulled back. I felt his fingertips trail down my inner thigh then back up and down again. His hand gripped my inner thigh as he lightly kissed the side of my neck. I was over the teasing game he was playing.

"Please!" I pleaded for reprieve. Honor finally took pity on me and started massaging my clit; I closed my eyes letting the pleasurable feeling take over me. His fingers sped up against my clit flicking it repeatedly causing pleasure to take over me.

I was right on the edge of no return, and before I knew it Honor had my body shuddering into an orgasm. My clit twitched underneath his fingers as he rubbed me from one orgasm to another.

My eyelids began to feel heavy as my body began to descend from my orgasm. I felt exhausted, and I hadn't even done any of the work.

"Go to sleep," Honor whispered in my ear and that was all I needed to hear.

I went back to sleep just as quick as I woke up.

****

When I woke up three hours ago, my hands were uncuffed. Instead of staying in bed, I got up cleaned the entire townhouse and showered. When Sayvonna woke up, I got her together before she could get loud enough to wake up Honor. Next, I made some chicken fried steak, gravy, eggs and biscuits by the time Honor had gotten up. My side and my foot were in pain by the time we finished eating.

Honor made me get back in bed and he wrapped an ice pack around my foot and he cuffed my wrist back to the bed.

"I told your ass you would do too much if you weren't cuffed," Honor stated as he placed one of my pills for pain on my tongue.

"You un-cuffed me just to prove your point, huh." I said after I swallowed the pill and he just smirked at me.

"Dr. Stephens is here. I'll be back after I let him in," Honor said as he looked up from his phone.

"Uncuff me before Dr. Stephens walks in; I don't want him seeing me like this," I begged. Honor smiled then threw one of Sayvonna's blankets over the cuffs before he walked out of the room. Sayvonna looked at me and crawled after her daddy. The second the two of them met it seemed like she traded on me for him. Wherever Honor was Sayvonna wasn't too far behind, if she wasn't already sitting next to him.

"I didn't know doctors still did house calls," I said Dr. Stephens when he walked in. I had tried to convince Honor to let me go to the clinic to get the stitches removed, but he wouldn't budge on his strong hell no.

"I don't know about other doctors, but I will always make house calls for the family of the person who made it possible for me to open my doors." Dr. Stephens answered then started looking over my wound. Honor stood behind him with Sayvonna in his arms watching every move Dr. Stephens made. I watched as he leaned forward as Dr. Stephens started to take out my stitches. His eyes were glued to every move Dr. Stephens made like he knew what

Dr. Stephens was supposed to be doing and could correct him if needed.

"You can start putting a little bit of pressure on your foot now and getting back to your routine; just don't overexert yourself," Dr. Stephens said as he gathered his supplies after taking my stitches out and checking my foot.

"Write what you need from the grocery store for Christmas, and seven days' worth of food for eight people." Honor told me as he handed me a notebook after walking Dr. Stephens out. The handcuffs had enough reach that I could sit up and write.

"I wanna do my own grocery shopping; you be forgetting stuff even with a note," I replied.

"We're going to Lake Tahoe for Christmas with Patch, Truly and the kids. We leave in an hour, but the people need our grocery list now to stock the fridge for us," Honor reported.

"Wait we're going to be in the cold snow? We need some new clothes before we leave; release me so I can go to the mall," I told him as I swung my legs over the bed.

"It ain't gonna be that cold, but Mama Brenda already went to the store. She got us all a new wardrobe for the trip, our bags are packed and, in the car, already. I already packed all the presents and wrapping paper you ordered; we just need to get some snacks, pick up Patch 'nem, then hit the road." Honor told me as he un-cuffed me from the bed. Truly did say Miss Brenda wanted to be a personal shopper, and she knew just how to dress each of her clients. I loved how she styled everyone for Truly and Patch's wedding.

I wrote out the grocery list as Honor packed a few last-minute items that I told him we might need. We left after I sent the grocery list to the company.

I was excited to be out of the house and getting a mini vacation in the process. There was just this bad feeling in the pit of my stomach that everything wouldn't be the same when we got back home.

Truly

Three and a half hours later...

"Are we there?" Truvon asked Patch.

"Not at the place we're staying, but me and Honor got a surprise for y'all." Truvon and PJ cheered when they heard that.

Everyone put on their puff jackets before getting out the car; a little bit of snow was falling. Patch had to carry the boys to the door because they were struggling in the snow. Honor carried Haven in because the snow was almost to her knees. Once we walked into the restaurant, the first thing I noticed was Christmas decorations everywhere. They had a sleigh in the middle of the restaurant, and some lit up reindeer attached to it.

Patch handed the hostess a piece of paper when she walked over and greeted us.

"Oh, VIP follow me," she told us. She reached over and grabbed three Christmas stockings with Sayvonna's, Truvon's and PJ's names sewed into them.

We followed her to the back of the restaurant to a private area. It had a large round table with seven place setting in the middle of the room.

"What can I get everyone to drink?" she asked us after we took off our coats and sat at the table. We all gave her our drink orders before she walked out.

A couple of minutes later Mr. and Mrs. Santa Claus walked in carrying platers of pancakes, sausage and eggs. Their little helpers came in seconds later with our drink orders.

"Truvon, what do you want for Christmas?" Santa bent down next to him and asked after setting the pancakes on the table.

"What's the best toy the elves make in the workshop and do they get paid?" Truvon asked, and PJ turned to Santa with a raised eyebrow waiting for the answer.

"They get paid in cookies and everything they make is the best," Santa answered.

"They only get cookies?" Truvon looked at Santa like he was crazy.

"But me and my brother want a swimming pool, some new games, nerf guns, and more board games; they fun. My baby cousin over there just want more girl toys," Truvon answered, and PJ sat next to him nodding his head. Truvon and PJ didn't know about the new house yet; we were taking them to see it when we got back home.

"We'll get right on making you everything you want," two of the elves said as they walked up and handed the boys cups with their names on them filled with candy canes. A girl Elf walked over and gave Haven the same thing for Sayvonna.

"Thanks, and y'all should be paid more than cookies. When me and my granny was watching the news, the teachers were on strike because they weren't getting paid enough. After this Christmas if Santa give you cookies for making the toys then go on strike too," Truvon said and everyone in the room laughed.

When Mr. and Mrs. Claus left with their elves we sat and ate our breakfast before heading to our cabin.

Christmas evening...

After dinner I ran up the stairs and changed my shirt while everyone was eating desert. Patch was on FaceTime with his mother when I came back down the stairs. We all had turned our phones off and put them up for the whole vacation, Patch had only taken his phone out to FaceTime his mother for Christmas. She said she wouldn't talk to us for a few weeks if she wasn't able to see her grandkids on Christmas.

"When y'all come back, we're going to open the presents I got y'all." The boys just nodded their heads to answer her because their mouths were stuffed with cake.

"Mom, read Truly's shirt," Patch said as he positioned the phone so she could see me. I pulled down my shirt so she could read it: *4 is turning into 5* was written on my red shirt in green glitter.

"What the hell, 4 turns into 5," she kept repeating and everyone at the table looked confused. Haven was the first one to realized what my shirt meant.

"Wait a minute…wait; am I having another grandchild?" she finally realized. When I almost got hit by the car Dr. Stephens made me take a pregnancy test. When he did the ultrasound to check me, he realized I was just starting my second trimester. Sometimes my periods didn't come for six to twelve weeks. So not having my period for that long didn't even raise red flags for me like it would for some women. When Patch asked me about the noise he heard, it was from the OBGYN at the clinic monitoring the baby.

"This time it better be a girl or I'm not babysitting anymore." We all knew she was lying.

"What's going on?" Truvon asked.

"You and PJ gonna have a little brother or sister in roughly six months," I answered him.

"We can teach the baby how to swim," PJ said and Truvon agreed. Ever since I started taking them to swimming lessons last summer that was all they talked about, teaching people how to swim and a pool.

"A'ight, Mama, me and Honor 'bouta take the boys out to play in the snow." After we all said goodbye to Brenda, Patch hung up his phone then turned it back off.

I made all four of them drink some of the homemade hot chocolate me and Haven had made before they went to put on their coats. The boys sounded like they were having so much fun; their laughter brought me, Haven and Sayvonna outside to watch them.

I sat on the porch next to Haven and Sayvonna with a cup of hot chocolate in my hands as we watched the boys play in the snow. Patch and Truvon were one team and Honor and PJ were on the other one; they were competing to see who could build the best and fastest snowman. Patch thought he was slick picking Truvon because he thought he could win with him since he was the oldest. Patch was all about getting a competitive edge and winning.

"It's getting too cold for her; we're going inside to sit by the fire place," Haven said shaking her head at Honor and Patch. They had taken to throwing snowballs at each other trying to make sure the other hadn't finished.

"I'll carry her in for you," I told her as Patch tossed a hand full of snow on the back of Honor's neck. Haven was using crutches, so I poured the rest of my hot chocolate out in the snow then took Sayvonna from her.

"You're so cute, you make me want the baby to be a girl," I cooed at the baby as we walked into the cabin.

"Yes, the baby needs to be a girl, so Say can have a built-in best friend," Haven said, and I agreed.

Thirty minutes after we walked in, the boys came in as well. We sat around the fire for another two hours having a Christmas movie night with desert and hot chocolate.

****

The next morning Patch and I left out of the house before the boys woke up. Patch said he had a surprise waiting for me.

"Oh, hell nawl, I'm dropping my location to Haven; your ass tryna kill me," I said as I took my phone out when we pulled up to deserted woods covered in snow.

"Sometimes I swea your imagination have you saying some of the stupidest shit I ever heard. A nigga out here tryna be romantic and shit, and your ass jump straight to me tryna kill you," Patch said to me just as a sleigh with Mr. and Mrs. Santa Claus pulled up.

We walked over to the sleigh and climbed in the middle seats. Once we were seated with a blanket secure around us the sleigh started to move. It was being pulled by some miniature horses that were dressed in Christmas décor.

I laid my head on Patch's shoulder, and he wrapped his arms around me as the people driving the sleigh started.

"Wow." The snow-covered trees looked beautiful as we passed them.

"You feeling this?" Patch asked me.

"Yes, the snow-covered mountains look even more beautiful close up," I answered. For an hour we rode, cuddled together, through towering pines and around a beautiful lake in the Alpine forest and meadows. The woods looked magnificent. Throughout the ride the tour guide stood up and explained what we were seeing around us. We got off the sleigh twice, once to hear the couple recite a few short stories, and the last time was to take pictures of me and Patch in front of the lake.

"You want to come back next year?" Patch asked as he helped me to the car.

"Yeah, and next time we can do more of the stops," I told him.

"Hell nawl, a nigga not doing that sing along shit; that's where I draw the line," Patch said while opening the car door for me. I climbed into the truck and he closed the door behind me.

"I really loved doing this with you, and thanks for planning it," I told him as he climbed into the car.

"It wasn't nothing, you already know it's anything for you, but is my baby hungry?" Patch said as he rubbed my stomach.

"Yeah, we want some pancakes," I replied.

We stopped at a café and got breakfast before we headed back to the cabinet. The boys were there waiting for us to take them to the carnival. We had a much-needed family vacation and I wasn't ready to leave and go back to the chaos the next day.

Haven

December 26th...

We left Truly and Patch at the carnival with the kids,
Honor and I were on a two-hour champagne sunset cruise.

"Where's everybody else?" I asked Honor as we went
to find our seats at the front of the boat.

"I bought all of the tickets, so it'd be just the two of
us," Honor replied as he sat down in a chair then pulled me
down on top of his lap. We were on the bow of the boat and
could see everything ahead of us; there was a table next to
the chair we were sitting on.

"Hi, I'm Greg and I will be your host tonight. The
view is beautiful from the inside as well if you want to
come in where it's warm. If not, I can bring a few blankets
out for the two of you," a man walked up to us and said.

"It's whateva you want," Honor said to me.

"I want to stay out here," I answered.

The boat started moving away from the dock as the
man walked away. When he came back there were two
waiters with him. They set down two glasses of wine, some
d'oeuvres and gave us two blankets. Honor wrapped the
blankets around us as the host told us that we would be

doing a wine tasting during the cruise and someone would be back with a different kind of wine throughout the cruise.

"They said we might need these," Honor pulled out two sets of binoculars and handed me one. During the cruise we used to binoculars to get a better view as we gazed out at the beautiful snow-covered mountain peaks surrounding us. We sailed around the lake as they gave us historic information about what surrounded us and how Lake Tahoe became a vacation destination spot.

One of the waiters from earlier in the ride brought us out champagne for our toast; as the sky faded from a beautiful blue to a range of crimson red and an exciting orange.

"To second chances," Honor said.

"And new beginnings," I added as the sunset made the water in front of us turn a beautiful pinkish red. We clinked our glasses together and drunk the champagne as we watched the beautiful scenery all around us. It was a romantic backdrop for us to cheers to our second chance with each other.

Layne

"I'mma need my money back because after two attempts I got no results, and now they are going to be after me. None of them post on social media anymore like they did so we can't even find them!" I shouted. They had pissed me off. I went to them for help and even paid but they fucked everything up.

"Bitch, this was supposed to be a simple snatch and grab, but you failed to speak on who we were fuckin' with. My brother is fuckin' dead behind this shit, so what you speakin' on is stupid shit at this point to me. Right now, this is about gettin' back at the people who killed my family and putting their family members in body bags. Hell, I don't even know where the fuck my brother is because there is no fuckin' body." He walked up on me and every step I took back he stepped forward until my back was against the wall.

"Aye, that's enough of that, I know somebody that can find them for us. We just got to give her some money and maybe lie about why we're lookin' for them." The oldest man in the room said.

"I can get some more money from my dad to pay whoever a nice amount for the information," I replied.

"A'ight I'mma hit her up, then I'mma get back at you." He told me. We left the apartment of the man whose brother got killed by Haven.

When me and the older man walked outside, we ran into a woman coming to the apartment we had just left. She smiled and waved at us, but I just looked at her and kept walking.

I looked around the parking lot for Patch or Honor and ran to my rental car when I didn't see either one of them. I wasn't crazy enough to still be driving my car knowing a psychopath was looking for me. I sat in my rental for a couple of minutes trying to figure out a place that I could go where they wouldn't find me.

I drove a few cities over to a hotel and paid for a few nights with the last bit of cash I had. At first, I just wanted the bitch to pay for taking my man, but it went too far. Now I had to get them before they could get me.

Haven

December 29ʰ

I walked out of the bathroom after caking on makeup to cover up my puffy eyes. My night was filled with more crying than it was sleeping. In the middle of the night, out of the blue, my body jolted awake and silent tears started pooling out of my eyes. A lot of emotions started pouring out of me, and I didn't know where they were coming from. Maybe all the emotions I kept letting build up without dealing with were bursting out of me from somewhere deep inside.

I couldn't decipher the different emotions boiling up inside of me, but I knew they were making me anxious to the point that a screaming fit, that no one could hear, was needed.

When I opened the door I noticed, Honor stood on the other side of the bathroom door and before I could cross over the threshold, he pulled me against him, molding me to fit into his strong arms and chest. Honor's arms were wrapped around me and the tighter he enveloped me in his arms the more secure I felt. With my head nestled on his chest, the sound of his heartbeat was soothing and made me feel as though I was home, but could I trust that home?

"Stop overthinkin'," Honor whispered. We stayed like that until Sayvonna's screeches got louder and louder and couldn't be ignored.

"Come on, we need to get her together so we can take her to her aunt's house, then I got somethin' you need to see," Honor said as he tugged me into Sayvonna's room. When we walked in, she was holding onto the bars of her bed, bouncing and screeching. She started laughing when she saw us walk in the room but quickly went right back to screeching.

"She got that shit from PJ, and just for that, we 'bouta drop her off to them and let her scream their ears off," Honor said as he picked her up. When the kids were playing in the snow PJ would stop what he was doing, take off one of his gloves, touch the snow and scream; now he had Sayvonna copying him.

I agreed with him as I picked up her diaper bag and followed them to the car.

"Where are we going?" I asked Honor after we dropped Sayvonna off at Patch and Truly's new house. He made me put on a blindfold before we pulled out of Patch and Truly's driveway and I couldn't stand it.

"You'll see when we get there," Honor chuckled, but I didn't find anything funny. I don't think we had been driving for a full five minutes before Honor parked.

"Don't move," were his exact words before I heard him fumbling with his keys and getting out of the car. Seconds later, he was opening my door, taking off my seat belt and hefting me out of the car.

"Lean back against me," Honor said when he placed my feet back on the ground. I did what I was told, and I could feel his hands on either side of my head. When he took the blindfold off, I was shocked about where we were standing.

"What are we doing here?" I questioned.

"This house was where the beginning of our story started, and it's only right that it's the place where we continue. I've been trying to buy this house since last year, but another bid was always better than mine, but those bids always fell off at the last minute. I got a call a few weeks after I read your letter about the house being back on the market, and Truly told me it was a sign that everything was meant to be. I don't think I believe in that shit but everything falling into place was kind of deep," Honor said.

We stood in front of the house we had fallen in love in, which was also the house I held him against his will for a few weeks.

"It's like we're rewriting our story from the beginning and making it ours. At first it had everyone else in it as main characters, especially your dad since he was the reason I kidnapped you. I don't want to move in here until whateva is going on with your dad and Layne is settled. I want all the negative shit chasing after us to be solved before we start our new beginning in our house. The bullshit they are trying to bring to us will just follow us into this house if we don't deal with them," I told Honor as we walked into the house.

"Don't even worry about them; they'll be handled before we move in here. I want us to paint Sayvonna's room and ours before we move in and change the countertops in the kitchen anyway. By the time all of that is done, we will have dealt with all the lingering shit from the past," he told me.

"I got some countertop samples in the kitchen; let's go choose." Honor swept me off my feet and carried me into the kitchen.

When Honor walked us into the kitchen there were bags on the table, but Honor steered us away from them.

He placed me back on my feet, and I leaned my back into him again. There were three countertop samples laid out and a rolodex with paint colors. I picked out the countertop I wanted, and Honor agreed with it. I decided that with the new countertop the walls in the kitchen and cabinets needed to be repainted.

When I told Honor he just said, "Pick out the colors for everything you think needs to be repainted. Once you do, write the color number on the wall of the room on this," he said handing me the blueprint for the contractor. I started doing what he said and I didn't even pay attention to him walking away from me. I could hear him pulling stuff out of the bags on the table, but I didn't pay attention because I was so into what I was doing.

"How did you know?" Tears poured from my eyes after turning around and seeing what he had been busy doing. There were two plates on the table with lasagna and fried chicken on them. In the center of the table was a small square cake with "Happy Birthday Mom, Dad, Savon and Haven," written on it. My mother's birthday was December 23rd, Dad's was on the 26th, Savon's was the 28th and mine was on the 5th of January. On the 29th of December the four of us always celebrated our birthdays together, just the four of us. We all had separate parties as well with family and friends but the 29th was our day. We stayed indoors together watching all the new movies we hadn't seen and pigging out on junk food.

"Your friend Amity DM'd and told me the significance of today a couple of days ago. She told me you'd be down today. You have a good friend," Honor told me. I didn't want to talk about it anymore, so I started eating my food. I could feel Honor's eyes on me for a minute, but pretty soon he started eating too.

"I thought your brother's birthday was in the summer time," Honor stated as he tossed the plastic dishes in the trash.

"When we were together, and I told you it was his birthday that was the day he came out to me and our parents. He said that day he felt reborn so that became a birthday me and him celebrated together. Truth celebrated it with us for a couple of years," I answered him as he pulled out a bottle of tequila; it was my parents' favorite drink.

"Did my brother celebrate one of those reborn days?" Honor asked.

"Yeah, his was June 10th," I smiled at Honor when he realized what that date meant.

"Truth started taking me to get ice cream to celebrate summer starting for like three years before he died. Damn, so he really didn't push me out of that side of his life; he just didn't give me full disclosure about it. Lookin' back on it, he gave me hints here and there without really telling me, but I didn't realize it until now," Honor said as he poured two shots of tequila.

After taking the shots, Honor put four candles on the cake and lit them. He sang Happy Birthday to all four of us and told me to make a wish and blow them out. I wished for my new family to stay safe and for us to get over all the hurdles in our way.

I felt so heavy with emotions as I blew out the candles, and I couldn't stop the tears from falling from my eyes.

"Come here, baby," Honor said as he pulled me down onto his lap. I curled up on him and sobbed into his chest. The sounds of my anguish echoed throughout the house. Honor wiped my tears from my face once I was all cried out.

"I'm sorry 'bout your shirt; I know my makeup looks a total fuckin' mess now." I started rambling and didn't stop until Honor kissed me.

I felt my nipples harden as they pressed into his chest and my arms wrapped around his neck. I sucked on his tongue as he stood up carrying me out of the kitchen and up the stairs.

He laid me in the center of the bed where we first had sex. Honor pulled my panties down then his tongue kissed my pussy. I moaned in delight as his tongue flicked up and down my bud. My hands locked around his neck pulling him deeper into my pussy.

He sucked on my clit and started indulging in my core. I moaned, bit my bottom lip and bucked my hips forward. He slid his tongue into my tight hole, dipping it in and out of me as his thumb wreaked havoc on my clit.

"Right there," I moaned. My pussy clenched around his tongue; I was about to cum. He pinned my legs all the way back and started licking and slurping my clit. He pushed two fingers inside me and pounded away as his tongue continued to lick and slurp me into oblivion. He held my hips still as his tongue licked and slurped up all my essence into his mouth.

I was in such a daze. I didn't even realize he came out of his clothes until he rubbed his dick around my clit causing me to shutter. My pussy clenched with need as the pleasure of his dick rubbing my clit took over all my senses.

"Put it in," I moaned. He groaned, slowly sliding home into my tightness, as my walls gripped him. He slowly pumped in and out of me.

I moaned as he sucked one of my nipples into his mouth. I lifted my hips and wrapped my legs around him. Honor started to slowly pound into my spot for a few strokes then he pulled out then put it back in. He repeated that method over and over until my body shook and I was coming again.

The pleasure took me completely out for a minute, and all I could do was lie there. He continued pumping in and out of me deeper, harder and faster with each stroke.

"Spread your legs for me, baby," he requested. I did as I was told. I cried out as he, grinded into me, and I dug my nails into the comforter. I swear he was balls-deep in me showing me how much he missed me with one deep stroke after another.

Honor leaned down and kissed me as his dick jerked inside of me and my pussy clenched around him. He grunted as his nut filled me up and my essence gushed out coating his dick and my inner thighs.

Honor laid his head on my chest and a short breather he was stroking in and out of me. We made slow sensual love until we both came again.

We finally got out of the bed three hours later, showered and changed into some of our clothes Honor had already sent to the house. After we got dressed, we packed up the cake, locked up the house and got back into Honor's car.

"Let's go get our baby," I said to him as I intertwined my fingers in his. Honor kissed my hand before he pulled off.

At the first stop sign he took a right turn, drove three blocks, took another right turn and we pulled into Patch and Truly's driveway. I was happy that their house was practically around the corner from ours.

"Bring the cake inside," Honor said before he got out of the car and made his way to the front door. I got out of the car with the cake in my hands and followed him into the house.

"Shut the door behind you and follow me." Honor was standing by a door in the hallway that led to a room I had never been in. I shut and locked the door then walked over to where Honor was standing. He took the cake out of my hands and walked down the stairs ahead of me.

It was starting to feel like I was in the middle of a scary movie, but I still followed behind him because I didn't hear any screams.

"Surprise!" everyone, who was at Patch and Truly's wedding, shouted with one addition being Amity.

"What's going on?" I was shocked and could barely see because the only light in the place was coming from their phones.

"We're having movie night," Amity said as someone flicked on the lights. I blinked a few times until my eyes adjusted back to the light. When they turned on the lights, I realized we were in the movie theater room.

Honor sat the cake on top of a glass cabinet filled with all the snacks a movie theater would have. To the right of it was a popcorn machine filled with fresh popcorn. And on the left of the glass cabinet was a Slurpee machine with blueberry, raspberry and lemonade flavor.

"Everybody grab your snack choices and pick a seat," Truly said and we all did. I sat in the middle of Amity and Honor with Sayvonna on my lap. We watched two of my families' favorite movies.

"I just want to thank all of y'all for this; I really needed it and I hope we can make this a yearly thing." I stood and thanked everyone after we watched the movies.

"Of course, sweetie, you're family now. I don't know how many times I gotta keep telling your ass that," Miss Brenda said before she ushered the boys out of the theater to get ready for bed.

Amity, Truly and I stood off to the side talking and Patch, Honor, Eagle, and Rocko were standing on the other side of the room discussing something. Sayvonna was lying on Honor's chest sleeping with his shirt clutched in her little fist.

"A'ight time for everybody to leave; I need to go put my wife to sleep," Patch said abruptly.

"Patchhh!" Truly screeched as she scowled at him; he just laughed at her.

"You gonna come up missing, keep saying shit like that around me 'bout my niece," Rocko said, throwing a fake jab at Patch.

As the girls and I hugged each other good-bye, Amity said she needed to tell me and Truly something but didn't want to on my family's day. Plus, Truly needed our help with something, so we all agreed to sneak away and meet up the next day.

Truly

The next day...

Haven and I sat in crack-head Bezzy's car while Amity knocked on Mark's door. We watched as Keisha opened the door and Amity pretend to be a new neighbor to get in.

"You should just turn your phone off like I did mine," I told Haven when she silenced another call from Honor. She nodded her head, then started fiddling with her phone for a couple of minutes.

"I texted him and told him we were alright, and he texted back saying him and Patch are lookin' for us. And if they find us instead of us coming home to them it's going to be hell to pay. I just texted back I love you too and turned off my phone," Haven said and we both laughed.

"How much longer do you think it'll take?" I asked Haven. Amity was supposed to be slipping Keisha and her boyfriend crushed up sleeping pills in a drink. She was pretending to be their new next-door neighbor. Amity acted like she accidently locked herself out when she went outside to get her food that was being delivered. Haven told her to tell them she would share her food with them if she could wait for her husband at their house. I didn't think it would, work but once they saw the food bags, and sodas they let her in.

"I don't know; it might take a while. She gotta cause some sort of distraction long enough to place the crushed pills in their drinks without them noticing and wait till the pills take effect to wave us in. Hell, we can be out here for thirty minutes to an hour," Haven answered.

"We gonna start lookin' suspicious just sittin' out here, so if she don't come soon we need to drive around a few blocks," I stated, leaning back and closing my eyes.

I must've fallen asleep because the next thing I knew Haven was shaking me to get my attention.

"Amity was just at the door; she left it cracked for us." We got out of the car with our gloves on and headed towards the house. When we walked in Keisha and her boyfriend were passed out in the kitchen.

Haven, and Amity dragged Mark to the garage and heaved him in Keisha's car. Amity and Haven carried Keisha to the car and placed her in the passenger's seat as I looked for their car keys. One of them had been smoking a cigarette so I took the still lit cigarette and placed it in the car with them. I started Keisha's car as the girls made sure all the windows and doors in the garage were closed.

Dear, Honor & Haven   Marqua'lla

I looked at Keisha passed out in the passenger's seat of the car one last time before I shut the garage door tightly behind us.

"We got one more stop to make," Amity said when we got back into the car.

"Okay, now what is it you had to tell us?" I asked her as we pulled off.

As we drove Amity told us about overhearing a conversation her boyfriend was having yesterday. She sat by the front window listening to part of their conversation until an older man and a woman our age left. She thought she heard Haven's name but wasn't sure, so she wanted to get more information. Last night, she pretended to be sleep while her boyfriend was on the phone. She heard him talking about everything that happened to me and Haven. He even told the caller where Layne was at and was begging the person to come to town to help him get revenge for his brother's death. The person on the other end must've told him hell no because he started cussing up a storm.

Amity told us how to get to the place Layne was staying, and I drove to the house. It was an abandoned house at the bottom of a hill on a one-way street. The entire street was abandoned because all the houses were condemned. I couldn't believe she would stay in abandoned houses that were probably rat infested.

"You guys go in and tie her to something while I get my tools," Haven said.

Amity and I walked in through the back door which was halfway off the hinges. The deeper we walked into the house, the more I wanted to turn around and run. We had to watch our steps because it looked as though the entire house would cave in on itself at any moment.

We found Layne asleep on an air mattress in the middle of the floor. She had a fold away chair in the corner and a computer sitting on it with a show playing on the computer.

"Let's just let her sleep until Haven comes in here," I whispered to Amity finally after watching Layne sleep for a moment.

"Okay, but shouldn't Haven be in here by now," Amity whispered back.

"Aahhhh," I screamed when I turned around and found Patch standing at the door watching me. My scream woke Layne, who jumped up and stared at us through bucked eyes.

"Honor's dad was helping me; I can tell you guys where he's at just don't hurt me!" she quickly informed us.

"We know he's been stayin' in the house two doors down; we already got his ass tied in the trunk, it's time for you to get in there with him," Patch said. Eagle walked into the room snatched up Layne and began to drag her out of the room.

"Good lookin' on the info," Patch turned to Amity and said.

"Wait, you told him we were comin' here?" I asked her.

"Hell no, I told them my ex was helping Layne and they went to snatch him up while we did that other thing. They must've got the rest of the information from my ex," Amity said as we walked out of the room.

"Fuck all of that; what other thing?" Patch questioned as we walked out of the door.

"Well Keisha and her boyfriend are slowly dying of carbon monoxide poisoning right now or maybe they're already dead. I don't know how long that shit takes," I told him.

Patch shook his head at me as we got in his car. Haven was already in the back seat of the car with Honor so Amity got into the car with Eagle. Patch drove us to a warehouse, and we all got out of the car and walked in. Me and the girls watched as Patch, Honor, Rocko, and Eagle dragged our prisoners out of the trunk and tied them to the chairs.

"Honor, you're just gonna let them kill your pops?" Richy started pleading for Honor's help.

"You killed my brother because he was gay; all bets are off, nigga," Honor replied.

"I did a lot of fucked up shit, like payin' for those dudes to jump you in high school. I had two dudes jump Truly while she was at her school and some other shit to the two of you. Hell, I even tried to suffocate your ass one night after you took your mother's side. But I didn't have Truth killed, that was your momma and that man she's fuckin' with now. Your brother found out your mom was stealing from me and Rocko and that she was cheating on me. He also found out that her boyfriend was the person stealin' from the connect, and that's why she went into hiding. Your mom thought your brother was going to tell me and Rocko, but the only person Truth told was his boyfriend. Savon came to me and told me what Truth learned after I told him it wasn't me who hired the dude to kill your brother. Savon thought it was his fault that Truth died, because he didn't convince him to tell me or Rocko what was going on." The whole room gasped.

"Your mother had all of y'all fooled thinking she was just this straight-laced person. I wouldn't be with a woman that wasn't just as *grimy* as me; she just snuck and did her dirt. Shit, she thought you knew too, that's why your ass was almost gunned down with Truth. She called y'all in the house at that exact time on purpose; he was supposed to get y'all walked in the apartment," Richy added.

"I don't believe you," Honor told him.

"Just pull out my phone; the video of Savon tellin' me is in there," Richy said. Honor pulled out the phone and everything Richy had just said, Savon was saying on the video. Savon even said Honor and Truth's mom was trying to get them to go off to college to make it easier for her and her boyfriend not to get caught. Their mom didn't know Truth was home when her and her boyfriend had that conversation, but she found out when he confronted her the next day with what he heard.

"You still got to die for what you did to my cousins and my girl's parents," Honor looked Richy in the eyes and said.

"Hell, one of them was your sibling," Richy stated. He was referring to when he burned down Rocko's house with his family in it because Rocko's wife wanted to end their affair.

"But I ain't do shit to your peoples, Haven, that was all on the home front. I don't know why your peoples or your grandparents ain't tell you what happened. They have known for years now and made the person responsible for it pay. Your mom left a message on your grandmother's voicemail a couple of hours before you found your parents. Your mom told your grandmother that she found Savon's journal.

"She found out that Drake, your dad's foster brother, had slept with your brother for two years while your brother was in middle school. Drake knew Savon was gay and used that shit to his advantage. Your momma felt like they failed Savon, so she killed your dad and herself. When you dad's right-hand man finally found out what happened, he killed Drake and anyone that knew and didn't speak up," Richy revealed, turning to Haven.

Honor walked over to Haven and held her in his arms as she silently cried. Both Honor and Haven were finding out information about their families neither of them wanted to believe.

We all stood back and watched Rocko torture Richy a little bit before he injected something into his arms. Haven shot Layne in her head and Honor finished off Amity's boyfriend. I think that was kind of liberating for the two of them.

"What did you give him, Unc?" I just had to know.

"I injected him with something to paralyze him so he can feel that fire while he's burning," Rocko answered before him and the rest of the men loaded the bodies into a hearse.

Eagle and Rocko pulled off in the hearse after the bodies were loaded inside. Haven, Amity, and Honor got into Honor's car and pulled off.

"You're lucky my baby is growing inside of you right now, otherwise there would be consequences for today. But check this out, you ever pull some shit like that again you'll be the one burning next," Patch said, walking off. I followed him to the car and got in.

"I'm sorry. I kept lookin' at those pictures of PJ on my porch like that, and I just got madder and madder each time. I couldn't let them live, especially after he told me they were yelling at him and his mom was pinching him," I told him as my tears began to fall; my emotions were all over the place.

"I understand that, but next time come to me and we can do that shit together," he told me as he grabbed my face and kissed me hard. I agreed to tell him next time and we pulled off heading home.

As we drove home it felt like a big weight was lifted off me and my family.

Haven

December 30th 7:30 pm

"You ready?" Patch asked when I got into his car.

"Yep, let's go finish this," I replied. Patch and I were riding out to Honor's mom Kimberly's house, neither of us wanted Honor to be the one to kill her. It was one thing when everyone thought his father was the parent who had Truth killed. Finding out it was his mother trying to protect herself and her boyfriend had a different impact than it being Richy. She was the one-person Honor thought would never let him down.

"How is he?" Patch asked.

"I think Honor is still in shock 'bout everything, so I just gave him one of my pills to put him to sleep. I'mma just need to get back before he wakes up," I answered. Honor wasn't doing good, but I didn't want Patch to know because that wasn't my place to tell him. If Honor wanted him to know exactly how he was doing, he'd have to be the one to tell him. I think for me to do it would be a betrayal of our trust.

"My mom said she's off so Sayvonna can stay as long as y'all need," Patch reported.

"We'll go get her as soon as we wake up in the morning. I'm sure your mother will be waitin' for us at the door by then. Ever since the vacation she's been screeching like PJ."

"Nah, my mama the type to screech right along with her. You might wanna get her soon 'cause my mama will have her screeching and makin' some weird farm animal sounds. When she read the farm books, she makes the animal sounds until the kids repeat her." I just looked at him and he laughed.

****

"We're almost there," Patch said snapping me out of my thoughts. I had gotten so lost in my thoughts that I hadn't even realized we had gotten off the freeway.

"I'mma park a bit of a ways away from the house, so we're going to have to hike it a little bit," Patch said.

"How you wanna play this?" I asked him.

"The connect wants it to look like a hit so that's what we're gonna do. After this, we're going to meet him at the warehouse and get paid," Patch answered, before we got out of the car.

"Can I torture her or not?" That was all I wanted to know.

"Hell yeah; both of them. We need to get as much information from them as we can," Patch said as he started picking the lock to Kimberly's house.

The minute we got inside, I pulled two chairs from their kitchen and placed them in the middle of the living room. I laid my tools out on a tarp in front of me like I was about to perform surgery. Then Patch and I went upstairs to wake the sleeping couple and bring them down to the party. It was a struggle to get them to the chairs until Patch pulled out his gun and placed it at dude's head.

They wouldn't talk until I gave Kimberly the same treatment I gave Nicki, and Patch pistol whipped her boyfriend.

"We just wanted a fresh start away from everyone, and we didn't have enough money between us. So, we both started stealing here and there to be able to disappear from our old lives. Truth and Honor could link us to the thefts so we disappeared." Trappy mumbled; he could hardly talk because of the beating Patch had put on him.

"I'm tired of the men in my life taking credit for all of my plans, first Richy then you. I was fuckin' tired of gettin' cramps in my hand because I had to do so much hair to take care of my kids. I had two kids by one of the biggest drug dealer in our hood and was basically taking care of our kids alone. All he did was buy them clothes to make them the envy of the hood and nothin' else. Then I find out he had a baby by someone that use to be my best friend, and was giving her enough money to pay all of her bills? So you damn right, I fucked up that little girl's life and made her pay for getting shit my kids didn't," Kimberly said.

"What you mean by that?" Patch asked her, but all she did was smirk at him. I grabbed my pliers and crushed her nipples; she gripped the chair handles and screamed out in pain.

"Answer his question or your clit is next, bitch," I told her and applied more pressure.

"I paid Trappy's cousin Damaria to rape Truly, and I paid his brother to kill Truth and Honor. The cousin who killed Truth was killed a year later by the nigga Trappy was working for because they were trying to find us." She said nonchalantly, like nothing she did was wrong.

"Why?" I asked her; Patch was still staring at her in shock.

"I didn't want to work anymore and I needed to get back at Jennifer and Richy somehow. I just simply wanted to live my life and I couldn't let Truth snitch on me. And I knew once Truth died, Honor would be sniffing around until he found out what happened, so I sent his ass off to school." She shrugged her shoulders like that was a good enough answer.

Patch finally snapped out of his shock, and I stepped back as he wrapped his hands around her neck. He squeezed so tight that she pissed on herself before passing out. If it was another situation, I would've stopped him from hitting her and did it myself. She crossed the line, so it was only right for him to be able to beat her ass. I went searching the house for things Honor might want while Patch finished the job. The connect wanted them shot in the back of the head twice, their hands cut off and their teeth knocked out, but I didn't want to see that.

I gathered pictures, Truth's diploma and his urn; she didn't deserve to keep that in her house even if she was dead. Afterwards, I waited in the hallway until Patch told me he was finished. We cleaned up our mess and headed out the same door we had come in. We put their hands and teeth in the trunk on a tarp.

"So, are we telling Truly and Honor everything we just learned?" I asked Patch as we pulled off and headed to the warehouse.

"Shit like this got a way of coming out one way or another, and I believe in all honesty. So yeah, we can tell them because what if the streets finally speak on why that nigga raped Truly. Best believe there are motherfuckas out there who know the real deal and might start speakin' on it. Then how are they gonna feel knowing we knew and didn't tell them. Plus, I don't want neither of them being caught off guard with the shit," Patch replied.

"I'll tell him tonight so it's not like after he gets finished processing one thing, I hit him with another and another," I said. Neither of us spoke the rest of the way; we were both lost in our own thoughts.

"Stay in here, I'll be right back," Patch said, parking in front of the warehouse. My eyes followed Patch as he got out of the car and headed straight for the trunk. He took the bags out and walked them into the warehouse.

I was milliseconds from going inside when Patch finally walked outside with two duffle bags. He placed them in the trunk and drove to the liquor store. We stocked up on Honor's and Truly's favorite alcohol before he took me home. Patch handed me one of the black duffle bags before I went in the house. I opened the bag once in the house and found out it was full of money. My mind raced with plans for the money to secure our future.

****

11:30 pm

I got in a hot shower and washed the blood from my body. The water was scolding hot because for some reason having her blood on me made me feel extremely dirty. Logically, I knew her ways couldn't rub off on me just because her blood got on me, but I still felt the need to clean myself thoroughly. I scrubbed my skin three times before I got out of the shower, dried off and put lotion on my skin.

When I walked into the room, Honor was lying in bed wide awake. I slid into bed next to him and I could see the pain etched on his face. Honor rolled over and positioned himself, so he was lying on top of me with his head resting on my chest.

"It's done," I told him, and he wrapped his arms around me. "I don't want to do this, but we found out more and I need to tell you."

"Lay it on me," Honor said, and I did. "I never thought I would say this, but I think my mother is more fucked up than my dad," Honor said after I told him everything. My mind had drifted elsewhere until I felt Honor start lightly biting and sucking on my breast. I rubbed the back of his head.

"Fuck," he groaned when milk squirted in his mouth after he sucked on my nipple. He wouldn't make the mistake of forgetting I was breastfeeding again, because from the look on his face he didn't like the taste too much. Honor kissed his way up from my breast to my waiting mouth. His tongue entered my mouth at the same time as his finger entered my center. His thumb pressed against my clit with just the right amount of pleasure and it drove me crazy. I reached down between us and grasped his dick in my hand. I knocked his hand out of my way then rubbed his dick around my clit as I stroke his tip. He groaned in my mouth and grinded his dick into my clit, it felt so good. I found my rhythm of stroking his tip as his dick circled my clit.

I was so damn horny my pussy was gushing on his dick, and I was seconds from coming.

"Put it in," Honor whispered in my ear. I raised my hips a bit as I moved him down to my opening.

My body writhed with need as he slowly entered me. My legs spread wider for him, and I wrapped my arms around his back pulling his body closer to mine as my pussy sucked him in deeper. He lifted up on his forearms and our eyes locked.

"I love you," he whispered as he slowly stroked in and out of me. He pulled halfway out of me then slowly drove back into my center repeatedly; I bit my bottom lip when his dick grazed my spot as he pushed back in. I could feel every inch of his girth every time he slowly drove inside of me.

"I love you too," I whispered against his lips before he kissed me with so much passion tears fell from my eyes. Every time he embedded himself deeper into me, his pelvis pressed into my clit causing me to tremble. Our bodies connected on a different level as he showed me how much he loved me with each slow, tantalizing stroke and kiss. When we came together it was on a cosmic level.

We took a shower together, slid into bed and cuddled. He laid in between my thighs with his head on my chest.

Something woke me suddenly in the middle of the night. I thought it was for no reason until I heard a noise and realized Honor was crying. For a second, I was stuck between if I should let him know I was awake or not.

I wiped his tears away while trying to hold my own back. It was hard trying to hold it together for him, and the muffled sounds coming from him made it impossible. Silent tears of empathy and sorrow poured from my eyes, his pain was my pain and I wished I could take it all from him. I knew I couldn't take the pain completely away; but giving him my unconditional love for the rest of our lives would lessen the pain of those who should've loved him without any conditions.

Honor might not have grown up with the perfect family, but he created one that was perfect for him. Where he was weak, was my strength; and where I fell short, he didn't.

"I love you with everything in me," I heard him mutter on the edge of sleep.

"I love you, too." I whispered as my arms and legs wrapped tightly around his body. Within seconds we were both drifting off to sleep.

Epilogue
Truly
2 months later

I wanted to celebrate everything I didn't get to with my first pregnancy. When I was pregnant with Truvon I was a scared and lost child just trying to make it in the cold world practically alone. There was only Patch and Mama Brenda in my corner, and, at the time, they were practically strangers. It was hard being a kid and depending on people; I didn't even know if I could fully trust that they would still be there for me the next day. There was always the fear that I would be out on the streets again with an infant.

In those days, I feared Patch was staying out all night and day because he didn't want to be around. I was scrubbing their house up and down and cooking, praying that they would let me stay because of it. But what I didn't know was that Patch and his mom were both working doubles to make sure my child wouldn't go without. Patch and Mama Brenda bought Truvon everything he needed and ever since then I knew I could count on them.

Even though I wanted to celebrate my second pregnancy, I didn't want a baby shower. We simply didn't have enough family and friends for that, and I liked it that way. Plus, for me I wanted everything about my pregnancy to be more intimate. Our circle might be small, but we still were a village standing together through everything and that was how I wanted the celebrations to be. I decided on having a gender reveal with our kids, and a mother's blessing dinner party with our family.

The mother's blessing was in two months, and Haven already had it planned. In the morning Amity, Mama Brenda, and Haven would take me to get pampered. Then we'd have an intimate dinner with the whole family where me and Patch would reveal the name of the baby. And everyone would give us presents for me or the baby which ever they wanted.

"Mommy, you ready?" Truvon asked as him and PJ stood in front of me. They were excited because they were about to reveal the gender.

"Go," I told them, and they both started reaching into their bags and stuffing the white cotton candy in their mouths. The white cotton candy would dissolve on their tongue and either leave their tongues pink or blue.

"A'ight that's enough, open y'all mouths," Patch said. When they did, their tongues were green; I was pissed. I had spent hella money to make this a happy and special occasion and they ruined it.

"Baby, don't cry just wait a second," Patch insisted when he saw the tears pooling in my eyes.

"Daddy is going to blindfold you; he got a surprise for us in the backyard," PJ said as Patch walked up to me with a blindfold.

Patch blindfolded me, then helped me up and into the backyard. He was excited and wanted to go all out, but I would have been fine with just revealing the gender to the boys with some cupcakes or something.

"This pregnancy is too special to do something so simple with just the kids," Patch said taking my blindfold off. My Uncle Rocko and his family, including Eagle, were standing to the right of the porch with my grandparents, Victor and Alisha. Of course, Mama Brenda, Amity Honor, Haven and Sayvonna were all standing to the left. Patch and I were standing in the center of the porch with the boys on either side of us. I didn't know how much I wanted them there until I saw them.

"Watch this," Patch whispered in my ear, wrapping his arm around me. I leaned against him as my eyes focused on the sky where he was pointing. The sun was just setting when, all of a sudden, a pop sounded then the sky was filled with pink fireworks that spelled out girl. Tears pooled in my eyes. I couldn't believe we were having a girl, something I was too scared to say I wanted for fear that my dream wouldn't come true. My thoughts were interrupted by gunfire.

"My bad, I'm just practicing for when a nigga try my daughter, but keep looking at the sky," Patch said as he walked back over to me when he saw the other men reaching for their guns and looking for the threat. A couple of seconds later the bomb sound ignited once more, and we all looked at the sky just as blue fireworks coated the sky with the words Baby 2.

Patch and I hid the fact that we were having twins from everyone; we kind of wanted to save one surprise for everyone, Brenda didn't even know I was having twins.

"Dad, can I practice to?" Truvon asked.

"Yes."

"No," we answered simultaneously.

"You bet not take him somewhere to practice shooting." I looked over at Patch but all he did was smirk at me. I was about to say something else to him but Brenda interrupted me.

"Sneaky motherfuckas," Brenda said as she walked up beside us with a glass of wine in her hand.

"PJ said he ain't sharing his room with no baby," Truvon said.

"PJ didn't say that, it was your ass," Brenda said.

"Grams, why you snitchin' on me?" Truvon asked.

"'Cause I can," she replied.

"Honor, do you have a house over here that I can rent? I need to be close to my grandkids," Brenda inquired.

"Nah, I don't," Honor answered, and we all could see the disappointment in her face. "But we all pitched in to put a down payment on a three-bedroom house a mile or two from here for you," Honor chimed as he handed over the keys to her.

Ever since we told Brenda I was pregnant, she had been hinting that she needed to rent a house near us.

"I got to figure out a way to pay for the mortgage now," Miss Brenda replied. Patch, Honor and I knew she wouldn't take the house if we had out right bought it for her.

"Eagle and Amity are each going to move into one of the townhouses and pay rent; that's how you'll make the mortgage payments," I told her. Last year, Brenda's father died and it turned out he had never taken her out of his will.

Instead, he lowered the amount she would receive. She didn't care about the money, but she did make an investment with it. Brenda had bought two townhomes in our hood for a reasonable price. Brenda had moved into one of them and Honor had moved into the other one last year. Mama Brenda was still mad she didn't get a chance to knock Layne out for breaking her window.

"In that case, Haven, you're helping me decorate my place, and you two," she said to Amity and Eagle, "can move in next week." Brenda was all smiles and I wanted to keep that smile on her face.

"There's a taco bar, drinks and cake in the pool house. After we eat, we can go see Mama's house," Patch announced, and everyone started making their way to the pool house.

My future always felt ambiguous to me, and I never thought I would have a family. On my darkest days I didn't think happiness would be in my grasp. Back then, I was still letting what happened or was said to me define how I felt and saw myself. When I finally realized those actions and words didn't define me, it only defined the people who hurt me physically and emotionally, I was able to see what was right in front of me and grasp my happiness. I might have lost a lot of stuff, but I gained something that was worth the world to me, and that was being a mother and a wife. I got a family that might not all be blood, but they all still loved me unconditionally.

"Baby, come on. I told these people they can't eat 'til you get in here and make your plate!" Patch shouted as he walked out of the pool house towards me.

My husband was brash, but I loved that about him and knew he loved the hell out of me without a doubt.

Haven

15 months later

"Maybe we should just go get her now," Honor said as he tried to FaceTime Patch's phone to talk to Sayvonna. She was at Patch and Truly's house staying the night to celebrate their twins', Rukiyah and Kasiyah, birthday. Rukiyah mugged every stranger that got close to her until they walked away; she was her father's twin in every way possible. Kasiyah, on the other hand, was calm and the sweetest little boy when he wasn't being sneaky.

"She'll be fine, and we can get her first thing in the morning. You promised me a night out where I could get dressed up and that's exactly what is happening tonight." Honor was acting like it wasn't his idea for Sayvonna to stay the night with Patch and Truly after the twins' party.

"I know, just go upstairs and shower but change into the outfit in the box. While I FaceTime Patch again to make sure Say good over there," Honor had become an overbearing father from the moment he held her in his arms.

"Don't go callin' them obsessively, because next thing you know, we gon' be out of another fuckin' babysitter," I called out as I headed up the stairs.

"We'll still have Brenda, and she wouldn't stop babysitting no matter how many times she threatens to after each of my calls." The first night we went out without Say, Brenda kept her, and I swear Honor FaceTimed that lady over ten times.

"Nigga, you not 'bouta be callin' my phone like you do my mama! This the first and last call I'mma answer of yours tonight." I heard Patch say when I made it to the top of the stairs. I just shook my head at the two of them and continued to the bathroom for my shower.

Thirty minutes later, I was out of the shower with my towel wrapped around me, adding my lashes on. I curled my hair as my fake and real eyelashes fused together, then applied a nice red glossy lip. I checked myself over one last time in my vanity mirror before getting up and heading to the bed. I took the top off the box Honor had left on the bed for me. There was a note on top of the tissue paper, I picked it up and opened it.

"Get dressed then come to the panic room," I read the note out loud. I moved the tissue paper and picked up the red dress. I knew Brenda must've picked it out for me.

The red, satin, top bustier, lace dress hugged every part of my body and accentuated my assets nicely. I slipped my feet into the heels at the foot of the bed and rushed out of our bedroom and into the panic room. I was anxious to get to the next part of the surprise for date night.

The first thing I noticed when I walked into the panic room was a bouquet of red Dahlia flowers and there was a note next to the flowers.

I picked up the note and started reading.

Dear Haven,

You came into my life like a tornado and wrecked it up in the best way possible. When you left, that shit crushed me, and a nigga turned slightly stalkerish for a minute. Man, a nigga ain't never did no shit like that until your crazy ass came along. I tried everything to forget you, but that simply wasn't possible because you nudged your way into my heart. The entire time you were gone, you took a piece of this nigga with you. And I didn't feel whole again until I saw you standing on the other side of my door.

You make a nigga feel invincible and like I can do anything in the world, and I will always do the same for you.

My promise to you is to always be there to protect you, make your dreams possible, and to love you not only when our love is smooth but when it is rocky as well.

NOW TURN AROUND!

"Will you marry me?" Honor was on one knee with a ring in his hand when I turned around.

I couldn't say nothing; all I could do was nod my head as the tears came down my eyes. Honor stood up, took my left hand in his and slid the channel set, princess cut, three-carat engagement ring on my finger. It had seven smaller diamonds on either side of the larger diamonds and infinity symbols cascading throughout the bottom of the ring. It was beautiful and so me, simple but not too simple at the same time.

"I want to have my way with you so bad right now, but we have reservations for that restaurant on the waterfront you've been wanting to try." When Honor said that it made me realize just how long he'd been planning this.

A new restaurant had opened on the waterfront a few months back, and it quickly became popular. Everyone wanted to eat at the restaurant made of pure glass with beautiful fish swimming beneath you. It quickly took off and within a few weeks there was a waitlist for months in advanced.

"Come on, we can go put those in water," he said referring to the flowers. "Then head over to the restaurant and come back and watch the proposal again," Honor said.

"You recorded it?" I asked as my eyes drifted back to my ring again.

"Hell yeah, I knew you would want to look back on it with everyone," Honor replied as he put the flowers in a vase. I loved the hell out of him and the way he knew me more than I knew myself at times.

I just stared back and forth from Honor to my ring in disbelief. Never in my wildest dreams did I believe I would find happiness after all the bad shit that happened in my life. Finally, I was getting my happy beginning.

Miss Brenda

14 months Later

My eyes were filled with unshed tears as I watched Honor and Haven have their first dance as husband and wife. Both of my boys were married now and had beautiful families to show for it. A couple of months back, we had a party to celebrate Truly officially adopting PJ.

After their first dance, Honor and Haven called Truly and Patch up to the dance floor. I loved seeing how happy my sons looked with their beautiful wives.

It made me think back to the day I lost the love of my life.

"Why the fuck you got that shit!?" Caden shouted. When he walked in my apartment and saw me with a pipe in my hand.

I tried to answer him, but all that came out was hiccups because I had been crying for days. I just felt all alone and so helpless.

"They took him from me," I finally managed to get out.

"Who CPS came?" Caden asked as he knocked the pipe out of my hand.

SOUL Publications

"No, Paevon's father came here and took him from me a couple of days ago. I went to get him back, but him and his wife had pictures of me from a couple of years ago. You know the ones of me doing drugs, and they threatened to give them to the police to get custody if I didn't leave."

"They always trying this bullshit when I get locked up." Caden must've come by my house as soon as he walked out those gates, and I was glad he did.

"Clean up this house, then we going to get your son back, and I'mma make them regret ever thinkin' they can fuck with you," Caden said, and I did what he said. An hour after he got there, we were walking out of the door to his car.

"Stay here, I'mma send Patch out to you," Caden told me before he got out of the car. I watched as he walked up to their door and started pounding on it. The man who raped me walked to the door with his chest puffed out like he was ready for the war Caden was about to bring on him.

"Patch! Come on, it's time to go!" Caden pushed past that pussy nigga and walked through his house. A few minutes later, Caden walked out holding Paevon in his hands then put him in the car.

Caden turned around and headed right for the devil himself. I watched as Caden started pistol whipping him and he wasn't letting up.

"Get off my husband; I called the police." His wife stood at the door crying with the phone in her hand. Caden acted like he didn't hear her and just started stomping the hell out of the nigga.

"Caden, come on; let's go. I can hear the sirens coming," I pleaded.

"Nah baby, they just gonna come get me anyway. Don't worry about me, my cousin gon' come drop some money off to you, I'll be fine. If he does this shit again just hit up my mans and he got you. Now take my car and get the hell out of here before the police get here." I didn't listen to him fully, I got out of the car and snatched the gun from him. My hands landed one last time on him as he sat down next to the body, waiting on the cops to get there and arrest him.

I got in the car with Paevon and drove to the marina to toss the gun. Paevon and I went home like nothing had happened.

I never thought that I would be glad the man who raped me was still alive, but I didn't want the man I loved to be in jail for murder. Caden got twenty-eight years in jail because he had an assault charge on top of having to serve the rest of the time that he was on parole for. I tried to see him, but he wrote me a letter saying he didn't regret it, but he needed me to move on. He wouldn't take my visits or anything and that hurt me like hell.

Caden was the only person who called Paevon, Patch, but when he went to prison for us, I started calling him Patch as well. The name picked up as a nickname in the hood and people assumed they knew where the name came from, but they didn't. Patch didn't even truly know why he was called Patch.

"Mom, come up here we 'bouta do a family dance." I shook my head, and it wasn't because I didn't want to dance with my family. But because everyone would have a dance partner, and I didn't want to be the lone person out. Even the kids would at least be dancing with each other. The kids were in one corner of the dance floor jumping up and wiggling their little bodies to the beat already.

"Okay, we got a few words to say to you, though," Haven said as she smiled at me. Truly took the mic from Haven and started speaking.

"Mom, over two years ago when we were helping you move to the house; we found some letters and articles that helped us learn a lot about you. We didn't read the letters; it was Patch who did. But anyways, you've always made sure all of us had everything we wanted so we got a surprise for you," Truly said.

"I don't need a surprise this is Honor and Haven's day," I told them.

"You sure 'bout that?" Wait, I knew that voice. I stood up out of my seat and started looking for him in the crowd.

Honor and Patch stepped aside, and there was Caden on the dance floor. Caden reminded me of Rico Ross, but he had a stronger jaw structure. He was a tall man with some dark-caramel skin with a few scars coating him from his face down. I sobbed as I got out of my seat and ran towards him and jumped in his waiting muscular arms.

"How?" I asked through my sobs.

"Patch found our letters, and he wrote me last March asking questions. I wrote back and next thing I know, I'm getting a visit from Honor the lawyer. He filed some paperwork based on the new laws that have been passed. And boom, a nigga was getting out a whole lot of years before I was supposed to," Caden answered.

"Aye Caden, I wanna thank you for being there with my mom when no one else was. You was just a young nigga and took on shit that you didn't have to," Patch said and dapped Caden up.

"You don't have to thank me for doing shit; as a man, I was supposed to do that for the person I love, but I appreciate that, youngin'," Caden told him.

"No seriously, thank you 'cause even though he might not have fully remembered you, I think subconsciously he did. And because of that, he was able to do for me and my son what you did for him and his mom." Truly looked over at Caden with tears in her eyes.

"I do remember some of the shit. I just always thought they were dreams of what I wished would have happened. But now I know I didn't just imagine this super hero coming in to save the day when certain shit happened. And that he really was there until a fuck nigga came and fucked shit up. I wanna thank that cousin of yours too one day."

When Caden went to jail, his cousin would come over to make sure we were okay, but I stopped that. My heart couldn't take seeing Caden's cousin, and I stopped him from even speaking to us. When I went on my benders, I would call Caden's cousin before I left, and he would leave food, money and water on my porch for Patch until I came back. All that stopped when his cousin got life in jail; that was when Patch had to start fending for himself during my bad benders.

"I know you don't need a father figure like you did back then, but just know I'm here if you need to talk. I'll just be like your friend or an uncle or some shit," Caden looked over at Patch and told him.

"Let's get back to this wedding, and on Monday I'll come through moms' so we can discuss business. Just when I come through don't be walkin' around naked and shit," Patch said while looking at both of us; the entire room chuckled.

I laid my head on Caden's chest as the song started, and we slow danced together.

"Who that man with my granny?" I heard Truvon say.

"That's her man," Amity answered.

"I'm watchin' you, and if you hurt my granny you gotta see me and my dad."

"And me too," PJ added.

I couldn't help but laugh at my grandkids' antics. I knew they would soon fall in love with Caden, just as their grandmother did.

"I don't want them problems," Caden joked.

"When I told you to move on that shit hurt me as much as it hurt you. I felt like I ripped out my own heart and stomped on that shit. It was just that every time you left the visiting room that shit hurt a nigga, knowing I couldn't leave with you, and I couldn't take that pain anymore. Even reading your letters hurt, and I told myself I would stop reading them, but I just couldn't. But I promise I'mma spend the rest of my life making it up to you," Caden leaned down and whispered in my ear. I wrote him once a month, but he only wrote me once a year on my birthday and sent me cards every holiday.

"Despite all that went down when you got locked up, my love for you never changed," I told him.

"I didn't stop loving your crazy ass either," Caden said.

My heart swelled in my chest and I felt safe, like my world was no longer upside down. Caden's arms wrapped around my waist tighter and he pulled me in closer to him. All of our lives were now filled with so much love that none of us thought would be possible.

We all had tragedy and pain in our lives that people just didn't come back from, and we all found someone that loved us so powerfully that the love overshadowed those tragedies.

Find Marqua'lla

Facebook: Marqua'lla L. Thomas,

Author Marqua'lla

SOUL Publications

CPSIA information can be obtained
at www.ICGtesting.com
Printed in the USA
LVHW111751130819
627498LV00002B/263/P